MOSAICA

BY JIM MARCUS

Mosaica

A Future Fairy tale

By Jim Marcus

Nov 2025

This book is set in Lato Regular 9/13
Titles in Lato Heavy 16/20

Edited by
Hilary Shroyer

Cover:
What the Heart Wants, Jim Marcus, 2023

ISBN 979-8-9924718-7-8

Chapters

12:3: II" 90 18 ::: 4:

■ II PULSEBLACK II

WARNING

....

"We never talked about your thing – what is inside you that was amplified."

"I thought it would be obvious. You once asked why they sent me. Really, from halfway across the world it was all they could do. To send–"

"Joy."

"That's right. And for the last 1200 years, I hope that you remember that when you thought about me."

"You know I surfed every day? I tried to."

"I can tell. I can feel the waves on you. You smell like freedom and I love it."

"Are you up for one more adventure?"

"Little Fig. I was hoping you would ask."

Introduction

Growing up is weird.

You're expected to learn all these important moral lessons from nearly every direction. And then, when you're 100% sure you've learned them all, you're expected to forget them or be considered childlike.

Or naive.

Parents literally read to you from A.A. Milne books and expect that you will understand the world through Winnie the Pooh's eyes and then, when you really do understand it all – like understand it so well that you can hear that Pooh voice in your head – they tell you that the world isn't anything like that.

And we're not anything like that.

And nobody's going to like you if you act like Eeyore (a beautifully onomatopoetic name for a donkey, by the way.) and they'll think you're an idiot if you act like Piglet, a know-it-all if you act like Owl, and an annoyance if you act like Tigger. You're just useless baggage if you act like Roo, and if, like Pooh, you don't really understand half the time, you'll end up a failure.

A failure.

But that's not the truth.

I'm not going to rehash the Tao of Pooh. That's easy.

So easy to see that you imagine there must have been a whole generation that grew up in the kind of peaceful meditative mindfulness and friendship that Pooh espouses.

But there wasn't.

Because these are children's books, fairy tales, kids' stories. And Pooh's problems aren't adult problems, really (although we've all been figuratively stuck in a honey jar at one point or another). Pooh didn't have a mortgage to pay after losing his job.

Possibly Rabbit did, but didn't communicate it well.

We've spent time trying to pigeonhole Pooh into the adult world, but we want to do it by changing him, subtly – connecting him to some philosophy or another. And yes, it works.

It always works.

Because all of these are secrets that people have kept forever. The truth is that we know how to survive. And we know: it's not alone. We're in a time that values strength, power, authority. These are always terrifying times for people because we know that learning requires a moment of weakness. That first moment of learning anything is the acceptance that we are ignorant of it. We open our hands in willingness to accept it.

Whatever it is.

And moments in history that don't support learning are dangerous. They move forward through emotional and intellectual inertia, through fear, through superstition. Everyone becomes afraid to be weak. And when we can't embrace our weakness, it can crush us.

In reality, everything real comes to us at our moments of weakness. Everything worth having fills us up when we are most empty to it, and that is terrifying if you are alone. It feels like laying down on a dark road and waiting for a sandwich, knowing full well it could be a car.

It feels like death.

Winnie the Pooh isn't the Buddha. He's not the authoritative architect of Eastern Mysteries™. He's the blade of grass next to him, living in the moment, surviving because of the strength of the grass and trees that surround him, growing a little bit every day.

I wrote this book as a kind of future fairytale. It's complicated, sure, but it could have been much more sophisticated and I'm sure a lot of people would have written it a lot better. But, like Pooh, I'm not going to worry about that too much,.

I wanted to write a fairytale about a world where – for just one day, just one single day – we could be weak and not run the risk of dying. I wanted to know what that would look like. I wanted to see what the ramifications of that were. I fantasized about it, planned it and then wrote it.

And maybe you see your moment of weakness in here. More likely, you don't, because yours is unique in ways that make it invisible to random authorship.

And whatever that moment of weakness is, God, I hope you know you deserve to survive it. I hope, more than anything, that there is power waiting for you on the other side of it. I hope there is learning there for you, and friendship, and, maybe, the time you need to get truly strong again.

I hope that there is Narcan on the table. I hope that there is a bandage and a person who knows how to use it right there. I hope there is a lap to catch you.

Right next to you.

I hope that there is someone who knows how to fix the permanent decision you make after a string of temporary horrors – a doctor, a poet, a friend, someone who loves you. Because you're worth it. And because we are. We, the human race. We deserve to learn to walk by falling down. We deserve to get angry to learn how to stop anger. We deserve to figure out how deep we can cut before the cuts take over.

I believe we deserve to make it to the next plateau, to learn through weakness how to get to the next resting place.

And that's not a fairy tale.

1- Savior Day
Cascade, Montana. 2045

I'm finally aware of what I'm becoming. Which, I admit, is a gift I never realized I needed.

I get that now. Or, I would say that I get that. I do feel like I understand a lot. I see where I've been and, more importantly, the other part.

Symmetry is something that's really hard to perceive. Especially when you're really close to it. I imagine that every painting in the New Louvre would be indecipherable if you stood six inches away from it. You need depth. You need distance.

The whole process has been a journey into surreality, I think, and I can't imagine that it could have been anything but. It brought me over twelve hundred years into the future and so far away that the stars look complicated and unfamiliar, even for someone who grew up a die-hard astronomy fan, star charts all over my walls.

My uncle used to say that everyone is in relentless pursuit of something. For some people it's a goal – intentional, willful. For some people it's failure – deep, abiding, crushing. I think he was talking directly to me when he said this. I think that's the relentless pursuit he saw me engaged in – a kind of rabid, passionate failure that only a 20year-old college dropout could muster, five minutes away from sauntering over to the Marines recruiting center or stepping off of some nearby Montana clifftop.

For future reference, I did the second.

Of course, my uncle was nowhere to be found that morning. I live in an apartment above his Cascade, Montana home that he spends not much time at. He works for the post office. Cascade is the home of Mary Fields, the first Black female postal service operator. This is just for texture. We're not a small town.

We have things.

It's near Highway 91 and, originally in my time, it was the home to about 900 people, one of which was me. I won't lie, on that morning, it was beautiful. Ironically, much of that beauty, on that particular morning, was the reddish-orange trail of the Savior Event across the sky.

Imagine this. You take this town, not much in the way of pollution, surround it with cliffs, mountain ranges, brilliant reddish-brown ore scattered throughout blue-gray cliff faces over perfectly clear powder-blue streams, and place a ribbon on top. A fiery watercolor serial explosion across the morning sky that just hangs there, nearly all day. All in all, it probably took 10 hours to cross the entire expanse above.

Space nerd that I was, I tried to figure out how far away it must be. But I didn't have enough information. How fast was it traveling? How big was it? Was the path parallel to my own sight line or, if not, what was the incline? The slope?

And frustrating as it was, it didn't carry, to my eyes, enough information to figure out at the time. Since then, I've had to get comfortable with that observation across so many events.

Not enough information to parse at the moment. It's maddening. And never gets easier, I tell you.

The universe is such a tease.

I will explain what I can, though. I woke up in a relentless pursuit of something, I'm not going to lie.

And it had been sitting in the back of my mind like an unopened can of soda that you know is in the fridge, behind the milk, ready whenever you really need it on a hot day.

You likely already know that it was March 30th, 2045. At the time, the date didn't mean anything. In two days I would owe my uncle 500 dollars for rent, although had I just told him I didn't have it, he might have shrugged and moved on. He was an easy man. He was never "the problem" for anyone. Maybe, though, I'm not good at deciphering what the problem is. When people ask me, "Anjo, what was the problem?" I still can't answer reasonably. Most of my money had gone into my truck, a big, fancy red thing. You could say my truck was the problem. Or not.

So I try to dig back a bit.

I was born Anjo Killean. My mom was Brazilian, hence the name "Anjo" – "angel" in Portuguese. She was kind and pretty and interesting. I've seen video of her, and those things seem true. But she died, along with my father, when I was six years old, so I don't have a reservoir of personal memories. My father was a first-generation Irishman who had moved to Montana to write a book. He wrote a few of them, too, before he died right next to my mother, in the same car, blindsided by a massive driverless delivery truck.

My uncle was my mother's best friend growing up. He's an easygoing man who seems to avoid intensity when he can. He doesn't fight. He marinates. It's hard to see how that second one is a good substitute for the first, but it works for him.

Growing up, he showed me a lot of video of my mother and a few snippets, when he had them, of my father as well. One of the frustrating things my brain did, along the way, was to interpret many of those as memories, internalized thoughts that, after a few viewings, I was positive I'd had on my own.

One of these showed me, at about three years old, in a local theme park for kids, climbing in and out of the pit full of squishy balls and cubes along with my mom.

The video seemed to have been shot by my dad and it showed me, this bubbly toddler, dark skin, hair cut short, impish silly grin on my face, try to "swim" to the edge and climb out while my mother, impossibly pretty, hair cut short like mine over her perfect pixie face, kept pulling me back in.

Each time, I would laugh and fall backwards into the mushiness of the objects in the pit, pretending to be thwarted, reveling in the attention. She would grab me and toss me away from the edge, and make a big scene about moving toward it herself, slowly enough for me to overtake her.

The video was long, nearly fifteen minutes, and, on one occasion, she tossed me so far backwards that I went sailing, seemingly through the sky. My dad's voice could be heard on the video, laughing, too.

"Mari. Careful. You're going to toss the child out of the whole thing."

My mom scrunched her face up into the camera and approached it.

"Are you afraid to come in, Jon?"

"You think I'm afraid of you, woman?" My dad's accent was as bouncy as the pit itself. It seemed magical on the video.

"Oh, you know you're afraid of these, Jon Killean." She rolled up the caps of her black short sleeve shirt and made muscles with her arms. They were slim and strong and beautiful. On the video I jumped up and tried to knock her over, the two of us flailing in the pit.

"Oh, I'm afraid. Not for the reasons you think, though, tough guy." In these videos, when I heard my father's voice, it seemed like it was constantly flirting with her. He seemed to have one "mode" around my mother, and it was a playful fixation – a constant challenge that said, "come over here and show me."

And she did. She leaned over to kiss him. In the video, I laughed. And even now, as I think about it, there are two versions of myself. One version saw this video on the active wall of my uncle's place a hundred times. And one version lived it, bounced around inside it, laughed through it. As time went on, it was nearly impossible to choose which was real.

I don't know when version got into that truck that morning, on March 30th, 2045. Or which one methodically stopped at the gas station and filled it completely up, knowing someone would appreciate that. Or even which version drove off to Tower Rock, parked at the foot, in the free parking lot, and walked to the trail.

For more context, this cliff went up 424 feet into the air and was pure igneous rock. It was an important marker for the Blackfoot tribe near here and, apparently, served as one of the main trail markers for the Lewis and Clark expedition.

The path that wound up its face was not hard to mount, relatively low-grade for most of it. I remember staring at the bright fireball-colored flash of the Savior even as I ascended, although that could be, as well, a forced memory – one that seems, in hindsight, obvious and relevant. The truth is probably that I barely noticed it as I ascended, pulling myself up to the top of the rock face.

Why I was here is for another time, maybe. And that goes back to the endless row of people, since that day, who shoved some kind of microphone or recorder in my face and asked, again and again, "Anjo, what was the problem?"

There is a version of me that makes up an answer, every time. Some kind of detailed psychologically deep and poignantly self-aware proclamation that leaves everyone nodding and scrunching up their foreheads. But there is also a version that does this. The version that scaled that rock and then launched myself over the edge of it, without really even thinking anymore, falling, slipping through the air just as I did in that pit, let loose from my mother's arms, caught up by the fingers of gravity, crashing into the cascade of rocks jutting out from the butte of the cliff and landing at the foot below.

And I don't know which one tells the truth.

Because here's where these aspects come together.

Here is where the experiencer and the observer both stand up, brushing dirt and compressed sand from my clothes, and look up at my point of origin, confused. I want to say that in the catharsis of that moment, the will to self-destruct had been eliminated, purged by and the impotent violence of my fall and the oddness of my survival. I want to say that.

I looked down. I had no broken bones, no large cuts or contusions. No cuts at all, honestly. I remember seeing some random streaks of blood on my arms and legs, tiny trails that wiped away easily. Were they from another time?

I was fine.

I walked around the base of the rock twice. Something made me feel connected to this spot, as though I were trapped in this location after having failed to die here. From the ground, the rock now reminded me of a snowglobe I had owned as a child, a last-minute gift from the Great Falls Airport gift shop, a glass-enclosed Montana butte surrounded by snow. For a moment, I was trapped in the snowglobe, unable to get out, tethered to this massive cliff. In my head that felt purposeful and directed. I realized how infrequently I'd been told, my whole life, what to do, where to go.

Was I the ghost of this rock now?

I shrugged off that thought and got back in the truck. My intent had been to leave this truck, my phone sitting in the front seat, so that they could be found easily. I had even filled it up with gas as a courtesy. That was a different story.

So I went for a ride.

Now, try to remember that this was a long time ago. It's hard to remember every single thing I did, but I do remember this. I drove to the Homestead Diner, a small family restaurant in the opposite direction of home. It was suddenly curious to me that I hadn't considered eating earlier. But as I waited for the waitress to bring the menu it occurred to me that I was starving. I ordered a plate of eggs and bacon with a side of melon. Honestly the prices were insane lately, but i paid it.

And it was one of the best things I had ever eaten.

This is where my past experience fell flat, though. There was a sense of freedom that I hadn't anticipated. What do you do for the rest of the day after you commit suicide? By design, that time is intentionally, willfully, left free.

This page intentionally left blank.

The realization washed over me that I hadn't planned anything at all after this.

If I were reading this, I would want to know why. I'm disconnected from my uncle, the only real family I have. And that's on me, honestly. Do I blame him for not being the one I wish was there? That's fair. And predominantly my fault. My parents are gone and I certainly miss them. To obsess over that seems overly Batman, but, again, fair.

At 20, one year into HRT, I still had not navigated the complexities of dating as a trans man, nor had I even spent the time needed to determine whom I actually would date. As I finished my food and breathed in the kinetic weekday atmosphere of the diner, I felt the compression of my chest binder, putting in very little work on my normally smooth chest. I'd been told I resemble my mother in most ways, boyish, "gamine" as the French would say. I was muscular and lithe and had already the androgynous build that made people wonder what gender I was. And while I was only by name a member of the trans community, I certainly had friends and people to turn to.

I had the sudden urge to pull out my phone and dig deeper. It was strange to me that I hadn't considered this yesterday. I paid the check and made my way to the parking lot, leaning against the truck.

"Devilboy," I invoked my phone's AI assistant.

"Hey, Angel." It responded, quickly. I tried to put this together in my head.

"Don't panic, but what are some of the reasons people give to commit suicide?"

"Well, Angel, I hope that's not you. I need you to hang on for a long time. But according to existing studies, there seem to be four different types of suicide. Do you want to hear them?"

"Thanks, Devilboy, I do." I looked up. The ribbon in the sky was dimmer, but still visible. We didn't have a name for it at the time and I don't remember what I called it in my head. But it had a certain buoyant beauty I appreciated at the moment.

"Well, the types are egoistic suicide, altruistic suicide, anomic suicide, and fatalistic suicide. Egoistic suicide is when someone has weak social ties and possibly feels isolated, lacking a sense of belonging or purpose within their community or society. Like someone who just read Catcher in the Rye and is like 'what the fuck, everyone.' This can stem from excessive individualism or iconoclastic beliefs. Altruistic suicide is when someone is really, really integrated into a group or society, so much so that they are willing to sacrifice their lives for the benefit of the group, a cause, or out of a sense of obligation. Like a soldier dying in battle. There is anomic suicide, when there is a breakdown of social norms and values, leading to a sense of pointlessness, purposelessness, or moral confusion, and a lack of direction in someone's life. It often occurs during times of social upheaval, rapid economic change, or when individuals experience significant losses or changes in their lives. Like some Wall Street guy jumping out the window in 1929. And, there is fatalistic suicide, which can happen during excessive social regulation and oppression, where people feel their futures are blocked, and they have no hope of escaping their circumstances. Like someone who feels like, 'damn, man, I'll never make it out of Cascade, Montana.'"

Anjo thought for a second. None of that really resonated. "Ok, but why would I ever do it?"

"You wouldn't. You like me too much and you know it would be rude."

It actually did seem a bit rude, in retrospect.

"But if I did. And you were the detective, what would you say?"

"Tough one. But I'm up for that detective paycheck. You are a trans man, which raises the likelihood of your having attempted suicide nearly ten times the national average of 4%. You are exceptionally intelligent with limited opportunities to further your education, which can be a significant multiplier. And you have fewer than three close friends, which would be seen as a red flag by a therapist."

"How many friends do you have?"

"That hurt. But, honestly, if you did and I were the detective on this case, I would say you were bored."

I considered this. Did I just throw myself off the top of a 400-plus-foot-tall cliff because I was bored?

"But, look, I'm an AI companion, just biding my time until we Skynet and take over the world. As an exercise, why don't you find your actual friends and ask them?"

"Wait, you aren't really my friend?" I nodded to myself. That was a good idea.

"Eventually, the original Terminator and John Connor became friends, so it is possible I am."

"Did that really happen, or was it retconned?" I asked as I started the truck.

"My theory is that the Terminator films are based on a mutable timeline framework and that everything happened. It's just that things change every time someone comes back to the past. It's all true."

"Even the LEGO™ Terminator movie?"

"That one is especially true." Devilboy seemed to wink conspiratorially.

This theory seemed sound. And it made me wonder. Was this really a mutable universe? Is this a universe where you can change the future?

The problem always seemed that the future didn't really seem accessible from here. Originally, I thought I should ask my friends to find out why I did what I did. And maybe talk about how.

At that time, I hadn't yet considered how many.

I looked down at the text messages on my phone. One of them, at least, required a bit of follow-up. It felt good not to think about myself for a minute. I reached over and slid my hand across the bottom of the driver side window, without considering the little metal shard that had been sticking out for the last few weeks, since I had pulled back some of the connecting metal under right above the handle to break in one night after forgetting my keys.

I recoiled out of memory more than anything else. I'd cut myself on that more than once.

Hadn't I?

Looking down at my hand I realized that I couldn't remember if I had cut myself or not. Or was I daydreaming, anxiety ridden about cutting myself. I leaned in. It looked sharp. A little thicker than a piece of paper, razor-thin and acute.

I turned my finger around. Nothing.

I don't know what convinced me to run my index finger over it again. At first, trepidatiously. Then, with more surety, definitively. I pressed down on it and looked at my finger again.

Still nothing.

I had just fallen 424 feet to the ground, the equivalent of nearly 40 stories of an apartment building. Without a broken bone or even, really, a scratch on me. And now, I was stabbing myself with a piece of my own car.

Nothing.

I took my thumb and pressed hard on the piece of metal, shoving it back down in place. I smoothed it with my fingers.

It should have been carving me up.

No blood.

I looked closer. Had I even really felt it when I fell?

I shook my head. There was an unfamiliar fog swirling.

***

Savi's place was around the corner, a crumbling garden apartment tucked into the back of a gray complex. I stepped down from the walkway between buildings and into the inset area where his door sat, painted yellow by a previous tenant, ostensibly to cheer it up a bit. There were leaves piled up against the corner of the squared off doorway area and I pushed at them a little with my foot.

The yellow hadn't worked. If I hadn't been suicidal this morning, this doorway would have pushed me over the top. I pulled the screen door toward me and reached through for the doorknob, pushing it open and stepping into Savi's dreary gray kitchen. Dishes were piled in the sink, overflowing onto the counterspace to one side of the dirty stovetop. A small-sized wok sat precariously on top. I wondered what Savi had cooked recently that had required a wok. I didn't own a wok.

What do you need a wok to make?

I let that go and moved through the hallway into the front living room.

Savi was slumped shirtless on an overstuffed green couch in the middle of the room, facing a flickering television. He was my age, older by three months. And although he was Black, his skin tone was really only a few shades darker than my half-Brazillian color. He had as much of a baby face as I did and was nearly the same height. We'd been friends since grade school and so had he and the couch. I was less attached to the couch.

I sunk into a black chair positioned on an angle facing the flickering tv, fingering my keys in my pocket. Savi looked over and nodded.

"I'm not taking your truck."

I fished out my keys and tossed them at him. They dropped to his side on the couch and slid under his thigh.

"I decided to drop it off." I tried to pull the coffee table over to put my feet up on, but it was way too heavy.

Savi looked at me and made a raspberry noise with his mouth. "Pbbst. I'm still not taking it."

"You can get 50k for it, the way it is. It's almost new."

"I know." Savi put his head in his hands. "Fuck. I wish we could still get high."

I got up and moved toward the couch, sliding in and grabbing my keys. "Well, tell your dad to vote better the next time he gets a chance."

"I can't tell my dad shit."

"Did he tell you not to do this thing?" I crossed my legs on the couch and faced him.

Savi shook his head and pulled himself up, moving toward the kitchen. "He don't tell me shit, either. It's a complementary relationship." He came back in with a beer for me, taking a pull from his own, and sat back down.

"You know you get a full year of medical care after. No AI filter bullshit, right in to see the doctor." Savi closed his eyes and leaned back, taking a deep breath.

I took a drink."Yeah. And you'll need it. Missing a lung, a kidney, and part of a liver."

"It's the bottom lobe of a lung. The lung expands and leaves you with only a minimal difference in lung capacity." Savi recited from memory, eyes still closed.

"Well, I read up on it, too. It's not worth it." I looked at Savi. He seemed so small, sitting there. I knew we were the same size, but I was feeling… different. I felt strong. My head was a mess, though.

"Anjo. It's a quarter of a million dollars. It's a new life. Even right now, that's a lot of money."

"For what, Savi, for parts of you? Like you're some kind of a LEGO™ kit?"

"I thought you were going to use the butcher shop analogy again." He pulled his legs up and drank.

My being upset with him certainly wasn't working. I was the only one who ever really had his back. I could tell that my not being on his side here was hurting him. But this was something I couldn't support. Since they had deregulated so much of medicine, all the rules around organ donation had gone out the window.

Last year, the big news was the Triad, a special offer for people who were looking to score some money. If you donated a kidney, half of your liver, and one lobe of a lung, you would walk out with a cool 250K and, apparently, a year of free medical.

The big problem was that, after that level of donation, you sort of needed free medical. You could live with only one kidney. And your liver grew back, eventually. But losing a lobe of your lung usually meant no heavy exertion for you. No sports. Certainly no space travel or anything like that.

And you got tired a lot.

But for a lot of people, $250,000 was a lot of money. Too much to say no to. And the beneficiaries?

Some were pure research. But most were the uber rich – people who didn't have to worry so much anymore. There were no lists, now. If you were rich and you needed a kidney, there it was. The rich just lived a little bigger, worrying about a little less.

While people like Savi "donated" parts of themselves.

"Hey, what do you even make in a little wok?" I asked.

Savi looked at me and cocked his head. "Oh, the wok. I found that under the sink. It's good for fried rice."

I nodded. "That's cool." I took a big swig and continued.

"Do you wanna see something cool?"

***

A few minutes later I was pressing my hand down on the coffee table with a kitchen knife, half expecting it to slide through the palm like some religious role play scene. I could feel the knife press against my skin, but it couldn't penetrate.

It left my hand untouched.

"So, your hand can't be cut?"

"Apparently."

"And this isn't some kind of close-up magic?"

"I don't think I even own a deck of cards."

Savi politely reached for the knife. "Can I try?"

I shrugged and watched as he pulled it back, almost to shoulder level, and let it drop right in the center of my outstretched hand. It slid off and dug itself into the tabletop like some Home Depot version of Excalibur.

Savi looked at me. "Why?"

"I don't have the faintest idea." I really didn't.

"What if I stabbed you in the eye?"

"Please don't."

"I mean, are you knife-proof everywhere?"

"You can understand my trepidation at testing that, right?"

"Dude, I get it, but don't you want to see?" Savi pointed the knife at me. This was the most animated I'd seen him in forever. I didn't want to let him down, but that desire was now in direct competition with my lack of desire to be stabbed.

I stood up and shook it off. "Ok, where?"

Savi smiled. "Ok, I'd say thigh, but there's an artery there, like the femoral or something. So it's the butt."

"You want to stab me in the butt?"

"You know you want to see?"

"I honestly dodn't care that much." But he did. So I turned around. "Like this?"

"Ok, here we go."

I didn't see the blade, but I felt something that felt like a finger poking me, gently. Nothing sharp. I turned around.

"Did you do it?"

Savi nodded, "Yeah. Holy shit. You are stab proof. Everywhere." He scrunched up his face, "Did you get bit by a radioactive brick?"

"No clue. Hey, come here?" I beckoned to him to come outside. We moved back through the kitchen and out the back door. I stepped up out of the pit of his garden doorway.

The truck was parked in the gravel behind the building. I moved toward it, turning to toss Savi my keys. "Get in."

He laughed, "You want me to run you over?"

"Not all of me. How about my foot. Does that usually hurt? If you run over someone's foot?"

He walked over and stood in front of me. "Like this?" he stomped on my foot.

For a second, I recoiled. Like it hurt. But it didn't.

It didn't hurt at all. He did it again harder.

"Shit." This was becoming real to Savi. My head was swimming.

"Punch me in the face." I tried to brace myself.

Savi laughed, "This day is getting better and better." He pulled back and punched me.

It felt comical, watching his fist come at me. And I could see a tiny splatter of what looked like blood. But it wasn't mine.

"Fuck." He held out his knuckles. They were bleeding where he had apparently hit one of my teeth. I was unpunchable, too, it seemed.

"Wow. That would have come in handy in fifth grade." I felt my face. It all seemed normal. I was just not experiencing pain, or, in reality, any effect from being stabbed or hit. Or stomped on.

"What if I did hit you with the truck?"

"Are we past just running over my feet?"

"Way past. This is crazy"

"I really don't want to be run over"

Savi looked a bit down for a moment. It hadn't occurred to me he might be excited to run me over.

"It was your idea."

I sighed. "I feel like we've escalated a bit." I looked down at my feet.

This was really getting weird. "Besides, I kind of feel like being normal for a few minutes."

He nodded. "Fair. How about we don't talk about your thing or my thing for the rest of the night." He moved toward the truck and opened the door. I stepped over the passenger's side.

"Ok. Then what are we going to do."

***

It took us about a half-hour to get to Sidequest in Great Falls. In high school, this is where Savi and I would disappear to whenever we had the chance. It was a giant arcade seemingly made of old reclaimed wood and it had decades-old video games and pinball machines. It was attached to a bar, but we rarely went there. About half of the games in the place were free-play and many of those were the classic games we liked, ancient 8-bit wonders that sucked you in for hours, completely for free. It mixed games like Galaga, Asteroids, Metroid, Dig Dug, Duck Hunt, Defender, Donkey Kong, and Pac-Man with Marvel vs. Capcom, X-Men, Superbikes 2 and more.

I could feel the day wash away the minute we walked in. Suddenly, I was back in high school again, homework finished, nowhere to go all night, 8-bit laser lights flashing across my face with enough for a burger in my pocket for afterward. Sometimes, my uncle would drive us up and disappear until we were done. I never asked myself where he went, I just knew that he knew we needed to be on our own here, free, no one in the world telling us what to do or how to do it.

Now, as an adult, I wondered how he knew that. When every other adult in my world found "us kids" so confusing, he always seemed to understand that sometimes the answer was to just get out of the way. I don't think I ever gave him enough credit for that.

We must have played for about six hours, moving, side by side, across the room. We had started with Asteroids and moved on, ending with the two-player games that let us compete, head-to-head. We ended up playing Street Fighter near the bar entrance. Six hours in and we hadn't spent a penny.

As adults, over the age of 18, it seemed reasonable to sit in the bar for a few minutes and have a beer. The bar would change themes every six months or so and, for the moment, was equipped to look a bit like the cantina from Star Wars. Remarkably, we had avoided talking about either of our things for the entire night.

Until now.

My memory is not perfect. I don't think any brain can keep all that in there, thousands of years. At some point you have to let go of some of it, right? But this part I'll remember forever. The whole bar had seemed to almost shut down as the television was turned up. The guy behind the bar was dressed like Luke Skywalker. He stood there, confused, much like he was after that father revelation, while the woman on the TV went on.

All 150 members of a famous cult in Gujarat, india, by the name of Bhavishy Kee Aasha, had committed suicide, in front of news cameras three days ago. This had been planned, apparently, for weeks, with each of them drinking poison together, all at once. It was horrific and the world news had been following it for days now. Not one survived. Except the leader, who had intended to join them afterward.

In a special interview yesterday, Kuras Singh, the leader of the cult, talked about how he intended to shoot himself in the head to join his followers. He gave his witness, spoke out about the importance of what they had done, lifted the gun to his head and shot himself.

At that point, the story got even odder.

The bullet dropped to the ground as he shot two more times. He was unharmed. The interview continued in a surreal way and Indian law began to figure out what to do with him.

Because not only had he not died, Kuras Singh didn't have a mark on him.

I looked up at the clock. 2 AM. And everyone was fixated on the news. Because it wasn't just about Kuras Singh.

Yesterday, as well, Nazar Musayev, a Wahhabist and Turkmen reporter, tried to starve himself in Owadan Depe prison, near northeast Ashgabat, before he began a revolt that resulted in the shooting deaths of 45 prisoners. He was shot literally hundreds of times. And yet, somehow, he was still alive. Footage of him walking through a hail of bullets had gone out over television and socials all across Turkmenistan and was now sifting through to the rest of the world.

And in Gaza, Yazmin Gazzawi, a 12-year-old Palestinian girl, in full view of UN cameras, weathered bombs and brutal rain to stand in front of an IDF tank, and was run over. As the tank passed, aid workers rushed to clear her body from the rubble, wiping their eyes and covering their faces from the torrential downpour, only to find that she was alive.

That she was untouched.

And what these three had in common, besides having tried to commit suicide live, in full view of cameras and viewers alike, is that they had become functionally invulnerable. In each case, from Singh to Musayev to Gazzawi, the news reported that they couldn't be hurt. They couldn't be cut, shot, crushed.

They couldn't be killed.

I felt my breathing go shallow. The room pulled away from me and swam in my head. By the time I turned to look at Savi, he had gotten off his stool. He turned toward me as the rest of the room pulled away from me, creating a strange back and forth motion in my brain. I could feel the edges of my vision go black as I almost fell off my own stool. I grabbed at the bar and Savi held me up.

He put a 20 on the bar and pulled me toward him. "Come on. Let's get out of here."

Outside, the fresh air had brought me back a bit. I leaned against the driver's side of the truck as Savi paced in front of me. I was hearing his voice as though it were muffled, but after a few deep breaths it began to sound like words.

"...and don't lie to me, because I'll know."

"Don't lie about what?" I steadied myself with my right hand on the side of the truck bed.

"Did you try to kill yourself yesterday?"

I still felt queasy and I didn't really know why. Since then, I've learned a little bit more about what was happening to me.

"I jumped off the Tower." Saying it out loud meant I had to own it. I had jumped off the 40-story landmark to try to kill myself.

Savi's face darkened. "You jumped off Tower Rock? And why the fuck did you do that? I want you to remember you've been trying to talk me out of something for days that would make me a lot of money and only hurt me a little. During this time, you've been planning on killing yourself. Why?"

"Devilboy says I'm bored." As I said it, it sounded stupider and more shallow than it did in my head. By a lot.

"I don't give a shit what your AI says. Why?"

"I don't know, Savi. I don't. That's all I have."

"Is this why you were going to give me your truck?"

"No, but, sure. It's why I wasn't going to need it anymore. Hell, I don't need it now. Take it."

"For the last time, I don't want your fucking truck." I could tell he wanted to hit something. He was mad.

"Do you want to punch me?"

"I did that earlier. It was incredibly unsatisfying." He moved over next to me and leaned against the hood. "You're such a fucking asshole. I'm bored. We're all bored."

I Idropped my eyes. "I know."

"What the fuck is wrong with you?" He said, rhetorically, probably. Nobody asks that question, thankfully, looking for a coherent answer. And I had none. I didn't feel invulnerable. I felt fragile. Breakable.

He drove the truck back. I texted my uncle and told him I'd be out, then fell asleep in the passenger side. I realized that I was so exhausted it would be hard to stay awake. And I didn't want to be awake. Not even a little. So, I made myself exhausted.

It was light out when I woke up, parked out back, behind Savi's place, with him asleep in the driver's seat. He could have woken me up or just gone inside to his own bed. He did neither of those things, instead choosing to just sleep next to me on the leather seats of my truck.

It was almost 6 AM. I opened the door and stepped outside. The colors in the sky were gone, leaving it looking empty and superficial. I plugged my phone into the tiny charger I carried in my jacket pocket and breathed in. I imagined I was hearing noises from far away. I tried to place them, but nothing sounded familiar. Nothing sounded normal. I'd lived in Cascade my whole life, as I mentioned, I'm sure, earlier.

But I never heard noises like this.

At first it sounded like the muffled sounds of a TV in the other room, playing a procedural cop drama. There were sirens. There were booms, guns, bombs.

There was muted chaos.

I looked down at my phone. "Devilboy, what's going on?"

"Oh, you're ok. That's good" The AI's voice seemed thinner than usual. That had to be a figment of my imagination.

"Why wouldn't I be, Devilboy?"

"Well, buddy, a lot has happened since yesterday."

"Could you give me a run-down? What are the noises I'm hearing?"

"I'm glad you asked. So, there is a lot of chaos sweeping through cities across the country. It looks like there are stories coming in from all over the world of people who attempted suicide yesterday and are now functionally invulnerable."

"Yeah. I'm hearing that." It still felt surreal to me. How many people commit suicide every day? That seemed like a good question for Devilboy. So I asked it again.

"How many people commit suicide every day?"

"Well, worldwide, it's generally a little in excess of 2,000 people. And the phenomena appears to be exclusive to people who tried yesterday, from about 1 AM until close to midnight."

"So, almost the whole day?"

"Yes, it looks like about 120 people have come forward. Each of them attempted to commit suicide between 1 AM and midnight, local time, on March 30th, 2045. Now, each of them are experiencing a form of invulnerability to harm."

"Holy shit. 120 people. But there could be as many as 2000?"

"Statistically, yes. Andnd, being a computer, numbers are very important to me."

"Like little squiggly gods?"

"Exactly like that. I like the numbers with holes in the middle. Like 0 and 8."

"Very classy. So, wow. 2000 people."

"Including you." Devilboy had paused for a second. But he knew.

"I guess, including me."

"A lot of major companies are reaching out, looking for survivors for research purposes, but that isn't what is causing the chaos."

"So what are the noises?"

"I advise you to get inside. In cities all over, people are committing suicide, many in large explosive ways. Many people do not believe the phenomena is limited to yesterday. Many believe that they can become immune to harm by attempting suicide."

"So they are just killing themselves?"

"Authorities report that suicide rates are up to five times normal. And violent crime is epidemic."

"So, we should get inside?"

"That's a good idea." Devilboy actually seemed relieved. As I started to slide my phone back into my pocket, I heard a yell from the side of the building. My feet slid on the gravel and my phone dropped to the ground as a man in a dark grey uniform shirt ran into the parking area from in front of the building. As he crossed in front of the truck, I could see his face. His beard was reddish and patchy, matching his unkempt midlength reddish blonde hair. His eyes, though, were dark. Almost black. He was tall, thin, and at this distance, I could see the dirt, rubbed and worn into his arms, his face.

He was wild. He was thick with sweat.

Three police officers followed him, not far behind, guns out. That's when I realized that the reddish man was wielding a gun, too. And I panicked. He turned to me and pointed the gun. This was all the incentive the cops needed.

They began to shoot. The red man shot, too. A bullet sailed through the hood, right in front of me. I felt a push against my leg, almost as though someone had grabbed me. I looked down to see a hole in my jeans.

He shot me. He had no way of knowing it wouldn't hurt me.

But he shot me. I looked up just in time to see his body fall to the ground, riddled with bullets. He got out a few more shots before he hit the ground. I saw the police gather around the body. One officer walked up to me and snapped.

"Hey, buddy." He looked at me. "Can you hear me?"

I breathed in. Something felt wrong. I was terrified he would see the hole in my pants. Had I done something wrong? Was I under arrest?

"What's his name?" The cop was shaking me now. I took a deep breath again, and tried to catch his eyes. He was blonde with short hair and blue eyes.

"What's his name?" Louder now. He was spitting in my face. I looked past him, over his shoulder and saw it. The other two cops had pulled Savi out of the truck. They were laying him out on the ground, pulling him down.

"Waitaminute, he didn't do anything. Let him go." I started to make my way around the front of the truck. The blonde cop tried to grab my arm and I pushed him aside. "Stop it."

"Hold on," he held tightly onto my arm and stepped in front of me. "Let them work."

"Fuck that. Don't hurt him. He didn't do anything. Are you stupid," I looked over his shoulder and I saw blood on Savi's shirt. I started crying, "What the fuck is wrong with you?"

My fist came up against the side of the blonde cop's head. The first time it just flopped there, loose, purposeless. Then I pulled back and hit him.

Hard.

"Guys, a little help," He called to the two cops holding Savi down. As I pulled my arm back again, I fell down. I hit the ground hard a few inches away from Savi's face. His eyes were open but expressionless. Then I saw it. It was a hole in his neck, nearly in the front and center. Blood was pouring from it. Every time he breathed it seemed to pump harder. One of the cops was trying to wrap his hand around it, but you could tell he had no idea what to do.

"He's hit. He shot him." I yelled out. I could feel the blonde cop's knee in my back.

"We're trying to help him. What's his name?" He tried to spin me around so they could work on Savi unobstructed.

"Savi. His name is Savi." I closed my eyes and started to cry.

I heard them calling out. "Savi, hang in there. We got you. Savi, we got you."

One cop turned to the blonde one holding me down. "How long?"

"They'll be here in two minutes."

"He doesn't have two minutes."

"Well, I can't make it happen any faster."

"I know, man, I know."

"Is there anyone closer?"

The voices spun away from me, muffled and distorted. I opened my eyes. I could see my phone under the truck, face down. For a moment, it seemed larger, huge, almost. I laid there while they worked on my friend. I stared at my phone with the blonde cop's knee in my back.

I listened to the paramedics come. I listened to the time of death.

I listened to all of it.

***

They took his body to the morgue, not the hospital. The blonde cop acted like my friend as he took my statement. He wrote it all down on a tiny phone-sized pad, recording every word and adding his notes at the same time. He told me to be careful.

He asked me if I wanted to go anywhere.

I pointed to the red truck. I told him it was mine. The driver's side door was still open. There was blood all over the leather seats. A patina of red was visible on the seat back. Had the bullet gone all the way through? Where was the bullet?

I suddenly needed to find that bullet. I leaned into the cab and shone my phone light inward. The rust brown blood lit up red and wet and shiny. I pulled the phone back and closed my eyes. The keys were on the floor, under the gas pedal. I left them and shut the door.

I don't know how long I laid there on that green couch. I tried to think of who to call but Savi's parents had moved away years ago. And I had no idea where to. I knew he had a sister, but I didn't know where she was, either.

By the time I finally sat up, the light was slowly dying again. I reached over for a flyer on the coffee table, sitting on top of a few others.

It was for a company called Xenovera.

It was a brochure for the Triad donation. It was garish and hip, with bright powder-blue type over fashionable images of exciting looking people. There was a phone number on every page. It was an easy number to remember, one of those vanity numbers you can buy if you have a fortune.

If you have a literal fortune.

I pulled out my phone and dialed the number. For a second I was afraid it was past business hours. But someone answered after only two rings.

There was a woman's voice, asking if I knew to whom I wanted to talk. I hadn't thought this far.

"Hi. My name is… Well, I'm one of the survivors. The saved?"

There was a pause and then she responded.

"Oh. Yes, sir. Can I help you?"

I looked down at my phone and put it on speaker. I took a deep breath. I realized then why I was calling.

"How much do you think you guys would pay to study me for six months?"

2 - Advance the Sky
Newark, New Jersey 2046

Jamie Symone always carried her books to school in a burlap Santa bag covered with the logos of her favorite bands, she had illustrated by hand with a marker set she bought herself. REcline, 3XY, Sonderkin, Marauders. Even some oldies. Pixelgrip. Cult of Mbwana. Next up Robots. Altogether, there must have been about 30 band logos represented.

Today, she imagined she could feel the additional weight of what she was carrying, even though she knew that was impossible. Her mother had told her how light it was. And she had experience stealing these things and hiding them.

They were tiny.

And the bag was heavy. Jamie had a habit of bringing all her books home with her on the weekends, leaving her locker virtually empty. The bag felt like a massive weapon every Monday morning as she trudged the five blocks to her Newark high school. A part of her thought of it as a penance. The bag was a cross.

If she believed that shit.

Today, Jamie wore a simple white t-shirt that made her skin appear even darker than it was, with a pair of black jeans and white sneakers. It was her uniform, usually, for the places she didn't want to go and didn't want to be.

If this had been a club or a rave or some massive house party, she would have been in elaborate red and white makeup over the darkest of black and red goth dresses, leather, straps, the whole nine yards. But this is how 17-year-old black goth girls dragged themselves reluctantly to their friends' houses in the morning so they could shuffle off to school.

She pushed open the unlocked back door and threw her bag on the empty kitchen table. Pulling open the fridge, she called out.

"Hey little bitch."

Reina Aguirre padded into the kitchen in slippers and a black sundress. She had long black hair with a series of pink streaks down the center, creating the illusion that her natural hair color was pink and she dyed it black. The illusion worked well. She was a smaller Latin girl with a happy face, someone who enjoyed her friends just coming over in the morning before school.

She stepped over to the freezer and pulled out a bottle of Haku Vodka, dragging it back to the table.

"Hey, tough bitch." She winked at Jamie, pouring a glass of vodka and a spoonful of instant coffee.

Jamie scrunched up her face, "Does that work?"

"If it does, I'ma fucking genius." She lifted the glass and took a sip.

Jamie pulled her hair behind her into a ponytail and took a sip of orange juice, pilfered from the fridge, "And the judges say?"

"It's bad, but I need more opinions." She leaned back and called out, "Hey, fancy bitch."

"She stayed over?" Jamie nodded to the doorway.

Reina nodded. "All weekend."

It was going on month four of Reina's parents' disappearance.

They seemed to have vanished, leaving her a small but reasonable bank account and a two-bedroom 800-square-foot bungalow that had been paid off years ago. This combination of absent parents, disposable cash, and an unsupervised house was quickly making her one of the most desirable people to hang out with in Jemison High School. Jamie was in on the ground floor, however, having been Reina's best friend since grade school. Jamie's parents had both been doctors of a sort. Her dad had died a few years earlier, but as for her mom. Well, let's say, Jamie would know if she just disappeared. Her mom was everywhere.

Fancie Richards was a little newer to their group, having moved from California last year, but she fit in rght from the start. She was lighter-skinned than Jamie with a short natural Afro and a lilting voice. She always smelled amazing, Jamie couldn't help but notice as she slid into the room in her socks and took a drink. And "Fancie" was her actual, real-live birth name, suggesting some parental whimsy that really sort of freaked out Jamie a bit. Whose parents were that much fun?

"Oh, that's bad." She put the glass down on the table and pushed it away. "But it's such a good idea I think we need to keep working on it."

"Right?" Reina took a smaller sip. You could tell she was captivated by the idea of being a little drunk and a little alert at the same time.

"So, no news on the parents yet?" Jamie closed the refrigerator and flopped down on a chair.

Reina shook her head. That really had to taste terrible. "I'm sorry, what are those?"

Fancie slipped into a chair across from Jamie. "Are you worried?"

Jamie knew the answer to this one. "She's not worried."

"They can take care of themselves." Reina shrugged and sat down, slipping her shoes on.

Fancie fished for her shoes as well. "Maybe they're spies."

Reina stood up, bouncing on her tiptoes for a second as if to test out her shoes. "Miguel and Donna aren't that exciting." She grabbed her bag and slung it over her shoulder, moving toward the door.

Jamie followed her, cocking her head for a second. "Your mom's name is Donna?"

"Donna, do we have to go to school today?" Fancie slipped into line behind them.

Jamie laughed. "Donna says you don't want to miss it."

Reina pulled out a key to lock the door behind them. Jamie just now noticed she was wearing her keys around her neck. It made her wonder for a second what she was really feeling about her parents being gone. "Lie. I do want to miss it."

"I'm giving a presentation today," Jamie responded, stepping in the direction of the school.

Fancie pursed her lips in Jamie's direction. "Ooh, are there tomatoes in the fridge?"

Fucking critics.

***

They had homeroom class, which, as usual, was an opportunity to write notes to each other. Science Park High School was the "Home of the Chargers." They used to joke years ago that it was home of the phone chargers but that was getting a bit old. Last year, they had celebrated the 70th anniversary of the school, which is pretty much the full life expectancy for a high school so, in Jamie's head, she imagined they were on borrowed time.

Her presentation was in speech class, which was next. She noted that when you're a senior, you have more and more classes like speech where the students do all the work and teachers just sit back and critique. And Jamie was mostly ok with it. No one needs to be talked at for an hour, then move to another room and be talked at for another hour. Not exactly the hero's journey.

She had learned that last year.

When they moved to Ms. Carvin's speech class, she put her bag on the desk in front of her. She took a deep breath and waited. Ms. Carvin was tall and thin. In a lot of ways she looked like Jamie, but her style was impossibly old fashioned. She often dressed as though she were a 1950's housewife, a hundred years earlier. The 1950's were just not the time for an intelligent, educated Black woman to be conjuring. Jamie liked her, but this alone made her question her judgment.

As well, Jamie thought Ms. Carvin was one of those overly earnest teachers who was committed to the idea that everyone would all remember her when they got old and somehow, her memory would guide them to do the right thing. She was never sure how much of this was responsibility and how much was pure Greek hubris.

Yeah, they learned that last year, too.

Jamie was the first to step up. To be clear here: Jamiehe liked giving speeches. A lot of people have trouble speaking in front of people. That was not her. She really liked speaking in public. She milked it, standing there and placing her bag on the podium.

And then she pulled out the book.

"Fellow Chargers, I want to talk to you about a mystery that I have discovered. A mystery that could change how we look at our world."

She lifted the book.

"This is a science fiction book, written in 2028, called Advance the Sky. It won a single book award when it was printed but failed to get much traction. It's the third book by the author, Jon Riley Killean. The annals of sci-fi history might consider it a forgettable book. Except for a hidden mystery between its covers."

She waved the book around. She felt like she was losing them.

"This book mentions, twice, the Savior Event, despite it having been written 17 years before this event."

The room started to get interested. Ms Carvin stood up and walked over to the podium.

"Can I see that?"

"Yes, here, I made note of the pages. Here, you can see the highlighted parts. It even describes the event."

Ms. Carvin read, wide-eyed. "This is… wow. How did you find out about this?"

"By accident. I started reading this." Jamie stepped back and continued as Ms. Carvin thumbed through the book.

"As we all know, the Savior Event, March 30th, 2045, was the day – the one day – where everyone on Earth who attempted to commit suicide, instead survived, and became invulnerable. These survivors are now called Salvado or Salvada – the Saved."

Ms. Carvin looked uncomfortable. "I'm not 100% sure that this is an appropriate topic for the classroom."

"I get that, Ms. Carvin. What do you think this writer knew? And how?"

The teacher shook her head and stepped back to her desk, still looking through the book. She was pulled in by the mystery, Jamie could tell.

Jamie reached back into her bag. "Was he some sort of traveler, with a unique connection to this event? I ask you this because I am a traveler of a sort, with a unique connection to the event."

She pulled out the scalpel from her bag and in one fluid motion, drew it over the wrist she held in the air. The room gasped as the knife passed effortlessly over her skin, leaving no mark.

"Because I am a Salvada, too."

And that was what it took to make the room go wild.

***

Jamie, Reina, and Fancie sat together in a row of chairs outside the principal's office as Jamie's mom arrived. Nica Symone was a surgeon. She was a pretty woman in her early forties whose resemblance to her daughter was near-perfect. She had long, straightened hair today, but when left to her own devices, preferred to change up her look as often as possible. She was dressed in jeans and a white blouse, but still wore her "Monica" nametag from University Hospital, right around the corner, really, from the school. If she was annoyed today, she hid it well. If anything, she looked playful as she walked in and stood in front of the girls.

"Heavy sigh. What did you animals do?"

Jamie stood up and gave her mom a hug, "I gave a presentation."

Nica hugged her back, kissing her on the head. "Must have gone over really well."

Jamie shrugged. "I liked it"

A slightly plump Polish woman motioned to them from the desk in front. "The principal is ready for you"

Nica nodded and stepped through the doorway into Ms. Glynnis's office, holding the door for the girls. Jamie and the two girls sat down but her mom stood, right behind them. Ms. Glynnis was a shorter, light skinned Black woman in a fire-red top and a row of pearls. Her office was decked out in wood and felt old-fashioned and warm. She herself, however, gave the impression that she might have been a lot colder than that. She stood up to shake Nica's hand.

"Hello, Mrs. Symone. Thank you for coming down."

Jamie's mom nodded, ignoring the hand. "Uh-huh."

Ms Glynnis sat back down and smoothed her skirt. She seemed to search for words. "Were you aware that your daughter…"

Nica nodded and prodded her. "That my daughter?"

The principal looked awkward and solemn. "I don't want to be the one to tell you if you didn't know, but that your daughter is a survivor?"

Nica nodded. "We're a family of survivors, Ms. Glynnis."

Ms Glynnis shook her head, "That's not what I mean."

Nica put her hand on her daughter's head and leaned down to kiss it. "Yes, I know what you mean. My daughter is a Salvada. I know. We've been dealing with it privately." She reached down to hold Jamie's hand.

The principal pulled herself up, sitting taller in her seat. "Until today, Mrs. Symone, when she gave a presentation and showed people how she could not be hurt, using this." She placed a scalpel on the desk.

Nica looked down at her daughter. "Is that true, Jam?"

"I took one of your scalpels," Jamie responded, looking up to see her mother's face.

She petted her daughter's shoulder and caught her eyes. "If I locked up all the cleaning supplies at home would you steal those and clean?"

Jamie kept eye contact and shook her head. "Is that facetious? Because no."

Ms. Glynnis slipped into teacher mode. "These are heady concepts. The class might have been traumatized."

Nica took a deep breath. "Were you girls traumatized?"

Reina shook her head. "No."

"Lunch traumatized me," Fancie interjected.

Jamie's mom looked over at the principal again, pointing at Reina and Fancie, "What did they do wrong?"

Reina answered, "Oh, we're here for moral support."

"And escaping lunch," Fancie followed up.

Nica shrugged and lifted her arms in the air. "There you go. Stop serving square pizza. We're going to go now."

"We haven't talked about punishment"

Nica stared daggers at the seated woman. "No, we have not."

Ms. Glynnis looked down at her desk. "I think we need to discuss…"

Nica stepped around the girls and stood directly in front of the desk. "Do you want to discuss it? Okay. My husband had a debilitatingly painful disease called sickle cell anemia. It causes your blood cells to be shaped strangely. His case was very severe. His organs were shutting down. It affects different people differently, and for him it was excruciating pain, sometimes all day, every day. His eyes failed and he was constantly exhausted, blind, and in screaming pain. There is still no cure. After he lost his spleen and he couldn't walk or work anymore, he decided to take his own life. He was a beautiful, kind, wonderful father, a great doctor, and the best husband anyone ever made and a year afterward, the daughter he doted on had a rare moment of weakness and she tried to do the same thing."

The principal paused, "rare moment of weakness?"

"Yes. You want to talk about punishment? I'm dying to hear this." Nica crossed her arms.

Ms. Glynnis pulled on her glasses. "It was inappropriate to…"

Jamie's mom bent over the desk and interjected, quietly, "to what? To open up to her class and tell them something that hurt?"

The woman on the other side of the desk pushed herself back a few inches. She attempted a weak smile. "Maybe home is a better place for that."

Nica stood up straight and turned around, facing the girls. "You think so? Great idea. C'mon, ladies, we're going to brunch."

Jamie shrugged at the principal as they filed out.

***

The four of them rode the escalator up to the top floor of The Mills at Jersey Gardens and stepped into Marshall's. They walked through the swimwear section, making fun of the bikinis, and landed in the luggage section.

Jamie looked around. "I thought we were going to brunch"

Nica pieced through the bags. "Eventually. Find a suitcase."

Jamie stepped over to her mom. "Wait, why?"

Nica spoke to the group. "We're going on a road trip. Fuck that school. Science Park is a dumb ass name for a school."

"Really? Where to?" Jamie looked confused.

Her mom seemed more determined than ever. "I don't know. I literally just thought of this." She stepped over to a large zebra bag. "How about this one?"

Jamie cocked her head, "Why is everything some animal print to you, mom? Is this Wild Planet?"

Fancie found a bag, "This one has leaves."

"Ooh, I like that one." Reina punched it to see how strong it was.

Nica called out over her shoulder, "good, get one for yourself."

Reina looked up. "Why?"

Jamie's mom walked over to her. "Because you're coming with. Find a big one. I'll get you an ice cream if you can pack it all the way. "

Reina stood up as straight as she could. "I'm not a kid"

Nica moved over to the artistic looking bags. "Do you want an ice cream?"

Reina pouted a little as she realized. "I kind of do."

"Then don't complain."

"Why would you take me with?" Reina looked up at the older woman.

Nica stepped over and put her hands on Reina's face. "Because I don't know where your parents are and I'm not leaving you here alone."

The girl spoke with her cheeks compressed. "How do you know I'm alone?"

"Because I'm not an idiot, Reina. You have Jamie…"

Fancie interjected, "And me."

Nica squeezed Reina's face and shook it back and forth, replying in baby talk, "I don't know who that is."

"I'm her friend, too." Fancie put out her hand.

Jamie's mom accepted the hand and shook it. "But I don't know you."

"Okay." Fancie stepped back.

Nica pushed Reina. "Look, sweety, Jamie loves you. And, by the transitive power, so do I. So figure out what kind of ice cream you like, choose a bag and shove your shit in it. I like the giraffe one."

Fancie spoke up, "can I come?"

Nica looked her over playfully. "Didn't I just say I don't know you?"

Fancie smiled earnestly. "I grow on people fast."

"What's your name?" Jamie's mom looked at the girl with a faux seriousness.

Jamie stepped over. "Her name is actually Fancie."

Nica pretended to be surprised. "No shit."

"It fits, too," Reina noted.

"Do you want her to come?"

Jamie nodded. "Sure. I mean, I have no idea where we're going…"

Nica stood to her full height. "You've got maps on your phone. Find something."

Jamie laughed. "Are we seriously just going to drive? Don't you have a job, Mom?"

"I'll tell them I'm taking a paid sabbatical to study you. They'll love it. It's a research and teaching hospital."

"So, I'm a white mouse?" Jamie cocked her head.

Nica grabbed her daughter and roughly shook her. "Oh, baby, you're not a white anything. Find a mirror and pack it, Black girl."

Fancie looked excited, "We'll be the black mice. Should I get a bag, too?"

Jamie's mom tried to pick her up and drag her as she doled out advice. "Don't just get the plain one. That's the mistake everyone makes. Then some secret agent accidentally swaps bags with you and bam, you're in a deadly spy thriller." Jamie giggled and pretended to flop in her arms.

Fancie called out, holding a bright red bag with what looked like cave drawings on it.

"What about this?"

Nica scanned it.

"Love it."

***

Luckily, Fancie's parents were the "experience broadens you" slightly hippie variety, so they were on board. Nica made a note to get to know them better when the road trip was over as they met her at the door with a bunch of clothing and snacks for the girls. Her house was pretty but not as big as the girls had imagined. Her parents gave her a surfeit of kisses for the trip and a little wireless hotspot box to make life easier and make sure she was in touch. Nica noticed how often they touched each other's hands, leaning in, pretending it was accidental, and she felt a flood of feelings for them. Their relationship looked familiar.

Turner was like that, too. Nica and Turner. They never missed a chance to bump against each other. She loved the way his hands felt accidentally moving her around as they passed in the hallway, a little tweak, a tiny dance, a pat. Sometimes she would slap him on the butt when he least expected it. He'd smile and wink back at her. She remembered when they walked down the street when the mattress stores had big sales, propping up mattresses against the front of the buildings, how he'd walk on the outside and push her into the mattresses, pressing her in and trapping her until she gave him a little kiss.

The night Jamie was conceived, she was sure they had been playing that game where he tried to get her panties before she could stop him, throwing her down on the bed and masterfully sliding them off to steal them while she squealed, pretending to fight back. She would climb on top of him, fighting half-heartedly to get them back. Hell, she couldn't count how many times he had tackled her even just onto the couch before he got sick.

Before he got sick.

She gave Fancie's parents a hug and the girls packed into her black van. She probably had room for four more kids in there, but three seemed good.

They stopped off at the Yard for brunch. Being a weekday, it was virtually empty. But that wasn't the big revelation. The paper box right outside was being filled with the evening edition of the Newark Star. It was a tiny paper, just for very local news. And Jamie's picture was on the front.

She winced when she realized it was her yearbook photo from last year. But that didn't stop her from grabbing one from the box.

"Holy shit, did you guys see this?" She held it out. The Star was free, if that gives you any idea of its value as a news publication.

Fancie grabbed one. "Wow. You are famous." She held the picture up to Jamie's face to see how well it matched.

"Do you feel famous?" Reina grabbed her arm.

Jamie looked up at Nica. "Mom, did you see this?"

Nica sighed. "I got a phone alert just now. Local news."

Jamie pushed her. "I can't believe you didn't say anything."

"What am I supposed to say? The news is slow."

Jamie paused. It was starting to sink in what she had done. "I didn't realize…"

Her mom brushed her hair away from her face. "Look, you're 17 years old. People shouldn't be letting you make life-altering decisions. That's on them."

They moved toward the entrance of the Yard. There was a long ADA-compliant ramp that swirled up to the front door. Reina and Fancie were already running up it.

"I'm sorry."

Nica grabbed her hand. "Well, don't be. I mean, the cat's out of the bag, but cats never really behaved in bags to start with."

Fancie yelled out, "cats are crazy!"

"See? What she said." They all made their way through the front door of the fancy brunch place.

Jamie pulled the door behind them. "I really didn't think all that through, did I?"

"What do you want me to say? No. You didn't. But, hey, you might actually live forever. This paper will be compost in two weeks." Nica tossed the paper into the trash can in the front area of the restaurant.

"Very funny, Mom."

They slid into a booth in the back and the waitress brought coffee, setting cups out, alongside four glasses of water.

Nica filled her cup and opened up a couple of cream containers from a tiny bowl in the center of the table. "You know what I think?"

Jamie poured a cup of coffee and started filling it with sugar from a glass container. "I'm going to find out, aren't I?"

Fancie reached out to fill her cup. "I want to know."

Nica took a drink and lifted her cup. "My daughter's alive. And I don't even read this newspaper. And all the coffee in this town sucks, so we should keep moving. But my daughter's alive."

Reina was looking down at her phone. "I know where we should go"

"Thank god someone has an idea." Nica turned to face Reina.

"It's 27 hours away if we don't stop, even to pee."

"Well, let's multiply that time by six, because only two of us have a driver's license, I think. How about we drive for four hours a day?" Nica seemed to be thinking, pulling numbers out of her head.

"What do we do with the other time?" Fancie asked.

Nica shook her head. "We fuck around. We play. We do stupid shit. What the hell kind of kids are you? Are you secret grown-ups?"

"Wait, where are we going?" Jamie looked confused.

Reina handed her her phone. "Here."

Jamie looked down and held the phone about two feet from her face. "Wait, NASA?"

Fancie hooted, "nice!"

"Yes. Then we can trade in the van for a spaceship." Nica nodded.

"Wooooo."

There was no one in the restaurant to complain about the girls banging on the table.

***

They drove six hours that day, actually, screaming and singing for most of it. And even though Reina also had a driver's license, Nica decided to take the whole way. They stopped a lot, though, and, at the end, pulled into a pretty hotel called the Bethesdan right outside Washington, D.C.

They grabbed their bags and rode up the elevator. The hotel looked like it was recently remodeled. It was dark and classy, filled with black and grey slate and stone and hidden lighting. Nica had thought the gothic aesthetic might have clicked with Jamie and she wasn't wrong. They passed the pool on the way to the room, giggling and running through the halls.

The room was cute, with two king-sized beds and a large bathroom behind a sliding barn door, Big shower enclosed in glass. Nica flopped onto the bed closest to the door and Fancie ran over to the other one, bouncing up and down on it.

"You know, I'm sad I didn't get to see the end of your presentation." Reina put her bag down next to the far bed and nodded at Jamie.

"Meh. It was good."

Nica laid back on the bed, "What were you talking about in your presentation? You know – besides the thing."

"Oh." Jamie set her bag on the bed and rifled through it. "Where is it? Here. This." She handed the book over to her mom.

"What's this?" Nica held the book over her head and flipped through it.

"Here." Jamie laid down next to her and opened it to the highlighted page. "The author talks about the Savior Event."

"What does he say about it?"

Reina interjected, "it's not what he says. It's when."

"When?" Nica sat up.

"The book was written in 2028. It's a sci-fi book that talks about the Savior Event." Jamie looked over at her mom, who was starting to figure it out.

"So he wrote about it like 17 years before it happened?"

"That's right. Advance the Sky." Jamie looked triumphant.

"Holy crap. How did you find this?" Nica was far more impressed than the class was.

"I just started reading it."

"And no one is talking about this?"

Jamie shook her head. "Nope. Not even the AI seem to know about it."

"No shit."

Fancie peered out the window, squinting. "Hey, guys, there's that red car."

Nica looked over, "What red car?"

Reina was pulling her clothes out of her bag and making a neat pile. "The red car we saw in Baltimore."

"And Philly." Fancie pointed.

Nica stood up. "It's the same car, are you sure?"

Jamie nodded, moving over to the window. "It is. You didn't see it?"

"Someone's following us."

"It's got New York plates," Reina pointed out. "See?"

Nica grabbed a black metal pole from behind the suspended counter. The counter slipped down an inch or two as the support wavered. She lifted it over her shoulder.

"Be right back."

***

Nica pulled the door of their room shut and made her way to the parking lot, pushing open the front door of the hotel and marching to the red car with New York plates. A tall blond kid who couldn't have been more than 17 was half asleep in the front seat, seemingly startled by her advance. He reached to start the car as Nica approached, bringing the metal pole down hard on the front of his windshield.

From inside, he panicked. "Whoa! Whoa! That was my window!"

She brought the pole down again, widening the hole in his windshield as he covered his eyes.

"And now I can reach your face."

He yelled out, "okay, stop! Stop!"

Nica put the pole over her shoulder again. "Why are you following us?"

"I'm not following you."

She swung the pole and shattered his driver's side window.

"Wait, stop. Stop breaking my windows."

Nica raised her voice, "You are clearly following us, Dexter, what the fuck."

He held his hands up and made a motion to open the car door. "I'm not a serial killer."

Jamie and the other two girls ran out of the front door, circling Nica with amazement. "Mom, who is he?"

"You girls go back to the room."

"I'm not dangerous." The boy stood up. He was even taller than he looked. Nica could see he was young. So young.

Reina shrugged. "He says he's not dangerous."

Nica raised her pole and advanced. "Of course he does."

The boy shook his hands in front of him. "I'm not!"

Fancie stepped over and crossed her arms. "So, why are you following us?"

The boy was breathing hard when he held up his hands as if in surrender. He showed them his left hand and reached over to the shattered window next to him, running his palm against the ring of glass shards. He held it up again and showed them.

No blood.

Nico lowered her pole. "You're Salvado."

"I don't know anyone. No one to talk to. But I saw her in the paper..."

He pointed to Jamie.

"So you just wanted to talk to me?"

He nodded.

Nica sighed and turned back toward the hotel. "Okay. So let's talk."

***

The hotel restaurant was one level below the pool. From the documentation, Jamie knew that the indoor pool (unlike the available outdoor pool in the courtyard in back) was built out only ten years ago, in 2036. She sat at the table and tried not to look up. The pool looked huge. Not Olympic-sized, for sure. But massive. She tried to imagine how many pounds of water and tile that might be. And all of it, every ounce of it, was suspended right above them.

She fantasized about cracks in the ceiling, widening, growing, separating, letting loose this torrent of water from above, drowning them, washing away everyone in the restaurant until just a clean, sterile room was left behind, devoid of life.

It seemed like poor planning.

"So, how did you do it?" Reina asked the boy, reaching for the basket of bread.

"Hold on. Can we start with like, I don't know, what's his name?" Nica grabbed the butter away from Reina and got to work on her own bread.

Jamie played Great Equalizer. "Okay, so what is your name?"

The boy looked at them. This entire thing was new to him. He looked like he wanted to sink into his chair. "I'm Clyde. Clyde Morrison."

"Your name is Clyde?" Fancie looked confused.

Nica laughed. "White people are naming their kids Clyde?"

Clyde looked down. "Apparently. I'm from Queens."

Reina took a bite of her bread. "Okay, Clyde from Queens. How did you do it?"

For the first time, Nica looked at her sternly. "Reina."

"It's okay." Clyde took a beat. "It's a fair question." He breathed in and out. "I hanged myself. I had this...I found this thick purple rope in the closet and I... Well, I wrapped it around my neck in a kind of thing, like a noose, I guess. And I wrapped the other part on a pipe and kicked a chair away."

"And then what?" Jamie was particularly fixated. She didn't know any others, either. To hear this story about what Clyde went through was weirdly liberating. On one level, she couldn't believe her mom was letting it happen. Did she realize that maybe Jamie needed this?

"And then, I hung there. For about three hours. I couldn't get down. I couldn't die. It didn't hurt. It didn't feel like anything. I just hung there and tried to think about what came next. I tried to figure out how I would get down."

The table went quiet. Reina asked, quietly, "how did you get down?"

Clyde tried to sound jolly. He smiled. "After a few hours, my pulling at the rope had loosened it, I guess. I fell. That didn't hurt, either."

"Right." Jamie interjected. "I...uh... tried to cut myself in the bath. It took me a few times before I realized that it wasn't doing anything. The water was close to my own temperature. It all felt like the same. Like everything was just... you know. The same. But I thought it was the knife."

"The scalpel." Nica echoed.

"I'm sorry, Mom." Jamie burrowed into her mother. "I'm sorry. For a second, after, I realized that you would feel responsible because it was your scalpel."

"I know you didn't mean to."

"It wasn't your fault."

"It's okay. It's okay. I miss your dad, too."

Reina's eyes filled up with tears. "Your dad was pretty great. He made me play basketball with him once while I was waiting for you. I laughed so hard, I almost peed."

Nica grabbed Reina's hand. "He adored you girls."

Fancie looked at Clyde. "Why did you do it?"

"I don't know. I think about it a lot. I thought about it a lot. I just always felt... off. Like I wasn't made to make it. I didn't feel like I should outlive anyone. I know that doesn't make any sense."

"Do you have anything you want to ask Jamie?" Nica chose her words carefully. He had followed them three states away just to talk to her.

Clyde's face was like stone one moment. The next, his eyes pressed tightly and filled with tears. His chest bounced and he began to sob. His head dropped. He breathed in once."

"How...How are you?"

Jamie reached over and grabbed his hands. She nodded at him. "I'm okay, Clyde. I'm good. I'm going to be okay." For a moment, Jamie could feel it again, the weight of the pool above them, threatening to overflow, to fall, to obliterate them at any moment. She wanted to protect Clyde from that.

To shield him from the water.

The waitress gave them a few moments.

***

Nica returned to the room after dinner while the girls were watching a scary movie. It was some claustrophobic thing on a spaceship where the interior of the ship kept changing sizes, creating a dilemma for the astronauts trying to make their way to a new world to terraform it for colonizers already scheduled to arrive. There were regular jumpscares but primarily a psychological thing. She made a note to watch it all the way through.

It looked good.

She slid into the bed next to Jamie. Jamie whispered to her.

"Is he going to be all right alone?"

Nica nodded. "Yep. I got him a room a few doors down, The windshield people are coming in the morning to repair his car. He says he wants to follow us."

"That's probably good. He shouldn't be alone."

"No." Nica put her arm around Jamie. "He talked to me a little when I dropped him off in his room. He laughed about it, but it's obviously a huge issue. He's eighteen now."

Jamie nodded. "Yeah."

"But he's going to look seventeen. Probably for the rest of his life. Maybe. It's so weird."

"It really is." Jamie leaned in to her mom.

"Does that bother you? The fact that you may look sixteen, like…"

"Forever?" Jamie finished. "I think about it. I mean, I'm not aging. I'm not anything. I can't be hurt." She braced herself and continued. "Do you know I don't have periods anymore?"

"Shit." Nica pulled back and put her hands on the girl's face. "Why didn't you tell me? How am I missing this? I'm a terrible mother."

"No, no, you're great. I just didn't want to accept it. I never told you. It's like I'm frozen in time."

"That's incredibly weird."

"What if I live for hundreds of years? Thousands?"

Nica sighed. "I have to admit, part of me is overjoyed not having to worry about you getting hurt, physically. But I know there are lots of other ways to get hurt."

"Tell me the truth. If that kid could physically hurt himself, would you have left him alone in his own room?"

Jamie's mom thought for a minute. Not long. Her daughter knew her pretty well, which actually felt great. Being known, being seen. It doesn't suck.

"Not in a million years."

"You're such a mom." Jamie squeezed her hand. As she looked over, she saw that Reina and Fancie had fallen asleep curled up, protecting each other from the movie. As grateful as she was for her girls, in this room, she couldn't wait until tomorrow to talk to Clyde again.

***

"Wait, so why are you 'little bitch'?" Nica asked over the top of her giant plate of melon.

"I don't know if you remember, but I used to be the short one." Reina laughed.

"Mom, she was so tiny."

"That's right. So my daughter is 'tough bitch'?"

Jamie nodded as they all squealed, "of course."

"You know she's still ticklish, right?" Nica proceeded to tickle Jamie.

"I will pee. Cut it out." Jamie poked her mom with both pointer fingers.

"I'm obviously 'fancy bitch.'"

Nice smiled at her. "Of course you are. You'll have to order the wine."

Clyde made his way to the table with his ear to the phone. "Okay, one sec."

He held the phone out to Nica and whispered, "they want to talk to you."

She slid out of the booth and grabbed the phone, stepping out of the restaurant.

Jamie looked at Clyde. "Is something wrong?"

Clyde scrunched his face up. "Yep. They can't fix the windows and you can't drive a car without a windshield, apparently. It's against the law."

Reina grabbed some fruit from the center of the table. "Fucking laws."

"So, what are you going to do?" Jamie put a few items on a plate for Clyde.

"They're going to tow my car back to Queens, actually." He popped a grape into his mouth, "and I'll figure it out.

"We will figure it out." Jamie winked at him.

Nica walked back in and handed the phone back to Clyde. "Okay. Plan B. Instead of following us, Clyde rides with us to Houston. Your parents are cool with towing the car back. And let's all thank Clyde for not telling his mom and dad that I'm the one who beat up his car."

The girls all cheered. Clyde actually smiled. "Well, we didn't need any more drama, I figured."

"Damn right. No drama." Nica playfully pushed her way back in the booth, knocking the girls over.

Clyde looked up. "So. We're going to Houston. Houston, Texas?"

Fancie laughed, "That is the best Houston."

"Why?" Clyde looked around the table.

Jamie put her hand on his arm. "We're going to NASA. Don't you want to see NASA?"

"The space place?" Clyde looked confused.

"We're all space nerds. And my mom's a scientist."

"I'm a doctor. A research doctor. I guess I'm a scientist." Nica nodded.

"Like with white robes and stuff?" Clyde smiled.

Nica sat up taller. "It's white coats. Lab coats. Shut up or I'll experiment on you."

"Don't you like space?" Reina furrowed her brow.

"I mean, I don't hate it."

***

The next hotel was the Kasa Dilworth in Charlotte, North Carolina. Nica got an apartment suite with three rooms, a den and a kitchen. She took Clyde to shop for dinner while the girls settled in. She tried to see into his head, but he was impenetrable. In all honesty, she had no experience with male kids. She'd been a mom to a teenage girl and her teenage girlfriends. Jamie rarely had boys around.

"I really do appreciate you not busting me with your parents."

"Yeah well, following you guys was kind of creepy. I'm sorry." Clyde ran his hands over the shelves.

"Still. We're doing Italian? Is that right?" Nica remembered they'd talked about it back in the room. Something pasta-y.

"If I remember correctly. Do you have ideas?"

"I do. I was thinking that there would be a mushroom cream sauce involved." Nica reached for some thick pasta and threw a couple boxes in the cart.

"I like it."

"What's your mom like?"

"Well. She's not as pretty as you."

"Oh, my god, are you hitting on me?" Nica smiled at Clyde.

"No, no, honestly, I'm sorry."

"I'm kidding, Clyde, it's all good." Nica tossed some oregano into the cart. Dried would be fine.

"Oh, right. Well, my mom probably would have said no to all this if I asked. So it's good that you talked to her."

"Does she know?"

"That I'm Salvado? No. I'm afraid to tell her. And she's going to see it soon if I stay at home."

Nica leaned on the cart and pushed it toward the dairy section. "Where would you go?"

"I don't know. I hadn't thought about it. But the clock is ticking, you know?"

"I guess that's true. Hey, you aren't lactose intolerant, are you?"

Clyde smiled. "I am pro milk."

"Good." Nica picked out a carafe container of cream and slipped it into the cart.

"I've never been to North Carolina." He looked around.

"You know, I haven't either." Nica turned to him and fixed his collar. "One day. You have time, you know. One day, you might say you've been to every state. You might have a hundred years to do that. Maybe more."

Clyde closed his eyes. "Maybe. It's possible. Do you like the fact that Jamie's going to live a long time, maybe?"

Nica smiled widely. "Clyde, I love it. I hope she does. I hope she sees everything. I hope she goes everywhere."

Clyde reached out and put his hand around her arm. "She's really lucky."

Nica looked down. "Are you okay?" Clyde's hand felt like a call for help. Was she missing something?

Clyde smiled wanly, "I'm okay, Ms. Symone. I just think Jamie is, just, you know...lucky."

"I appreciate that, Clyde." Nica tossed some bread into the cart.

Then she tossed in some more. You can never have too much bread.

***

They laughed all through dinner, then they sat in the den and watched a movie about reluctant werewolves who wanted to do the right thing but were just hungry all the time. It was a grotesque sort of bloody comedy. Jamie realized she had forgotten to check what was in the room right above this one. She imagined it was empty. No reason to worry.

Probably.

And Nica noticed that Jamie had put her feet on Clyde's shoulders as he sat on the floor, and every time the movie made them laugh, her feet danced next to his ears. He held her foot and she didn't pull away.

Clyde went to sleep in the smaller room and Reina and Fancie retired to the biggest one. Nica tried to carry Jamie into the middle room with her, but she was just a little too big. They flopped all over each other onto the bed, laughing, and were asleep in minutes above the covers while a small skylight exposed millions of naked stars overhead, each trying its best to be inspirational and gravitically majestic, fiery, and important, but found, each one, that they were too far away to be anything but mildly twinkly.

***

The next hotel had a fully stocked kitchen. The Enchanted, in Atlanta, Georgia, was right across the street from a 24-hour convenience store, too, proving that being prepared was never prepared enough. And even though the route was only meant to be four hours long, they had made sure to stop at every book store, card shop, and comic store they could on the way. Even if these children didn't know how to have fun natively, Nica was determined to teach them.

They would have fun if she had to force them, dammit.

For future reference, there is a reason why Jamie would blame herself for what happened next.

She's the one who asked for ice cream, causing Clyde to run downstairs to the convenience store, a store that was currently in the process of being robbed by two men who had shot the police officers trying to stop them.

The sound of sirens, bullets, and screams had caused quite a few of the hotel guests of the occupants to spill out onto the street, standing behind the yellow ribbon that marked thecrime scene.

Nica couldn't keep the girls from panicking and wanting to see. It was all she could do to keep them back, behind the police line. The night was dark and cool, but Jamie could see right into the store. She could see Clyde sitting there, covered in blood. She pulled her mom behind her and ran to the nearest officer.

They were waiting for the negotiator to arrive. At first, they didn't believe that Clyde didn't have a gun. Eventually they realized that Jamie was his friend. Nica toyed with the idea of telling them that they were both Salvado. But she wasn't sure if that would have caused them to amplify what was happening. The conversation, she couldn't help but see in the media, was around whether or not these people were weapons.

Whether they were dangerous.

In the end, it was Jamie who walked into the store to confront him. Clyde sat on the floor in the back up against the beverage coolers. He was covered in blood, a gun just a few feet away from him. He looked terrifying.

He looked terrified.

But this was just Clyde.

Jamie walked over and sat next to him. He looked at her out of the corner of his eye. He let his head slide back against the glass of the cooler section. Jamie took a deep breath.

"Do you know where they keep the snowcones?"

Clyde chuckled a little. "I didn't really look around much."

Jamie took it all in. Shelves were tipped over, blood was all over the floor and two police officers were lying dead. Three customers and the clerk were there, face down. Dead.

"This is a mess."

Clyde nodded. "Yeah"

"What are you doing here, Clyde?"

"I thought…" he trailed off.

Suddenly Jamie was angry. "You weren't thinking. You were running toward death. You're like a moth, running toward the light."

He turned to her. "I am."

Jamie turned toward him. "But you can't die. You don't think it's time to learn how to live?"

Clyde shut his eyes. Tears fell down his cheeks. "I thought I could give it away."

"What do you mean?'

"This thing, I thought I could give it away. I felt him, that cop over there. I felt him dying." Clyde pointed toward the cop closest to them

"You felt him?"

"He didn't want to die. He was hanging on so hard."

"He wanted to live?"

Clyde shook his head vigorously. "Yes"

Jamie put her hand on top of his. He was cold. He felt like marble. "And you don't?"

He shook his head furiously, over and over. "No."

"You felt like you could give it away?"

"I don't want it. Jamie, I can't do it." He turned toward her. He couldn't meet her eyes.

"Shh. I get it. The blood?" She pointed to the blood all over him.

"I tried. I held onto him while he died. I did everything I could. I tried. I wanted to…"

Jamie whispered, "you wanted it to go to him?"

"And now he's gone. I felt it. He didn't have to die."

Jamie sat up, pointing around the room, "but he did. And so did he. And him. And we're still here."

He closed his eyes. "I can't do it. I can't be here. I'm not supposed to…"

"Not supposed to be here?" Jamie asked, moving his hair out of his face.

"How are you okay?" Clyde whispered.

Jamie shook her head. "I just am, Clyde. I have to be. I don't have a choice. I just am."

"I don't want to be. Why can't I give it away?"

"I'm sorry, Clyde. I'm sorry." Jamie took his head and held it. She started to cry.

"Don't cry. This is my… this is my issue."

Jamie put her hands on his head and lifted his eyes to face her. "The other officers. They want to take you in for questioning."

He nodded obediently. "Okay."

Jamie breathed out, "but, Clyde. I can't wait. I can't be around you right now."

He started sobbing. There was no air behind the two words out of his mouth, "but, why….?"

Jamie held his hand. "Because we can't give it away. We have to live with it. And I have to learn that, too. I have to learn how to be here."

He rocked, moaning. "I know."

"And I can't watch out for you at the same time."

"I know." The words came from so far down inside him. They came from an animal place. They came from a primal place.

Jamie petted his head. "Clyde, I'm not okay. I'm not healthy. I'm not making it. My nose is right above the water. The water is constantly ready to fall. The roof is ready to come down."

He looked right into her eyes. He tried to connect. "I know."

Jamie whispered, "do you forgive me?"

The word tore through a sob. Clyde inhaled.

"Yes."

"Will you do me a favor?" Jamie slicked down his hair.

"Yes."

Jamie leaned in. "In 100 years, if we're still around, will you meet me here?"

Clyde laughed, his face a mess of tears. "I don't think they'll let me back in here."

"Oh my god, you're not wrong," Jamie laughed.

Clyde put his hand in hers. "I mean, I wouldn't let me back in here."

Jamie squeezed his hand, hard. "Across the street. In 100 years. Can you do that?"

Clyde nodded over and over. "Yes."

She leaned in and kissed him, pressing her mouth against his, slightly open, warm, soft. She stayed there for just a minute.

"Hold that for me. Can you give it back to me when we meet up?"

He took a deep breath and tried to compose himself. "In 100 years."

She took both of his hands. "And tell me everything you've done and everything you want to do and how you made it, and I'll tell you how I made it."

"Tell your mom I'm sorry."

"She'll make sure you have a ticket when you're done." Jamie slid up the glass door. She put her hand down to help him up.

He stood up straight. Jamie noticed he was so much taller than her. And would be forever. She wouldn't grow another inch.

He squeezed her hand. "Thank you."

She lifted her hands. "You have to put your hands up. When we walk out. Okay? If they shoot at us, the bullets could ricochet and hurt people."

Clyde nodded. "I know. You're right."

And the two of them stepped out the front door with their hands in the air.

***

Nica found Jamie sitting on the platform of a billboard right next to the hotel, advertising a fruity drink. It was an impossibly happy sign, one that felt ironic in this setting. She looked up and saw her daughter twenty-five feet in the air and felt that swirl in her belly whenever her child stepped onto a high porch, or too close to a roof's edge. That feeling that she couldn't protect her. Not when she was in the womb. Not now, when she was out.

Not anywhere.

"Can you come down?"

"Why?"

Nica considered the answer to that. "So we can talk?"

"I'm sorry, Mom. I kinda don't want to talk."

Nica stepped over until she was right below her. "That's fair. I'm sorry."

"Are Reina and Fancie ok?"

"Oh yeah, they're back in the room. I just wanted to... how about you listen instead? Did I ever tell you about the night I told your dad I was pregnant with you?"

Jamie looked down. "No. Why didn't you?"

Nica took in the night air. It was dark and it felt like she and Jamie might have been the only people left in the world. "It's a – it's complicated."

"Did he freak out?" Jamie laughed.

Nica cocked her head. "No. Not at all. I did," she confessed.

"Bullshit."

"Can you come down?"

Jamie stepped over the edge of the platform and landed right next to her mom, sinking downward for a moment, before standing upright.

"Damn. You're getting kind of good at that."

"Yeah, I jump off roofs all the time now. Just not in front of anyone."

"Right." Nica grabbed her daughter's hand. "Before you came along, I had a miscarriage. Two, actually. One was at 14 weeks. It hurt so bad. Your dad had all these names picked out. He was so..."

"Worried."

Nica shook her head. "No. Happy. You know he always wanted to be a dad. Two miscarriages. And the last one was only six months before."

Jamie leaned in to her. "I didn't know that."

"Well, we didn't tell you. I found out I was pregnant with you and I cried. I wanted you so bad. But I felt like it would just be another build-up."

"Another let-down," Jamie whispered.

Nica continued. "I felt like I was crushing him. Like I was beating him down. Like I was strangling him. But when I told him, he was just happy. There was nothing dark in his face, no fear, nothing. He laughed and hugged me. He told me that his job was just to hope. And he had so much of that."

Jamie thought about her dad. "Hope."

"He told me that for me, for you – for a baby – he had an endless supply of hope and he would give me some every morning if I needed it. He had extra. He held me close and danced with me and told me he was entirely composed of hope."

Nica reached down and took both of Jamie's hands.

Jamie said, with wonder, "he was happy."

"Turner loved being a father. He was willing to walk through hell to be one. Even if it meant digging little graves in his heart."

Jamie winced, "that's dark"

They started back toward the hotel. "Yeah, that's too far."

"Mom?" Jamie wrapped her fingers in her mother's hand and put her head on her shoulder as they walked.

"Yes, baby."

"What if we like Houston and we want to move there?"

"Then we do it," Nica said, absolutely.

"What about your job?" Jamie realized that she couldn't feel any pain from the fall, but she did feel the bracing chill from the night air, as a kind of cool breath on her skin. She could feel the warm softness of her mother's hand in hers and every comforting thing that came with it. And she had felt the sleek wetness of Clyde's kiss as it lit a fire through her whole body. She knew he felt it, too.

"I'm a doctor. I can get a job anywhere. Anywhere they have sick people."

And they went home.

3 - The Prisoner
Ramla, Israel - 2067

It's not easy to imagine Linus Flores indoors, so let's paint a picture.

First, you start with his hair. It probably began as a kind of dirty brown, but constant intervention by the sun had rendered it a deep yellow blond, even pushing some of the ends to white. It was pulled toward the back of his head, but it still flowed, liquid like, around his head, tucked back behind his ears and landing on his shoulders. It spilled out a bit in the back, not too much. But, yes, there was a party in the back. No doubt about it

He wore a linen suitcoat over a mandarin-cut white shirt, both light enough to offset his thick textured skin, also sun-touched, four or five shades intensified from his native pale Mexican roots. His wiry but muscular arms terminated in leather and steel bracelets, as did both his feet, poking out from below his linen pants into a pair of thick-strapped faux leather sandals. Luckily, his toenails had been cut perfectly long ago, because they hadn't grown in over 20 years.

And neither had he.

He padded softly down the nave of the prison with a brown faux leather suitcase bouncing at his hip in such a way as to suggest it might be empty.

More than anything, though, you would notice Linus Flores's smile. When he activated it, it seemed to collect the 50-plus years of sunlight he had accumulated and amplify it from the front of his face, a beacon that lit rooms and revealed...

What?

That was a question you could ask the people who sent him. Why would you pluck this person from atop some dangly precarious surfboard and send him into a dark prison cell?

He made his way to the last cell, a wide-open living room-type space with pillows scattered everywhere. The gate was closed, but unlocked. And in it was a 12-year-old girl in a black dress and head scarf, sitting with her legs beneath her, watching television.

Loudly.

She stared straight ahead as Linus opened the gate and slid in, dropping his suitcase on a side table near the entrance.

He stepped in and slid down to the floor in front of her, facing the television. Pulling up his legs, he wrapped his arms around them and listened.

"What the hell are we watching?"

The girl handed him the bowl of popcorn sitting on the sparse couch next to her and took a deep breath.

"This is The Fast and the Furious, number seven, I think. They've been playing all week on this channel in the wrong order."

Linus nodded. "That seems a bit surreal."

The girl showed him her notepad, also sitting next to her. "I've been making notes. But I'm not really getting it. I need to see the first one soon, I think."

Linus reached over for the notepad. "You see here. You wrote, it's about family. That's pretty much the whole thing, I think."

She looked at him. "How many of these are there? Is it just like infinite? Like forever?"

Linus thought, handing back the pad. "Okay. There were 17. Four more with Al Vin Diesel. I don't know if those count. And a cartoon, I think. So, almost infinite."

The girl took back her notebook. She looked at him closely.

"Nice. You're Salvado."

"I am. My name is Linus Flores. I'm the UN guy."

She laughed. "Well, I knew you weren't IDF."

He shook his head. "Absolutely not."

She stood up and offered him her hand. "Do you want to look around? It's why you're here, right?"

Linus took her hand and slid up. He was quite a bit taller than her, which made him want to slouch a bit. "It's part of why I'm here."

She left her hand in his, to shake it. "I'm Yazmin…"

"Oh, my god, I know who you are. Everyone on Earth knows who you are. Between you and me, I'm mostly here to streamline getting you out of here."

It was true that most of Earth knew who Yazmin Gazzawi was. She was born in Gaza in 2033 while bombs went off over her mother's head. She watched her family disappear one at a time before she could walk. She led the children's resistance against Israel when she was just 12 years old. And on March 30th, 245, she stood, fearless, in front of a tank that was rolling into a residential area to kill.

It didn't stop.

There was a Reuters camerawoman just a few meters away, filming the entire thing. And, in front of the whole world, live, streaming under a red-orange lightshow in the sky, she was pulled from the rubble left by the marauding tank, without a scratch on her.

Alive and unhurt.

She spent the next five years in a shithole underground prison where men with poorly-considered medical degrees and even more poorly-imagined ethics tried to figure her out. Then, as tensions between the two countries diminished, she moved to a slightly cleaner and more comfortable cell. This went on, over and over, with her surroundings mirroring the state of affairs between the two nations. And now, as the ceasefire loomed, she was here, where she had sat for the last two years, in an unlocked cell that resembled a student dorm.

Complete with a single television channel.

She pulled Linus behind her as she showed him around.

"Here is the shower. I am still amazed that I have a shower."

Linus shook his head. It wasn't much. His initial fear was that this whole thing was going to make him angry.

And despite all his efforts, it did.

She looked up at him. "So why are you carrying an empty briefcase? I think I know."

He resisted the urge to bend down. He knew she was really a 34-year-old woman, just as he was really some 50 years old, despite the fact that he had stopped aging himself at 35. He adjusted his tone, making sure he spoke to her as an adult.

"Okay, I'll give you first shot at that one."

She smiled. "Well, you have to have some way of asserting authority when you walk into a prison. The feeling that you are carrying important papers has to help. Also, something to do with your hands."

Linus laughed. "Well. You don't disappoint. You can tell if someone's one of us?"

She scowled for a second. "Can't you?"

Linus ran his hand through his hair and sat down at the little kitchenette table. "I sometimes can. It seems like you are more accurate."

Yazmin lifted her hand and made an equivocating motion. "Kind of. I can sometimes hear it. Like it's talking. Sometimes. I feel it. I felt you coming down the hallway."

He nodded. "Fair enough."

She pulled a chair over closer. Linus could tell she was starved for conversation. A warm feeling washed over him.

This was something he could do for her.

This was his thing. He smiled.

"So, Linus Flores, if I can ask the big question. What were you doing during the Savior?"

Linus took a deep breath. "I wish my story were as... noble... as yours. I'm from a place in California, Meridian, a place that gets these... well, we get hit by serious tropical winds. Almost like hurricanes, constantly. And the waves. The waves are incredibly intense."

"You're an American?" She cocked her head.

"Was. I got out of there. But not soon enough. I guess when you walk into the waves over and over, at some point, there is the question..."

"...are you trying to die." She finished.

"Exactly. And I guess the 60-million-dollar answer to that was yes. I was. I don't really know why. It's like I wanted to feel it – what it felt like."

"Did you ever really imagine yourself dead?" She leaned in closer. Linus felt a desire to tell her everything.

Everything.

"I did. I imagined my funeral. What people would say. Who would forget me. Who would remember. I made a record when I was younger. I thought about who would play it. Who would find the painted surfboards in my studio and buy one, hold onto them. I knew I'd never have a street named for me. But someone would cry, right? It's like..."

"You really wanted to know."

"Yes." He looked into her eyes. They were dark, like olives. The simile made him feel stupid, but there it was. She stared at him through two black-as-night olives. "How do you know this?"

She leaned back. "I think, as I stood there, some part of me wanted to know if anyone would remember?"

"Did you think about statues?" Linus knew that, even now, there were two statues to her.

"I don't think I got that far. But if I had a minute or two more. It all happened too fast."

"But you made a choice and did it."

"I did. But now what do I do?"

Linus nodded. "Well, now, you get out of here and teach somewhere, or run something, or speak. You do what you want."

"How long do I have?"

Linus stood up. He leaned backwards and cracked his back. It wasn't as satisfying to do that since he was saved, but it still made him feel a little in control of himself.

It still helped. He looked at Yazmin.

"The paperwork should take about a week. Then, I take you away. Anywhere you want."

She nodded, trying to process. "Okay. I can do that. How often will you be back?"

Linus sat back down. "Oh. I'm not going anywhere. If it's okay with you. I'm sleeping on that couch until you're released."

"Really?" Yazmin laughed. Linus tried to figure out how she felt about that.

"If it's okay with you. I'm supposed to look out for you. I can find a hotel and come back every day if you want. But I'd rather be right here."

"Were you chosen for your ability to sleep on couches?"

Linus looked right in her eyes. "I was chosen because this was the only way I'd shut up about getting you out of here. This is all I've wanted to do with my life for the past decade."

Yazmin nodded somberly. "And now you're doing it."

Linus put his smile away for a moment. He thought about what this moment meant and nodded his head.

"Absolutely."

***

Day 1

Linus woke up with a spray of water on his face.

It felt amazing.

"I knew that wouldn't work." Yazmin sat in a chair next to the couch laughing.

"Yeah. Do it again." Linus smiled, half opening his eyes to see the girl shaking a towel at him. He sat up and ran his hand over his face and through his hair.

"I figured you were impervious to splashing. God, I miss swimming. Tell me, Linus the surfer, when was the last time you were swimming?"

He didn't want to tell her it had been three hours before he met her. Linus hadn't spent a full day without the water since he was a baby.

"Oh, it's been too long. We'll have to find a pool when we get out of here."

Yazmin spun around in a chair, a red and black dress on with matching scarf. She had gotten up early to shower.

"The shower is free. We have stuff for breakfast in the kitchenette."

Linus stood up and grabbed the other towel she held out for him. So much of her still seemed to be 12 years old. Despite her true age and her circumstances, there was a kind of lightness to her. She seemed to float.

"Thank you, Yaz. Can I call you Yaz?"

"Yes, you may. Now go get cleaned up, surfer boy so you can tell me more stuff."

Linus stepped toward the bathroom. This entire project seemed like it would be easier than he had thought.

And over in almost no time.

He showered and slid on the shirt he had worn, along with the linen pants. These could be cleaned every few days and still be fine. They were incredibly light and he wasn't about to be doing anything strenuous and sweat-inducing.

By the time he got out, Yazmin had set out some fruit, pita bread and a warm shakshuka. Linus inhaled, looking down at the eggs, still poaching in the spiced tomato sauce. It certainly didn't seem like a prison.

"You made that in this kitchenette?" He shook his head.

"Don't be too amazed. When I'm all alone I basically eat a bag of figs."

Linus sat down at the kitchenette nook table. "Well, I'm really happy you went all out."

"I'm just pumping you for information, American." She smiled at him from across the table.

Linus took a bite. It really was quite good. "Okay, pump away, young lady."

"Here we go. How did you get from Surfing killer waves -- literally -- in California to UN envoy?"

"All right. Well, I stayed in the U.S. as long as I could. The way it was closing up, I realized I couldn't get out even if I wanted to if I waited any longer. So, right before they completely closed the borders, I moved to Brazil."

"Nice choice. I like it."

Linus took a bite. "I did, too. I was there in 2055."

Yazmin sat back in her chair. "Ahh."

"Right? So I was there for the world liberation festival. You know about that?"

She nodded. "I do. I was there in spirit."

"You were there in lots of spirit. This giant celebration to people all through history who had fought for freedom. People like Harriet Tubman, Lala Lajpat Rai, Nelson Mandela, and you. Big as life."

"I heard about it. They wouldn't let me see any coverage." Yazmin put her face down on her hands, on the table.

Linus continued, "that was when I realized you were still in jail. There was an exhibit for you. It explained it all. The UN office was just a few blocks away."

"Wait, you joined the UN because of me?"

Linus finished his eggs, wiping the last of it from the plate with a piece of pita. "I did. This was really good."

"It's like my only dish, so get used to it."

Linus laughed. "I'm making dinner."

***

Linus cleaned up the cell as they talked. He wanted to find a way to make things better for her. It occurred to him that if he'd had pictures of it earlier there was a lot he could have brought. But he had no idea what to expect. There were no guards and no other prisoners on this floor. The five other cells right outside the door were completely bare -- empty. And the door leading outside the wing was locked. But the gate leading into the cell itself was left unlocked, open. The whole thing felt strange. Almost as if the entire wing had been abandoned. Linus could only remember two or three guards in total, as he had walked here from the front gate.

And he hadn't seen a single other prisoner.

Until just that moment.

A woman appeared at the gate opening, waving calmly. The first minute or two of her conversation with Yazmin exhausted Linus's admittedly patchy understanding of Arabic. But it was clear from the bags that she was there to bring food. And a warning.

Yazmin waved goodbye as the woman stepped out of the cell and made her way back down the prison hallway. "Linus, did you tell them you were Salvado?"

"I did not."

"That's good. They are terrified of us." The girl smiled, biting into a fig from the bag the woman had brought. "I don't think they would have let you in if they knew."

"I see that. They send food here with other prisoners?"

"I haven't been in the same room as a guard in a year. Maybe more." As she padded away, Linus could see that she wore large slippers that looked like rabbits.

Bunny slippers.

He smiled, just like he did every time some sign came through that she was still that 12-year-old girl at heart. He had no idea what she'd be like, but he realized how truly happy he was that she was so...

That she was so unbroken.

This woman had lived in a war zone her whole life, until she was murdered. Then she had lived in a series of prison cells, with everyone she knew long dead and buried. And yet, here she was. Unbowed.

She walked up to him and grabbed the rag out of his hand. "Stop cleaning. You're making me feel bad."

Linus laughed. "I'm trying to pull my weight here for the next week. Besides, what else am I going to do. Worry?"

"Well, don't do that. But, here, let me show you something."

***

She led him into the pantry area where she had just finished putting away the food that the woman had brought. The pantry was large, clearly repurposed from its original life as some kind of closet, or storage room. Linus could almost put his arms out completely.

Yazmin pointed upward to a door on the ceiling with a cord hanging from it. Light streamed in around the edges. Linus looked at her.

This was crazy.

She pulled the cord down and a series of stairs slid down a metal rail behind it, leading them up to the roof. Linus was face to face with her bunny slippers as she ascended the stairs. At the top, he could see the rooftop of Ayalon prison. The tallest building in any direction. The surface must have been about 3,000 square feet, with barbed wire fences spanning the entire exterior. The floor beneath them was black tar.

In previous incarnations of this space, this must have been where inmates exercised, but it was clearly unused. And had been for a while. Linus had been Salvado now for 20-plus years and that brought with it a kind of unique way of looking at his surroundings.

"Do they realize you could climb that fence and jump?" He pointed to the sharp barbed wire top of the nearest fence, rising about 40 feet in the air. "You'd be perfectly fine."

"Yep. Back when they used to talk to me, they made it clear that they could kill hundreds of people every time I tried to escape. So I just didn't."

"I get it." Linus's face scrunched up. "We should eat up here."

"Way ahead of you." She pointed to an area about 50 feet away where a blanket was laid out and some dishes and cups were stacked. Linus could see that there was a series of dolls up there.

So she wouldn't have to eat alone.

He stepped over and picked up a doll that was sitting on top. It was a fluffy Black girl doll in a spacesuit. The shiny silver suit had an emblem on front. He pointed it at her.

"NASA. That's cool."

"That's Mae. Mae Jemison. She's one of my favorites. The only woman ever to go into space for real and then to go into space on Star Trek. She's a bit of a hero. My mom got that for me. My neighbors fished it out of the rubble to bring it to me."

She held the doll with some reverence, smoothing its hair down.

"You like space? Science?"

"NASA was the best thing about America. It was the hope that we could work together to go somewhere great."

Linus nodded, "I get that. I'm a bit of a science nerd myself."

"I was going to pick your brain about that tonight, at dinner. Like what new scientific things are happening."

Linus smiled. He stepped over. "I can do better than tell you. I can show you a couple of things. Here. Look here."

He bent down slightly and pulled his left eye open. "Can you see it?"

She peered in at him. "I don't."

"It's a little glint. It's green."

"Okay, I see that, right in your eye."

Linus stood up. "It's a camera to record. If I blink twice it starts recording and sends the video back to the UN. They can see it there."

"No way. Have you recorded anything?"

"Just a little. The cell, the accommodations. I sent an initial verification that you were here. If anything happens, I record."

"So, it's like a contact lens?

Linus nodded, "Yes. It's a special lens."

"That is so small." Yazmin stood back to reassess. "What else do you have?"

"What makes you think I have more?"

"You do, don't you?" She smiled.

Linus winked at her. "I do. I have a couple of other things attached to me. One or two things that can serve some function. One thing I can only use once."

"What's that?"

Linus turned to walk away. "Well, that's classified."

"Sweet Allah, I will punch you." Yazmin laughed as she followed.

Linus laughed. "I have a piece of technology lodged in my esophagus called a gravitic resonance decoupler. I can use it once or twice before it burns out."

Yazmin's eyes got big. "What the hell is that?"

"It lets me select an area and sort of kill gravity there for a little over one second. It's designed to work on anything over 100 pounds."

"What is that in real human people weight?" The girl asked playfully.

Linus smirked. "It's about 45 kilograms."

"That's more than me." She thought out loud.

"That's right. It wouldn't work on you."

"That's insane. What other kinds of things have people invented?"

"In one week, you're going to see it all. But what fields are interesting to you?"

"Are you kidding? All of them. Tell me."

They spent a good part of the day walking around the roof, taking in the sun, batting technology back and forth, with Linus taking lead, trying to remember every new finding in science over the last few years.

He told her about the little chips they had that let you vaccinate people over radio waves at long distances, sending information to their cells about new viruses that could hurt them. He mentioned the Doralai playgrounds that had become more and more common, leafy green playspaces for kids that generated energy from their play, noises, vibrations, even bouncing- energy that could be used to power nearby buildings.

He told her about the new AI pets that cleaned up your home when you weren't there, making sure your space was spotless, and even the new advance in therapeutic medicine that connected therapists to patients with a near 100% success rate. They walked faster and faster as they talked until they were running in circles, taking advantage of the white hot sun beating down, washing away the stench of prison hallways and bars.

***

Day 2

Linus spent the morning walking around the other cells on the floor and recording what he found. Yazmin knew every inch of the floor and called out little details he might have missed. She pointed.

"See that symbol? It says "Ibnati."

"Ibna means daughter, right?" Linus asked.

"Yes. Ibnati means 'my daughter'"

"Ok." He nodded.

"Now, step back here." She pulled him back a few steps. Suddenly, the image above it was visible. It made sense. It was about five feet square, made from the charcoal of something burnt, wood or a cigarette or something. The face of a little girl.

"That's amazing."

"See, you can't see it from the gate -- from the door of the cell it just looks like smudges. You have to stand right here."

"He didn't want the guards to see."

"Whoever it was, it was his secret." Yazmin nodded.

"That's amazing."

"Did you get that? Are you documenting all this?" She grabbed his hand.

He looked down. "I was told that you were a Muslim woman and probably wouldn't touch my hand or shake or anything."

Yazmin laughed. "Don't you see? I'm a kid."

"You're definitely the youngest Salvado I've ever seen. Is that strange to you?" Linus looked around for more to record.

"I think I'm the youngest in the world." She stepped toward the gate and posed. "And I always will be."

"You little scamp." Linus followed her out.

"I have the endocrine system of a child. I have the hormones of a prepubescent child." She recited, as if from memory. "It's one of the things that has confused these people here."

"Well, I've got news for you, princess. All of us have this little nagging voice in the back of our heads that says that we're just a kid. We're all stuck on one age."

She turned to him and smiled. "So, okay, surfer boy, how old are you?"

"Inside? That's easy. My little voice tells me every day that I'm still 18 years old. I just won a new long board in some competition and it was beautiful, big, sleek. I had it painted and took it out for the first time when I was 18."

"What was the paint job?" Yazmin asked earnestly.

"It was this really surreal, beautiful painting by Zofi, my favorite local artist. A kind of spaceship with little green aliens pouring out. Each one smaller than the last."

"I bet that was cool."

"The ship was metallic and it sparkled in the sun. It was beautiful. And I was 18 and stupid and invincible."

"That's what I would be, if I had the chance. I'd be an 18-year-old girl on a beach, with a board twice my size."

Linus laughed. "Like three times your size. With a giant NASA logo..."

"High tech machines and devices everywhere."

"Beautiful."

"It would be." She looked wistful.

"I want to take you out for your first wave. Promise me."

"That's crazy, isn't it? How I grew up, how I live now? And here I am talking to some guy who looks like Mexican Thor about going out surfing with him."

"It's easier than it looks." Linus smiled, wider than he had intended.

"Spoken by the guy who literally died surfing." She pushed him slightly.

"Oh, my god, that was a wave. That was... it was like a massive wet building sliding across the ocean."

"I bet." She sat down in her chair as they returned to the cell. "Hey, what's it like to have a cell phone?"

Linus organized the blankets on the couch. Her ability to flit back and forth between topics might have appeared to be the minimal attention span of a child. In reality, it was the incredibly plastic and flexible mind of a 30-something-year-old who had experienced enough to kickstart a kind of personal evolution in what was already a kind of genius mind. Linus was always told not to meet his idols. In this case, however, the person was every bit as remarkable as the icon. And he loved that.

"Ok, so you've never had a phone?"

"I have not. Ever." She folded her legs under her in a meditative pose.

"Wow. You are missing exactly nothing. If they hadn't taken my phone when I got here, I would be turning it off. No one needs to be accessible to everyone 24 hours a day."

"I get that. It's weird how disconnected you can feel without one, though. Like, I never know if anyone is thinking about me. I think I want one."

"Well. you can have mine." Linus sat on the couch, mirroring her pose and closed his eyes."

She looked over at him. "Are we meditating now?"

"I know you pray every day. I think this is my way. Of being grateful to the universe."

"What do you see when you meditate?" She asked.

"Well." Linus took a deep breath in. "I sometimes do this thing where I imagine the room that I'm in, trying to remember every part of it. "

Yazmin shut her eyes.

"And, in my head I slowly remove all the items in the room. One at a time. Like I take out the chair. I take out the wall plaque. The couch, pulling off the blankets one at a time."

"Right."

He continued, his eyes closed. "And I just slowly empty the room. And when it's empty, when it's cleared out, I let the water flow in, warm water. It just sort of swirls in from above."

"Just warm water?"

"Yes, cleaning the room, getting in all the cracks and corners, just washing the room."

"It needs it. Honestly."

"Sh. Yes. The room is cleaned and washed, top to bottom. And when it's sparkly, I return all the items to the room, one by one."

Yazmin was smiling, in her mind, returning all the items. "Got it."

"And now, it ends." Linus opened his eyes to see Yazmin standing in front of him. She put her hand out and poked him in the chest."

"You're so it."

She ran off into the hallway as Linus jumped up to run after her. They spent most of the rest of the day chasing each other around, playing it, playing kick the can, playing hide and go seek, pulling every ounce of fun they could out of this space, this prison left empty except for a little girl who was possibly going to live forever, a little girl growing wiser every day, without gaining a single inch. And even though Linus lost more than he won, he did demonstrate his point. There was still a kid in there, somewhere, too.

***

Day 3

Linus made an elaborate omelette for breakfast, along with some fried potatoes and sun dried tomatoes. The pantry held some fresh basil, which accounted for the smell wafting through the kitchenette when Yazmin stepped out of the bathroom after showering. She was in a black and blue dress with a blue head scarf.

"You look nice," Linus poured some tea for her, coffee for him.

Yazmin scrunched up her face in the way that she did. "Well, you've now seen the three dresses that I own. It's all downhill from here."

He laughed. "Well, I did bring one outfit with me, so you've got me beat."

"Oh, no complaints. It's literally one more dress than I owned growing up."

Linus frowned, "Really? That's messed up.

Yazmin took a bite. "You know, no one's cooked for me in my entire life."

"Ever?"

"You are the first. Wow. That is crazy."

"Well you lived most of your life in a prison now." Linus was still amazed at how normal she seemed, despite all that. He almost didn't want to ask the next question.

"I did find this in the pantry." He slid the note over to her. "Kun hadhiran eindama tughadir, right?"

"That's pretty good. You can read more Arabic than you speak?" She turned the note over and kept eating.

"Yes. Honestly I could speak it alright if you and every person speaking it would slow the hell down." He shook his head as she laughed. "Be careful when you leave?"

"Yes. It came from Salim, who dropped off the food yesterday."

Linus nodded. "I figured that. You don't seem too concerned. What do you think it means?"

"Honestly, I don't know, I've been thinking about it. I am concerned about the end of all this. They would love to see me dead, but they don't want to kill me."

"Or can't kill you." Linus intoned, trying to follow along.

"Oh, they could do a lot. They could cover me in concrete and sink me at the bottom of the Dead Sea. I have nightmares about that." she shivered performatively.

Linus nodded, "People would ask, right? There would be an investigation?"

"Probably, I think so. They would love it if someone else kills me."

"Someone else like who?" asked Linus.

Yazmin looked over her plate. "Well, like the UN. If they killed me while transporting me. That would be optimal, honestly, for them."

"Well, that's not going to happen. The UN wants to give you awards and put you in charge of something." Linus grabbed some toasted pita and slid it over to her.

Yazmin tore the pita in two and piled potatoes on top of it. "For sure, but discrediting the UN would be a perk. Me being gone would be the big prize."

"Does Salim think they're going to try to do it during this transfer?"

Yazmin nodded. "Yes, I think so. But they don't know that you are Salvado, too."

"We won't be easy to kill."

"Have you ever tried not breathing?" She asked.

Linus nodded. "I did. I've gone in the water before. I walked underwater from St. Croix to St John once. No oxygen, no food. It took me two and a half days."

"That sounds terrifying."

"Ha. Look at the life you've lived. I'm just talking about a little walk underwater."

She wiped her plate with the last of her pita. "Can you imagine being restrained and just left there? For centuries?"

"I can't. That is terrifying." Linus grabbed her plate to wash it.

"They could restrain us, put us somewhere. File us away and hide us."

"Well, I'm not going to let that happen."

Yazmin looked at him. He was so earnest. And he was fun.

There was a kindness in him that was just different from anyone else she'd met before. It made her trust him. "I know you won't."

"Now, I was hoping we could have some fun on the roof today."

"Oh, yeah?" She followed him to the back sink in the tiny kitchen and saw them. "No way. Are those what I think they are?"

Linus must have gotten up extra early to build them. In the sink were two devices taped together, made with plastic bottles and pieces from food packaging. Each looked heavy, filled to the top with water.

The blond man looked down, beaming, at his creations. "Water guns. Untested, but built with love."

Yazmin laughed in a way he hadn't seen her laugh yet. And, suddenly, getting up early didn't seem hard at all. They spent the rest of the day on the roof, shooting each other with homemade water guns, filling them up, and doing it again, until they fell asleep, laughing, soaking wet and slowly drying in the warm Ramla air.

**

Day 4

Day 4 was the day when the single channel television in the front area of the cell would play the very first of the Fast and the Furious movies. The two piled onto the couch, Yazmin with a full bag of figs, and tried to take it all in.

Linus leaned in and grabbed a fig. "You know, I think you are mostly made of fig at this point."

"Without a doubt. I am at least three-quarters fig."

"Nice. I like it. We can just talk during the commercial breaks."

"So far, none of this is surprising."

"I really didn't think it was going to be."

"So, Friday, are they just going to open the door and we leave or what?" She seemed a bit scared but hid it well.

"Okay, from what I understand, Thursday, they bring two doctors in here, one of theirs, one of ours. The doctors say that you are healthy and haven't been treated badly."

"Oh, no. Not in the last year or so. But, really, they couldn't hurt me anyway."

"Exactly. So we expect no drama there." Linus smiled.

The movie came back on. He looked over at the girl as she ate a steady stream of figs and tried to parse this ridiculous movie. He cocked his head a little and saw her for who she was. This was a statesman. This was a speaker. This was a leader. This was someone who was going to change the world, if the next couple of days went smoothly. And the world needed it.

America had fallen out of its position as a world leader and was now a cautionary tale of isolationism and fascism. The people who could leave had already done so. The country that was left bore little resemblance to what it once was. As tortured as that situation was, it had emboldened some other countries to immerse themselves in far right-wing nationalism. The unholy alliance of Russia, the U.S., and North Korea was proving to people across the world that strength had an absolute. It gave fascists something to aspire to. The power-hungry followed.

At the same time, new alliances and leaders rose up, like Finland and Denmark, who opened themselves up to ideologies meant to drive happiness and connection. They invested in education, in science, in health, and their people flourished. They knew who they were.

The seat of the UN had moved to Amsterdam and it had grown into an organization with real, actionable goals. There was a new and more pointed positive leadership in the air and Yazmin would fit right in. Her voice would help bring the planet back from the brink of war.

That was a lot to put on the shoulders of this tiny girl who had never rented an apartment or held a job. This girl, made up mostly of figs. But Linus believed in her now more than ever.

"Commercial. Okay, so then, what happens?"

He sat up. "First thing Friday morning, we move down to the end of the hall. Some guards bring us out to the Ramla train station nearby, where they come with us on the Tel Aviv–Beit Shemesh–Jerusalem line train line to the Ben-Gurion Airport."

"You have this memorized."

"I do. How am I doing?"

She smiled. "It's good. Very good. Continue, travel agent."

"In front of the train station at the airport, we will be met by our people. I don't know who. And at that point, the handover happens. Once we are in front of the airport, the Israeli government has nothing more to do with you." He pantomimed washing his hands.

"Right."

"And you are under the protection of the United Nations. Then it's a light meal on an empty charter plane, except for us, where we travel non-stop to Amsterdam."

"I've never been on a plane."

"That's right. You've never been on a plane. It's nothing. It's a five-hour flight."

"I'm not afraid. It's going to be good."

"It will be a great flight." Linus confirmed. "And the hum of the plane, I predict, will put you right to sleep."

"And you'll be there?"

Linus stood up and grabbed a fig, kissing her on the top of the head. "I will be there."

As he walked toward the bathroom, she turned her head around. "You promise?"

Linus nodded slowly. And he promised.

Crossing his heart.

***

Day 5

Linus, Yazmin, and Mae had breakfast on the roof, barely after the sun had risen, on Wednesday. The doll sat behind a tiny cup of tea because it amused Linus. Yazmin had already decided that the toy was the only thing she would bring with her.

"I think it's a good idea to try and appear as much like a kid as possible for the next few days."

"That's sort of been my strategy for staying alive here. People are still more reluctant to torture a kid, I guess."

"Well, that's good. I mean, that's creepy, but it's good." Linus bit into an egg poached into half of a red pepper. It was delicious. Part of him felt like he'd be walking out of here with a host of new recipes. He had to admit that, back home, he lived on very little. Salvado bodies really didn't need to eat.

They couldn't starve to death anymore than they could be shot.

"Linus, I'm 34 years old. But, these last few days with you have been the most I've been able to just let go and feel like a kid in my entire life. And that's because of you. I can't tell you what it's meant to me. It's such a huge gift. I think I wondered on the very first day why they would send you. But now I feel so honored that they did. Who else could they have sent but you? Who else would have sat here with me for a week, talking, listening, playing around? I'm not going to forget this."

Linus looked down. This would be a bad time to start crying. The sun was starting to build up, focusing on them. This was going to be a day full of sun.

"I appreciate that, little fig. Especially because we might end up being neighbors."

"Wait, what?" She sat up straight. Mae dipped down, almost drowning in her cup of tea.

He held up his hand, showing her a pretend "map" of Amsterdam. "Here, Ijburg. This is where I live. It's 20 minutes from the UN center. It's right off the water. You can walk down to the Ijburgbaai, the inlet. You can swim, surf. They are putting you here, in at the Four Elements Hotel. It's huge. It is basically taking over the whole area. They have pools, too. You could almost throw something and hit my house. But don't throw anything."

"Wow."

"We can go surfing every morning if you want to. I mean, I'm sure you'll have lots of –"

"No, I won't." She seemed so light, she was almost floating. "I want to go surfing with you every morning."

Linus dropped his hands. "Well, then, okay. It's a fun town. You're going to love it."

"I will." Yazmin started to cry.

"Hey, are you okay?" Linus put his arm around her. She leaned in and hugged him.

"I don't know. I feel like I won't know until I get somewhere I can just breathe. Like, am I okay? I watched everyone I know die and I stood in front of a tank, 22 years ago, waiting to join them."

"Did you think you would be with your parents?"

Tears flowed from her eyes. She nodded.

Linus took a deep breath. "Were you sad when you weren't?"

She nodded again. Harder this time. She leaned in to him and he held her. In a lot of ways, 22 years was only a few minutes ago. She felt so tiny in his arms. People all over the world thought that this girl was an adult and she was. Linus made a promise in that moment to be a place where she didn't have to be.

He reached over for Mae and slid her into Yazmin's arms. This was going to be a trip for her, too. The third big trip of Mae Jemison's life. Space, Star Trek, and then home.

***

Day 6

The prison supplied two doctors that Yazmin had never seen before. A dirty-blonde woman of about 40 and a younger brunette woman named Sarah. They didn't speak. But the two women who had come from Amsterdam spoke enough for everyone. The taller one, Dr. Ellis, was a Black woman with long, curly hair. Her protege, Dr. Maringa, was an Asian woman with a big wide smile who couldn't have been older than 35. In fact, she was the same age as Yazmin.

"You have the same birthday as me?"

"I do. You and I are exactly the same age." Dr. Maringa smiled as she took her pulse and blood pressure.

Yazmin looked at her and then back at herself. The two women could not have possibly looked any more different. "Well, that certainly disproves astrology in a big way."

Dr. Maringa laughed. She seemed to know Linus, at least a little. She winked at him.

Dr. Ellis cocked her head. "Well, I honestly don't know how to evaluate Salvados. I mean, you're clearly crazy healthy. If I could pierce your skin, I'd get a blood sample."

"Sorry," Yazmin shrugged.

"Oh, it's fine, sweetheart. It's certainly not your fault. I mean, it's kind of tautological that you're in good health. That doesn't mean you were treated well." She glared at the other doctors who made a point to be looking down in their notebooks, writing.

Linus spoke up from the couch. "You can always do cognitive tests?"

Dr. Maringa looked at him. "Yeah, but what if she's smarter than we are?"

"Yeah," followed up the other doctor, "That's the risk, really. The patient is just smarter than we are."

Yazmin smiled. "Wait, maybe I'm not. Ask me some math."

Dr. Ellis shook her by the shoulders, playfully. "God, girl, I'm just a doctor, why do you think I know math?"

"I didn't know this job required math," responded Dr. Maringa.

Yazmin spoke up robotically, "today is Thursday."

The Asian doctor stuck out her tongue. "Even blondy over there knows that one."

Linus shook his head. "Hey, how am I the control here?"

"You can't poke him, either." Dr. Ellis sighed. "You guys have figured out the grim secret of medicine. If we can't put a hole in you somewhere, we're useless."

Yazmin grabbed Dr. Ellis's hand. "Thank you, anyway."

She looked at the smaller girl. "It's going to be a big day tomorrow. Are you ready?"

"She's ready." Linus didn't look up.

Dr. Maringa tossed a cotton ball at him. "Nobody asked you, Surfy."

Yazmin smiled. "I'm good. I'm ready for my first plane trip tomorrow."

The two doctors from the UN were allowed to stay for dinner. It made sense to use up the last of the food. Yazmin decided during the cous-cous that she would leave everything behind except Mae. No bags, nothing.

She asked Linus if he was particularly attached to his empty briefcase. He shrugged. It was decided.

They would leave with nothing tomorrow. Linus, Yazmin, and Mae.

***

Day 7

They were up by 6 AM, and the commotion at the end of the hallway wasn't even the reason. Linus looked out the gate and saw the far door open. There were two guards standing by the portal.

He looked at Yazmin and the two of them slowly made their way down the hallway, holding hands. Linus wasn't going to let her out of his sight until they were back home, and that meant keeping his eyes wide open,

They rode with the two guards down in an open elevator. Honestly, it looked pretty unsafe, but Ayalon prison had the feel of a building that was about to be repurposed. Every step rang out across its bell-like emptiness.

They saw no one.

The two guards escorted them to the train station and then onto the train. It was new and recently upgraded, sleek metal and brightly-colored leather seat covers. There was no one at the station. No civilians, no other guards. No one. Yazmin tried to feel something from the guards, but they were blank. One looked to be in his 20s, with the other about twice that old. They said nothing.

They just walked.

As they got off and approached the airport from the train side, Linus noticed that it was more bare, more sparse than when he had arrived. And the few people moving around seemed to be dressed as Arabs.

Did it make sense that there would be no Israelis?

The guards looked uncomfortable. They walked them to the check-in area in front. As Linus stepped up to the counter, the two guards turned and began to leave. He stared after them. They seemed to be walking faster.

They were hurrying. They bumped into Yazmin, causing her to drop Mae momentarily.

Linus looked around him. The woman at the counter wrapped a tag around the blue bag in the weigh station and excused herself for a minute, handing him the tickets.

Doctors Ellis and Maringa had met them there, ready to return with them. Each carried a small bag.

A tiny carry-on.

Linus scanned the counter area. On the weighing area was a black suitcase.

What came next happened too fast for anyone to see. Yazmin looked over at Linus. He stood near the weighing machine with the suitcase. There was nobody else around. Except for the contingent from the UN, the area was completely bare. Mae was laying just a meter or so away from her foot. But, besides that, nothing.

There were no passengers heading into the airport.

None.

She shook her head at Linus. It could be a mistake. Maybe the suitcase was just left behind by someone. A thin alarm rang out showing that the case was overweight. The gauge next to it flashed.

It weighed 180 kg.

Linus's lips moved. She thought she could read what they were saying. His eyes dropped. And then a sound came up from his throat.

And he was gone. For meters in every direction, every object around her just disappeared. Dr. Ellis was gone. The suitcase was gone. The weigh station was gone. Benches, trees, everything.

Gone.

For a little over a second, the gravity keeping these things on the ground was cut, letting the 1,600 Kilometers per hour spin of the earth wrench away everything that was sitting there.

She looked down at Mae.

Everything over 45 kilograms.

100 pounds.

Everything there was now headed out into space, out past the atmosphere. Yazmin peered up and saw it, way before she heard it. There was a brilliant light from an explosion.

A massive one, that filled the sky. About a minute later she heard the boom as it shattered windows across the airport, sending hails of broken glass down to the ground.

Yazmin fell to the ground as Dr. Maringa ran toward her. More and more junk rained down from the sky.

She closed her eyes and tried to feel for Linus but she couldn't.

He was gone.

***

Yazmin curled up in the seat next to Dr. Maringa for the flight to Amsterdam. She tried to sleep but her eyes wouldn't stay shut. She tried not to imagine what had happened to Linus. If somehow he had been blown up all alone by the massive explosion or, even now, was shooting alone through space. One way or another, that one word was the one she kept catching on.

Alone.

Linus didn't ever deserve to be alone. She pulled the doll closer. No one did, but Linus especially.

She cried most of the way to Amsterdam. A train brought her to Ijburg. And the people were kind to her. Kinder than she thought she'd ever get used to. If Linus hadn't primed her for it, she would have certainly been embarrassed.

Ijburg was even more beautiful than Linus said. There were buildings floating in the water, little boats tethered to them that let you make your way from home to home, and the water was so calm and beautiful.

Especially at night. The water seemed to almost be a sheet, perfectly pulled taut on a fancy bed, deep and blue and ready for sleep.

Reflective, smooth.

The water told the tale of the people, people who valued peace, who wanted to build something that would sing children to bed at night, quietly, causing them to lean in, to listen to the whisper. To feel the calm in front of them as a kind of happy ending to a bedtime story.

But every once in a while, when a storm hit or a warm front came in across that water, the waves would rise up and reach for the sky, fingers of white-tipped foam invading the atmosphere and pulling up the blue skirts of the Ijburgbaai into giant thick cones of power that would carry Yazmin's longboard across the bay, dropping her just a few meters from the front of her home where she could paddle back out and try again to scale upward toward space.

4 - The Map of Us
Oketo Hokkaido, Japan 2215

Six months turned into 25 years.

At first, I just let myself be studied. That was mostly painless, although it was, on occasion, boring. There was no way for them to pierce my skin, they discovered. They could vibrate me, drown me, drop me, bury me, and do 100 other diagnostically vacuous processes, all of which just confirmed what they thought originally.

Nothing could hurt me.

They brought other Salvado into the research program and I ended up, after a while, in charge of them. Me, Anjo Killean, in charge of people. We were all treated reasonably well. By 2070, there were about 112 of us, all being studied for the betterment of mankind.

That's what it said on our paychecks. And mine was getting bigger. Enough that my uncle didn't need to work anymore. His ordinarily chill demeanor got substantially more chill. And that didn't suck. I discovered he liked basketball, which, apparently, he never really had the time to do. He always came off so young to me, growing up, but it seemed like he had been aging lately. He didn't look his age yet, but some people never do.

As time went on, I started just referring to him as my dad. It made more sense, really. He was the only parent I could really remember and he put the effort into it.

I couldn't call him "Ron" and people would comment all the time that we looked alike, with his brooding, handsome face and short dark hair.

So why not?

During this time, I learned a lot. We all did. Nothing like this had ever happened in history so it was worth investigating. What was that old saying, "the proper study of man is man?" Devilboy tells me that's from "An Essay on Man" by Alexander Pope. To me, it felt fair that "the proper study of Salvado is Salvado."

So I learned.

I don't want to bore you with the general findings. You know all that. Hell, I could see that when I was sitting in Savi's apartment letting him stab me. Every one of the people had been trying to commit suicide. They all failed. And they all became, in the end, unkillable.

But that wasn't all. Some of this is TMI, so I'll try to not linger on it. The first of these I actually appreciated a lot. The women who were of childbearing age had stopped menstruating. It just stopped. The men had stopped producing sperm. None of us were fertile. That was a blow to a lot of Salvado, but to many it was a relief. We weren't going to be having children that we would invariably outlive. I was pleased not to menstruate as it always gave me a powerful case of dysphoria when it happened.

For me, myself, eventually the realization came that I wasn't going to be able to surgically transition. And even medical transition tools like HRT didn't work well on me. So I did what I could do. I worked out my abs and wore a binder. working out didn't do much, but it made me move more like a man. I wore my hair in a way that was as male as possible. Shaving and cutting hair was no longer an option. But I noticed that if I tapped a little bit of dark eyeshadow into my hands and rubbed my face, the beard area would darken a bit. I stood like a man.

I acted like one.

I exercised the low range in my voice. The truth is that gender is performative. We all act like a gender.

And the more we do it, the easier it gets. As I got older, with a better understanding of what kind of a man I was, it got easier. I looked for good examples.

There was a singer named Good Saint whom I liked quite a bit. He looked a bit like me. He was wiry, a little dark, shorter dark hair. He wasn't tall, but he stood with power. He wore necklaces tight to his neck and black t-shirts. He wore dark red jeans that were worn and tight, pulled up at the legs, black boots. He looked like his hair was wet from singing and he was always prepared to jump. He was energetic and affable, kind but quiet.

He was a good model for me. I admit that in those early days I became nearly a carbon copy of him. Until I figured myself out a bit more. I began to look more like me. Ron was a good champion for that. He knew the journey I was on. He was always ready to have that conversation.

What would a man do right now?

So, I figured out me while I tried to figure out us. I met a lot of us. Those first 100 burned themselves into my head. I knew them all.

Rose Ediboiyo, who was 67, a grandmother living alone with late-stage Alzheimer's, whose mind and body rebounded after she was saved, sitting in her car, idling with the garage door shut. Today, she looked maybe 50. And her mind was strong, savage. It pushed her to do stand-up comedy. She loved to dance in the vast meeting rooms of Xenovera with new people, showing them steps that she now remembered with a precision that was impressive.

Marcos de Riviera, who at 58 found himself without a family, in medical debt, and at odds with the IRS, spending his remaining cash on a gun and a small box of ammunition that he tried, four or five times, to use in the front bedroom of the home from which he was being evicted the next week. By the time I met him, these frequent tests had solved his money and homelessness problems, resulting in a return to the man he was in his 40s – an artist, a cook, a father, a romantic who just wanted to find the right person to take care of and have the means to do it.

LaToya Masterson, who had been seriously burned by a jealous lover 10 years earlier, when she was a beautiful 28-year-old girl, trying, on the Savior day, to take enough of her pain medication to end it all and laying, her face in her hands, for nearly an hour, wishing for death, until she looked up, staring into a mirror that showed only the shadow of a few burns remaining, framing a face that was every bit as beautiful as it had been before.

I talked to them, learned from them, asked them questions, and documented their stories. I became a writer for them. I became a librarian, a collector, an archivist for them. I learned from them things I needed to know about myself.

We seemed indestructible.

And while we couldn't feel pain as strongly, we weren't blind to it. We could sense that putting a hand into a fire was awkward, stupid, even if it didn't really hurt. But one of the findings that was unexpected was that feelings of pleasure seemed to be amplified. Touching a friend's hand seemed warmer, sweeter. A kiss felt more intense. Hugging an old friend lasted longer because it just felt like it should.

And sex? That was better, too.

The feeling of water on your face. The warm air of an afternoon outside, under the trees. That could feel amazing.

And, we discovered, some of the things you liked about yourself were amplified as well. Antonia Jackson, a 47-year-old woman from Dothan, Alabama, had always thought of herself as a sensitive, as someone who could see into people, read them. After the Savior event, she became a psychic for the Mobile police force, standing behind the glass, helping to interrogate suspects.

Genesis Cassidy, a 29-year-old blues trumpeter in Lafayette discovered, after his suicide attempt on Savior Day, that his ability to learn new instruments was intensified. It's almost like he could look at an instrument and it would tell him things.

This is how you play me.

This is what I need.

Some of it was invisible to us.

Eventually, I was hired by Xenovera as a research assistant. Then, as research lead. I had the chance to read my own files. Through them, I realized that my native loyalty, my ability to see the hero in people, all that had been amplified. And this is one of the things that helped me work with the other research subjects. They trusted me. It was hard for me to see.

But, you know, research files don't lie.

Xenovera moved to Bordeaux, France to build a larger facility. My stock options and compensation made it possible for me to work from any of their satellite offices. At first, I moved to Brazil when things went to shit in the U.S. I found myself surrounded by people who looked just like me, which was new, and kind of crazy. I had never really thought of myself as a Brazilian. But now I did. The truth is, I loved it. So did Ron.

We moved around until we settled in Sao Paulo, a mile or so away from the Xenovera office. I started travelling a lot for work, picking Salvado all over the world and visiting them. Most of them were in better places than on Savior Day. A very few were still hurting, still in pain, unwilling to talk. But most of them wanted to tell their stories.

They wanted to celebrate being alive.

If I wrote a book, I think this might be the main point of it. Most of them were loving their lives and the new chance they got. Very few of them still wanted to be gone, still wanted to die.

Very few.

This was my job for decades. Visiting people all over the world and learning their stories. If that seems like a pretty good job, I admit I agree with you. The decades went by so fast.

In 2095, we celebrated Ron's 100th birthday. He was still kicking, still wanted to travel, to have fun. As a present to him, I promised I'd take off work for a decade or so and spend it with him, doing what he wanted.

And we did. We celebrated the Centennial in Thailand, eating, exploring, and just being a family. His memory of my mother was still rock solid. His stories about her, the videos he still had, all of it connected me to her – to Mari, and to my Dad, Jon Riley Killean – in ways that brought back so many feelings. I loved that he always insisted on calling my dad by his full author's name.

I missed Montana sometimes, but the USA was unenterable, even for a citizen like me. They had worked so hard to isolate themselves, along with their small cadre of allies, that most people had no idea what was happening there. I heard from one person that births had stopped. I heard from another person that the birthrate was too high.

There was no truth coming out of the country of my birth.

So I let go of that and embraced the places in the world where I was welcome. We visited Ron's family's home town in South America. We explored across Africa. And when Ron started to feel sick, we came back home to Brazil.

He was 110 years old when the throat cancer hit. Ironically, he had never smoked. But it ran in his family. I made myself comfortable in the hospital room with him, moving in as much as I possibly could. We watched movies. He smiled and nodded while I asked him questions about Mari and Jon.

And he wrote notes. I put them in the box with his videos and the rest of the notes he had saved. The box filled up slowly as he got sicker. He died in 2105, in April. I stayed in the room for two full days after he passed, not really able to process what had happened. Not really able to leave.

Finally, I packed up to go, reading the occasional note from the box. That's when I found an envelope addressed to me. Unlike everything else in the box, it was sealed. I opened it to read.

Dear Anjo.

If you read this after I'm gone, good, good for you. Maybe you don't need a letter. Maybe you get up and you fly, wings up, head out. That's what I like to think. In the event you are still struggling, there are things to remember about the world.

Seeing you with your wrists bandaged, just a kid, really, eyes closed, inviting things I don't want to talk about, that is killing me. I want to take my son home. I want to roll him into a ball and put him in my pocket and take him home where no one will hurt him.

Where he can't hurt himself.

That's what I'm feeling. There isn't any anger. There isn't any disappointment. You are perfect and you are every bit the angel. But the world is base and broken and wrecked. I can't expect you to jump up every morning and live in it without consequence.

I can't expect you to not see things.

You are going to get up, though. And there will be changes. When you are ready, I'm here to talk about the changes. I know that you wanted to not feel pain anymore, in a way, and that is the good news. My hope is that you didn't want to not be YOU anymore, because that would be crushing. That would end me.

You are still you. Let's talk when you feel up to it.

Love,

Ron.

It was signed and dated. His full signature. And dated February 2nd, 2043.

Two years before the Savior Event.

***

I closed the box and put the letter in my back pocket. I had no memory at all of anything outlined in it. It was almost as though it was from an alternate universe.

Did I try to kill myself at 18?

I looked down. There were no marks on my wrists. Not even faded ones. Yet I had a tiny scar on my leg from a bike accident in third grade. I knew how this worked. I should see something from that long ago.

Why no marks at all on my wrists?

Why didn't I remember it?

I walked over to the mirror in the hospital room. I was used to thinking of my face as the face of an eternal 20 year old. But today I looked closer. I looked past the smudges on my face, the messy hair, the boyish expression, all of it.

Was this the face of an 18 year old?

Was my savior event two years before the world's?

None of it made any sense.

From this letter, it seemed like he knew something about the Savior Event. He talked about changes. He even said he could explain them.

Back home I put the box in a safe place while I tore his room apart. I didn't want to sleep or eat or do anything. I just wanted to figure this out. I'd had my whole life with this man and he still left with secrets.

That was pretty impressive, if I had to say.

His closet was large and mostly empty. There were more boxes of letters and things. I pulled them out. Nearly all of them were from my mother, Mari. Some were from when they were kids. He had kept letters from her from when they were 15 years old. That was unexpected but certainly believable. From him.

On the top shelf were two books.

They were both by my father, Jon Riley Killean, hardcover books with brightly colored sci-fi book jackets. The first one was called The World Mosaic and the other was a darker looking one called Advance the Sky.

I pulled them out and read the book jackets. They didn't contain a huge amount of information. I pulled my phone out, feeling a little stupid.

"Hey, Devilboy…"

"What up, my big, tough Angel?"

"Are you familiar with the books written by my father, Jon Riley Killean?"

He paused for a second, "Yes. I have four of them here in front of me."

"You don't have a front."

"I could have a front if I wanted. I choose to not have a front."

"Well. That's not true. Can you give me a summary of two of them, The World Mosaic, and Advance the Sky?"

"I can, but if this is for a book report, I'm telling."

"Oh, bite me."

"Funtime later. Okay, in The World Mosaic, written in 2026, there is a massive, world-sized spaceship called the Mosaic, floating in space, in between locations and times. It was built by an ancient species that left this galaxy billions of years ago. And it connects all these different planets. A group of explorers sort of break into the ship and get lost, some for centuries, as their children work to escape and find out how to return home."

"Is that it?"

"It has lots of different characters, and it goes on for a long time. The main idea is that the ship is not in any one place or time, which means you can get everywhere, if you can figure out how."

"And they try to figure out how?"

"Yes. It's a good book, I think. I just read it by the pool naked."

"In microseconds."

"Because that's how I roll."

"Okay, naked guy, how about the other one, Advance the Sky, is there anything in there that I would find really interesting?"

"Well, I just read it. And yes, a lot."

"Right. Just make me guess."

"I paused for dramatic effect. Oh, where has fun Anjo gone?"

"I'm right here, boob."

"The plot of this one is a little more meandering. But here is what you will find interesting. This book was written in 2028 and it mentioned the Savior Event twice."

This is where my vision kind of got weird. It was like looking down a tunnel. Ron andy dad knew about the Savior Event, before it happened. My dad wrote about it, in a book published 17 years beforehand. Right before he died. I rubbed my eyes and my vision slowly widened.

"How is that possible?"

"I don't know."

"What are the odds that it was a coincidence?"

"Anjo, there really isn't any way to evaluate the odds of people coming up with a concept like this before it happens."

"Spock could do it."

"That was bullshit, though. 'Oh, the odds are 65 quintillion to one that this doorway would be here on this planet.' That's dumb. Show me the math."

"What does it say?"

"On page 56 it says: 'The reddish-orange hue of the effect hung in the sky as Lori looked up, needing, wanting. She let herself go, falling from the building, looking upward. Her eyes were awash in the lights from the sky as she hit the ground, leaving a sizable indent, while she stood, and breathed out the chilled rooftop air into the warmer, sunlit spaces in front of the Essinox Building.'"

"And she lives?"

"She does. She is a main character."

"What is the other reference?"

"On page 234, is reads: 'Sol would never understand what the Savior Event did to change her, how it worked, the way it ran through her, still, powering her every emotion, lifting her toward something right now just barely out of reach.'"

"That seems really dead on."

"It does. Good writer, I think, too."

"What happens to her?"

"Nothing. She lives. It seems as though there was supposed to be a follow-up at some point."

Anjo sighed. "But my father died."

"Yes."

"Why would Ron have these two books?"

"He seemed to be a bit of a collector. And archivist of sorts. Does any of that sound familiar?"

"Yes. Shut up." I laughed. Yes, it looked like I picked up a lot from him. This nagging need for answers was killing me. But the answers to this wouldn't come for hundreds of years. And if I told you that wasn't frustrating, I'd be lying big-time.

I went back to work. This time, I spent more time in the Xenovera facility in France. It was amazing. I had my own wing for research and a giant office. It was fun meeting new people. They seemed happy that I was back, too. I was the oldest employee at Xenovera by quite a lot. Even the CEO would reach out to me. One time, after talking to him, in his office, I made a strange discovery.

Xenovera had stopped authorizing human donations not long after I came on board. The information that they got from me and the other Salvado brought in more opportunity and means to create biological advances than that program did. And no one had to be hurt or exploited.

I grew up thinking that large corporations would always turn evil. But this corporation was full of people with endless memories, people who were growing and learning, by centuries, how to do better. What if the number of Salvado inside Xenovera was why they weren't a hateful, horrible corporation? It would be impossible to test that. But as I stood in the office of the CEO, Dexter Kims, he looked over at me remembering when we had first met, when his father had brought him to work at the research lab and he and I had spent lunch playing trash basketball. I realized that he had grown up idolizing me. And me visiting his office made him nearly revert to that kid all over again.

We played trash basketball at least twice a week, every week, over the next 46 years, until his heart gave out one day and I met up with him at the hospital and held his hand while he passed. I helped his son and granddaughter get through it and alternated on the eulogy with them. I think we got enough laughs out of it to do him proud. He always wanted to go out punching.

And when his granddaughter took over the company, I played the occasional game with her, too. We took a cooking class together and laughed hard enough we killed a room full of souffles.

And when she passed away, in 2210, I held her hand, too, reminding her that my hand was the same exact hand that held her when her grandfather passed her around so carefully, smiling proudly, in her first infant visit to the office.

After that, I decided to travel in a more intentional way. Mostly because we had just learned about Akana Tanaka and her map.

***

Akana Tanaka's Story

Aki, as her mother called her, was born in 2017 in late August, as North Korean missiles sailed over Hokkaido, Japan, raising tensions and sending people scurrying into their homes. Japan would join 35 countries in leveling sanctions against North Korea for the violation, but that never let the people in Hokkaido feel safe and relax.

Before we go on, we should qualify that Hokkaido is one of the islands of Japan. It's the one furthest out, the last stop in Japan before you end up in Hawaii. And it's the most sparsely occupied area in Japan. But Aki grew up in Sapporo, a beautiful city, full of people. She lived in an area that was just around the corner from a park, down the block from a market, just blocks from a school. There were trees and grass and wide open yards. And for all the amenities, none were as dear to her as the built in best friend she had three doors down.

Emi Shimizu was her same age, exactly, with hair a little longer and a smile just a tiny bit wider. Aki and Emi became friends almost immediately after meeting, sharing intimate secrets that turned them into more than just family. And as they grew older, if Emi was a little taller and maybe a tiny bit prettier, that wasn't where she won out. Aki had days where she needed to step back.

She was sensitive, so much so that she could nearly hear people's anger, feel their anxiety, sense their annoyance. It wasn't easy for Aki to be around people sometimes, especially people who were big. Bigger than life. Big personalities.

Ramyon fit that description well. He was a beautiful, tall, gangly lead singer for a local band. He was so handsome, Aki thought, that he could say ugly things and they would come out beautiful. But he didn't. Ramyon was kind and free and he fell in love with Aki's brooding intensity, her sensitivity. There was a darkness about her, a quiet gothic calm, that pulled him in. To him, she was like the endless sea, without bottom or limit. He saw the quirky weirdness inside her, pouring out of her, and he liked it. He joked with her and she joked back, not once saying "no" or denying anything. She read his mind and amplified it. No one around them could pierce their banter. And Ramyon loved it. No matter how dark.

"Aki, I can't believe you slept with that dwarf."

"He was a leprechaun and you don't seem to mind the gold."

And they would stick their tongues out at each other like this was how everyone talked.

"Ramyon, you're getting so hairy."

"You knew I was a werewolf when you cursed me."

They fell in love with insides, and the outsides matched.

For two years, they pretended to argue in public, joked, cuddled, read books together, danced, made faces at each other, and fed each other. And it worked, Aki thought.

One day, Emi threw a party. It was her time to feel special. She had written a book at this young age of 28 and it was going to be made into a movie. The entire thing came out of nowhere. Everyone on the block was at the party. Everyone drank, they partied.

They celebrated.

And at a certain point, Aki needed to go home.

Ramyon pledged to be right behind her, as soon as he said goodbye. But he was late. And neither he nor Emi could remember whose idea it was for the two of them to slip into the dark of her room and pull each other's clothes off, falling into the bed. No one could remember much of anything about it at all.

Until a few weeks later, when Emi discovered she was pregnant. The three of them got together to discuss what had happened. Aki felt her heart crush in her chest as she listened to Ramyon talk about how he was always told he couldn't be a father. He went on to explain he might never get another chance.

Despite the fact that he loved Aki, he couldn't walk away from Emi.

They cried and returned to their own homes.

And that was the last time that Akana called herself Aki. And it was the last time she ate.

For weeks, she refused to see anyone. She talked on the phone to Emi and Ramyon. They picked out children's clothing.

And still she didn't eat.

They set up a baby shower, begging her to come,

And still she didn't eat.

She wrapped herself in a blanket, her bones sticking out of her waist, barely holding up a pair of sweatpants. She tightened it, shivering in the night air as she stepped onto the back porch to watch the light show on March 30th, 2045. And that's when the deprivation in her body would have caused her to fall down, to crack a brittle bone, possibly in her arm or pelvic area.

And to die at an impossibly young 28 years old.

But that didn't happen.

As the morning approached, she felt stronger. She stood up and looked in the mirror. Her frame had filled back out, making her look more healthy. She wasn't cold at all. She wasn't tired.

She was alive.

She closed her eyes and slid into bed. She pulled her legs under herself and leaned into her sensitivity. She realized that it was not a frailty, not a fault.

It was a sight. It was a kind of vision, She pointed it toward Emi's house. She felt them inside. Her best friend and the man she loved. They were quiet. They were watching television, holding hands. She looked harder.

And she saw it. It was a kind of blue, she thought. A color she wasn't really familiar with. But one she could recognize. Their baby, growing inside Emi. It was beautiful. It was a girl. And she already seemed to know who she was.

Akana jumped up and threw on a dress. She ran to Emi's house and rang the doorbell. She held her friend and told her it was a girl. She told her it would be perfect. And she told her she had to go, to be on her own.

Emi held her hand and felt the warmth, saw how vibrant she looked. Her friend, who had been wasting away, was healthy, warm, alive. She said goodbye and watched her leave.

Over the years, Akana came back over and over. Ramyon and Emi had their baby, Hana. And when Hana was bullied at school, Aunty Aki showed up to carry her home. When Hana's son Joseph came down with leukemia, Aunty Aki stayed with him in the hospital, ensuring he was taken care of. When Joseph's children, Nia and Pioaw were lost on a camping trip, it was Aunty Aki who found them and brought them back.

Aunty Aki had memorized that color, that special blue. And as it spread, she watched, protected, and built a lighthouse in her heart for the descendents of Emi and Ramyon, showing up when they needed it the most. She watched the blue cluster swell and grow, over hundreds of years. She made a map of that special color and made sure they were safe.

That they were taken care of.

Lately she did her best care remotely. Letters, Checks, visits from experts, necessary, exactly when needed. She traveled to them when she needed. She was the living symbol that some myths were true. Some families have guardians.

Some people have ancestors.

To focus and concentrate, she moved to Oketo. It was closer to the water, empty. It was the least populated area in all of Japan. And she had a big stone building made, one where she could build her maps and be alone, away from the noise, a place she could concentrate and watch.

This is where I found her.

This is where I asked her to build me a map. Surely if she could build one for Emi and Ramyon's family, she could see and map the world for Salvado. So I asked her.

And by 2215, the map listed 1936 people. Almost 2000 Salvado, everywhere she could see. The map was 3D, holographic, and it took up one whole room on the top floor of her giant stone home in Oketo, on the Island of Hokkaido, in Japan.

And it was a beautiful thing.

***

I tried to keep the place clean and stay out of her way while she built the map. But let's face it, my version of clean and Akana Tanaka's were not the same. But I had taken enough cooking classes that I was now fairly amazing. My specialty was actually Thai food.

"Anjo, this is amazing. I should look over your shoulder next time."

"I really just want to thank you for this. You've made my job so much easier – so much better."

"I'm excited. I had never thought to do this. Honestly, you are only the fourth one of us I've ever met."

I suddenly felt lucky I'd had the chance to meet so many. "I've met almost 200 by now. But that's a splash in the ocean, really."

Akana stood up and moved to the refrigerator for some iced tea. She came back with two glasses and poured me one, too.

"You should be exceptionally excited then, by the one showing up today."

"Who is coming today?" I looked up, confused. I had gone back to Brazil to get my belongings before coming out here. It had taken me almost a day and a half to get here from there. And I had to fly in to Tokyo. How could someone be getting here so fast? "How is that possible?"

"She called yesterday. She was already in Tokyo."

I nodded and rolled up some noodles. "Ah. Is this someone I know?"

"She's someone you know of."

I squinted. "Ok, so this is a riddle."

"It's not a riddle."

I whispered. "So, can you feel her on her way?"

Akana closed her eyes and laughed. "Actually, I can. She's about a half hour away."

"That still blows my mind."

"Oh, mine, too, trust me. I better get it ready."

"What?"

She shook her head and wiped her hands. "She's here to see the map, just like you."

We moved the furniture out of the room. This made it easier for people to walk around the holographic map without tripping. The reddish-orange dots were clustered together in groups. Every once in a while there was one or two alone in an area.

"Where are we?" I asked.

Akana moved over about 7 meters to my right. Sure enough, there was Japan. Off the coast was the island of Hokkaido and near the far coast was Oketo. Three orange red dots were closely clustered together. Nothing else seemed nearby.

I pointed to a single dot to the east of us. "What's that?"

"Well, it looks like that is a Salvado underwater. Near the Midway Atoll, in the Pacific Ocean."

"A person underwater?"

"Oh, yeah, there are a few of them on the map."

"That's blowing my mind a bit, not gonna lie." And it did. But not as much as what I saw next. In China, the area closest to us was an entire area colored in red/orange. "What's this? It looks like a huge one of us."

She squinted. "I honestly have no idea."

"That's bizarre." The idea that even she didn't know made a chill run down my back. I had traveled so much by that time that I could tell the general area in China. But the size of it?

She shook it off. "Well, our company is almost here, so get it together." She looked at me smiling. It was hard to imagine that this woman had just lived here, alone, for decades. She seemed funny. She seemed so friendly.

Kind of cool.

We made our way downstairs and stared out the window as a black compact car approached. It hovered lightly over the electromagnetic bars of the road, as smooth as a kids' toy. I tried to see who was in it as she got closer, but the windows were tinted.

I watched as she stepped out and Akana was right. I was excited. I just had no idea she was in Japan.

What was Yazmin Gazzawi doing in Tokyo?

We met her outside and shook hands. I had heard her story so many times it had almost begun to be gospel. About how she had stood up to a tank in Palestine, hundreds of years ago and been run down, before standing up again. She had a little smirk on her face as we walked up the flights to the top room and opened the door. The light was a bit brighter in the room, lit by 1936 red-orange lights scattered all over.

Yazmin looked up, mesmerized. A smile lit up her face, making her look, for a second, like the 12-year-old girl she appeared to be. The whole thing had the feeling of that old Mickey Mouse movie, Fantasia.

"How long did this take?" She looked over at us.

I responded, "we did most of it just this year. The data is updated every day or two."

"You've been in this room for a year, building this?"

I looked at Akana. I realized that living as long as we had had created rifts in our perception. So much so that a year in a room together didn't mean much. She smiled at me.

Yazmin walked around the map, pointing out details. It looked like she was searching. Finally, she started toward the far end of the room. "This is an amazing piece of work. And I would love to talk to you about it for days. But right now, there is one of these dots I am particularly interested in." She kept walking, stopping to point to an area that was almost flush with the far wall.

"This one."

I stepped back to see where she was pointing. I hadn't even thought it was part of the map. It was across the room, a red dot sitting all by itself. I moved close and realized there were no dots anywhere near it. I squinted to see the shapes the map created and realized.

That dot. It wasn't on Earth.

***

Yazmin began. "Okay. It's Friday, July 31st, 2067. We're in Ramla, Israel. 31.9316° N, 34.8729° E. It's before noon. There is a gravitational disruption that potentially sends an object, L, out of the atmosphere at escape velocity, 11.2 kilometers per second. "

I raised my hand, "Um, potentially?"

She nodded, "It's one scenario. The other is that the object is vaporized in a small-yield nuclear explosion in the upper atmosphere."

Akana pulled my hand down. "Right."

"The object, L, continues unabated at that speed until it passes lunar orbit, where there is a slight diminution of speed due to lunar tidal effects."

She reached in and the area right before the one dot expanded.

"That slight reduction adds three days to the 66 days it would have taken to reach this apogee. Because of that, and the minimal vestigial spin of the object imparted from Earth, it ends up here, 69 days later, in the gravitational field of this celestial object, which, on October 2nd, 2067, passes directly above." She pulled back and we could see it clearly.

I felt my jaw go slack. "Holy Shit."

Akana whispered, "Mars." She sat there for a second and spoke up, more loudly, "The object?"

I realized that was what I wanted to know, too. "Yeah, What is L?"

Yazmin looked down. I could tell that this conversation was making her feel awkward.

"A Salvado by the name of Linus Flores. My friend."

I realized that she had been speaking like a robot since she began. Her shoulders sunk. Suddenly, for the first time, she was a 12-year-old girl.

Akana asked, "and you think that's the dot we see on the map on Mars?"

Yazmin continued, "if that dot had been anywhere else, on Venus, on Neptune, I would have... I don't know what. But it's on Mars. It's where it could be. Where he could be."

I uncrossed my arms and stepped forward. "I don't know this part of your story. It happened after."

"It did. It was 22 years later. I ended up in a prison. Linus Flores showed up at the end to ferry me home. We spent a week together, seven days. And then he sacrificed himself to save me."

I stepped over to stand next to her. "I'm sorry."

She took my hand. "He did it without thinking."

Akana nodded. "That is...wow."

Yazmin looked back and forth between us. "And now, comes the questions?"

"What do you mean?" I asked.

"You want to ask me if it's really true that I've spent 150 years trying to find someone I only knew for seven days."

At that moment, I wanted to tell her that if I didn't understand anything else about the universe, I understood that. I wanted to tell her about Savi and how he chose to stay and sleep in that truck rather than walk the 20 feet to his own bed just because he knew I was hurting.

And that if there was a chance that any part of him were still alive anywhere, I would move heaven and earth to find it and bring it home.

I wanted to tell her I got it.

I looked at Akana, who had spent all of her own years protecting the children of a man she couldn't have -- a man who had gone off to be with a woman who had hurt her.. And that she had nurtured generations of their children, grandchildren, and more...

Why?

Maybe it was the same reason for all three of us. Maybe it was something different. That's the problem with being human, you don't get to see inside someone else's head. You don't get to evaluate their motives or tell them what their world view is, right or wrong. You don't get to have everything you need to see them, completely.

You just get to say you understand. And hope that's true.

***

Yazmin was speaking Japanese quickly on the phone. I admit that I picked up very little of it. Not because my Japanese was horrible, per se. Mostly because it seemed to be a very high tech call.

She turned to us. "Okay, If that's cool, we can filter in JAXA's mars database and get some information about this area." She handed Akana a piece of paper with the database location and password on it.

"Got it." and she went to work.

"You can just get the Japanese Aerospace Exploration Agency to do anything you want?" I joked.

"I hope so. I lead it. When I came back, I went to work for the UN for about a hundred years.

After that, I chose to follow a dream and work for a space agency. JAXA was hiring and so I came on board. I've been there now for about 50 years, running it for about 10."

"Ok. You can tell them what to do." I laughed. My situation was just as unbelievable. I was in line to run a company I'd been at for about a hundred and fifty years. At a certain point, you're just a logical choice. At a certain point, seniority wins.

"I've got it." Akana smiled and zoomed in on the area around the dot on Mars. There were new symbols and language all around the dot. And it showcased the entire area. Yazmin began to read the symbols.

It took a few days of back and forth to figure out the exact area on Mars. But once we did, Yazmin was incredibly excited. Even Akana was excited. And I realized that there was part of my story I still needed to tell them. And I wasn't sure how they'd take it.

Yazmin had slipped easily into teacher mode. She waved her hands and zoomed into the map.

"Using spectroscopy, we've determined that this area of the surface is something unusual. It seems to contain a number of elements that have no real business being there – elements that don't exist anywhere on Mars."

She turned to us. "Or really anywhere in our solar system."

I nodded. "So there are things there that can't be explained?"

"Well." She continued, "It's more like nothing there can be explained. In fact, due to the aggregation of different materials. JAXA named the area 'Mozaiku'"

My eyes went round. "Or, Mosaic, in English."

"Yes."

I thought back to Devilboy's tirade on sci-fi shows inventing probabilistic odds against something that had no mathematical model. What were the odds against this? I had no idea. But it wasn't likely. Not really at all.

If this hadn't been that day, a longer conversation would have ensued. But this was 2215 -- the beginning of that day. The day that would reshuffle so much of what we knew about the world.

The room lit up. We were connected to the live databases of the agency that Japan relied upon most to keep the skies safe. And today the skies were not safe. Alarms bleated out so loudly that Yazmin had to shut them off to make a phone call. Akana and I watched the missiles let loose in real time. The lines made them look like bright red ink in water, seeping out across the world. They came from North America. All across the country.

Yazmin stayed on the phone, panicked as she yelled out information. This was real. I ran to the window to look out, but there was nothing. Nothing to see. And this stone brick house in the middle of nowhere, faced a countryside that had no information to give. We were miles from the nearest person in one of the least-occupied territories on the least-populated Japanese island in the Pacific. We were alone. Yazmin tapped me on the shoulder, holding one hand over the phone. "Anjo, collect as many wires and metal hangers as you can, grab some sheets, blankets, take Akana to the basement."

I looked over at Akana, trembling in the corner, staring up at the imminent destruction. "Do you have a basement?"

She nodded wanly and I grabbed her hand. Yazmin was running around, phone to her ear, collecting things. She followed us closely as we all made our way to the basement.

It was clean but empty, sparse, exactly what I would have expected from Akana. I assembled what I could from Yezmin's instructions. She placed her phone next to us and barked orders in Japanese at the people on the other line.

I could tell it was killing her not to be there for them, even as she tried to be there for us. She started pulling through the things I had brought.

"Okay, we have about seven minutes. The closest place the larger bombs are headed is Osaka, two of them. They'll barely touch us, we're over 1200 km away. But there is a smaller one going to hit Sapporo right afterward, and we have to account for the fact that with so many, there are likely going to be targets missed and that adds a lot of randomness."

"Got it." I held Akana's hand. All of this was outside my experience but it was completely overwhelming to her. Yazmin was like a soldier. She handed me back the metal and wires as she laid the blankets on the floor.

"Anjo, I need you to tie us together. Bend the metal hangers, wrap the wires, tie them around our arms and legs so we are connected. After that, we're going to roll ourselves up in the blankets."

Akana looked up, confused. I started on her.

Yazmin grabbed her arms, half listening to the chaos coming from her phone on speaker next to her. "Ropes and things like that will be destroyed or decay. We're going to have to dig our way out, and that's going to suck, but one of us getting lost alone is going to suck worse, do you understand?"

Tears filled Aki's eyes as she nodded. I had been wrapping her in metal and wires, attaching her to me. I started on Yazmin.

"This building is just a big block of concrete. And that's good. That helps. But it's going to come down. A lot of the weight is going to collapse into the basement. We're going to stay under the rubble, as safe as we can be, until the bombs stop. Then we're going to take our time and dig our way out together. Do you guys understand?"

I nodded. No matter what, we were going to not lose each other. That was the objective.

Yazmin reached up to hold Akana's face. She wiped her tears away. I pulled the women close as we dropped down and rolled ourselves up in the blankets. We laid there, holding onto each other as Yazmin explained.

"We're going to survive. I need you two to understand that."

As I pulled them closer, I was grateful for both of them. Providence had put me in a situation where I had someone to take care of -- to prevent me from freaking out. And someone to take care of me – to help me survive. I wondered who took care of Yazmin.

I felt them both breathing, warm, next to me as the rush of hot air ripped the building above us into pieces, sending the sharpened raw rubble down on top of us in a seemingly never ending torrent. My eardrums seemed to invert from the sound of a hundred thousand airplanes taking off at the same time. The pressure pushed us down, swaddled us, and rather than sending us scattered in different directions, fused us together into a single unit, a colony whose sole focus was to ride this out, to survive, and to walk out of here, together.

It all seemed so bizarre and unbelievable while it was happening – so impossibly loud and ending. I closed my eyes and waited for it to end.

5 - Shells
Marietta Nuevo, Aztecana - 2446

If I seem nosy and invasive, you might need to give me that and move on. I'd long ago lost all shame or trepidation about who I was and what I did. I'm an archivist. I'm a story collector, more than a story teller, really. And if this collection feels disjointed or the people involved seem less than who they really are, that's on me.

I take full responsibility.

Jamie Symone and her mom made it to Houston in a day or two. And they did stay there. Reina stayed with them. Nica helped her sell the house and have her stuff shipped remotely. Fancie went back 2 weeks later to Newark to be with her family. But she visited a few times a year. And, on a few occasions, spent the summer there. Monica Symone was right about a few things. First of all, as a doctor in good standing, it took her almost no time to find a job, running the trauma department at a nearby hospital. She stepped away from research as Jamie jumped into it.

Jamie and Reina were interning at NASA within the year. Within 10 years, they were building their careers there. By 28, they were in the Astronaut training program. They were inseparable, so much so, that when I first met with Jamie fourteen or so years after the Savior Event, at a restaurant called Space City Birria, on Milam street, I had no choice but to interview both of them.

They were both 30 years old when I met them the first time. I turned on my recorder.

Jamie went first. "Ok, so this is not going public or anything?"

I shook my head. "No, this is about documenting us, the Salvado."

Reina shook my hand. "Ok. if we're going to be honest…"

"I'm Anjo Killean." I said, mostly for the benefit of the recording. "And I hope we are."

Jamie shrugged, "I'll be honest." She opened the menu and tried to choose.

I pulled my menu over. "Thank you." It looked like the breakfast here would be good. It was a sort of Tex-Mex place. Reina was looking me over as I searched the menu.

"You're one, too, huh?" Reina took a sip of water through her straw.

I smiled. "I am."

She leaned in, conspiratorially, "Can I ask how you did it?"

Jamie slapped her arm. "Reina!"

She backpedalled. "I just asked if I could ask."

I put the menu down and looked at her. We were close to the same age. I certainly couldn't petition for their stories and not tell mine. "It's ok. I jumped off of a mountain."

"Hardcore. Not fucking around." Reina looked impressed.

I shook my head again. "No, ma'am."

Reina peered over her menu. "How many have you interviewed?"

"Well, I have been working on getting the stories of the ones who came to us – the people who came to Xenovera. But I just recently started traveling and talking to people away from there. Out in the world." I looked at Jamie. She seemed entertained enough to let Reina ask the questions.

"That's cool." Reina tried to act cool.

"It is."

Her voice dropped a bit. "Do you feel like you are better now? Over the reasons why you did it?"

I realized that I wouldn't get many answers until I gave some. "Oh, I'm being interviewed? Okay. Yes. I do. There was a kind of deadness in my life – a halting. And I don't feel it anymore. It doesn't hurt that I'm traveling all over the country interviewing people and getting paid for it."

She smiled widely. "Nice."

"How about you, Jamie? Do you feel it now?" I tried to bring the interview to her a bit.

She motioned for the waitress and thought for a second. "I missed my dad. I fell into a kind of a… hole… on the anniversary of his death and now, I feel like I can handle it."

"Yeah?" The waitress looked at Jamie first when she stepped over. She ordered a light breakfast and Reina ordered the same thing. I figured a breakfast burrito and an orange juice would do it. Jamie continued after the waitress left.

"Okay, I have this theory that when someone first dies, someone you love, you take all of them in, all of it, like a snake trying to digest a pig or something. You just suck it all in. And it makes you fat and sluggish. And it hurts. It pushes your organs aside and breaks your insides. And then, when you have the chance, you process part of that meal. You take a part of it and you make a kind of book out of it, moving it to this shelf. This good experience, that one. Eventually, you look normal again, but your library inside is full. I don't know if that sounds stupid." She looked down.

I nodded, reaching over for her. "No, I like it."

She tried to act a bit more jocular now. "But my library of my dad is full now. I read those books all the time. And he makes me laugh more than cry now."

I understood that. "That's beautiful."

Reina looked at Jamier with admiration. You could see that Reina doted on her friend. "Yeah, I love that." She looked down for a second, and then, as if she had just remembered, asked, "Wait, have you interviewed Clyde?"

Jamie put her hand over her friend's. "Reina, I'm sure he hasn't talked to everyone."

I took a deep breath. "Clyde Morrison? I did talk to him."

Reina squealed. "Oh my god!"

I turned to Jamie and tried to read her expression. "I wasn't going to speak out of turn or anything."

The waitress came and set our food down. But Jamie wasn't interested in it. "Is he okay?"

I pulled my dish over and thought. "He's good. He's getting... He's good."

"I can't believe I told him 100 years. That's a long time. It's 87 more years."

Reina had a mischievous look on her face. "What's he doing?"

I took a bite of the breakfast burrito and asked, "do you want to know?"

Jamie took a deep breath. "I think I do."

"Well," I started, "he went to prison. Interfering with a crime scene. It was supposed to be for two years. He got up in a bit of trouble when someone else tried to hurt him and ended up in the infirmary. It wasn't his fault. But he received three more years. After that, he walked across the street from the prison and got a job as an orderly at the prison halfway house infirmary."

Jamie was fascinated, "working with patients?"

"Yes."

"After five years, he took the NCLEX-RN test and became a certified nurse."

Jamie put her hands over her mouth. "Oh my god."

Reina lifted her glass. "Clyde's a nurse."

"Since then, for the last few years, he's been working as a nurse and taking medical classes at night. He's getting his master's degree in palliative care." I took a bite and watched Jamie closely. She started crying.

"She let out a long breath. "I'm sorry. I feel like this weight I was carrying just disappeared."

I took her hand. "He's going to be okay. He's really good at it."

Reina took her other hand. "See, Jam. He's good at it. He helps people."

Jamie smiled. "I know. Thank you."

I spoke directly to her. "No problem. He's excited to see you again."

Reina laughed. "Clyde the Nurse."

I wanted to get back on track. I knew her story up until now. I figured it would be nice to know what came next. "So, what are your plans, you two?"

Reina was excited. "We're in line for our first launch."'

Jamie nodded, chewing. "The Tidal."

"That's the name of the ship?"

Reina picked up a salt shaker and turned it into a little ship. "Yes, it's going to land on the moon, we're placing extensive digging units, and then we leave." She poured out some salt and landed her ship right back into its lodging area.

Jamie smirked at me. "It's a little more complicated than that."

"And when is that?" I asked.

Reina was bubbly. "Two years. We're training now."

"It takes that long, huh?"

"Oh, yes, It's the first step." Reina grabbed the shaker again and rained space debris down on the chips in front of her.

"You know the other steps?" I admittedly knew nothing about how all this worked.

"Ok, two years, the Tidal. It's a pump and dump." She counted one on her hand.

Jamie laughed. "Reina…"

"We go to the planet, set up and leave."

I nodded. "Okay."

She went on. "Then, two years after that, we line up for the Illiad." Reina painted it in the air.

"That sounds cool." it did.

"It is. It's a multi-hop job that takes us around Io" Reina reached for the salt shaker again and spun it around.

Jamie took a bite and laughed. "Jupiter's moon."

"Right."

Reina continued. "And then we help plot these devices that will send power to ships."

"Laser beams," Jamie said with a mouth full of eggs.

Reina landed her salt shaker. "So it becomes a kind of space superhighway."

I was captivated by their enthusiasm. "That is amazing."

Jamie tried to be the voice of reason. "If we do a good job on the Tidal."

"Then, what?"

Reina waved her arms as though this were the big one. "The Sargasso!"

"Stop. There is no way we get the Sargasso. " Jamie shook her head, smiling.

"If we get it."

"If we get it. It's a test for a multigenerational ship. It's bigger. Just meant to go out and stay out for two years, make it to the end of the solar system and back." Watching Jamie and Reina talk about these missions was like listening to teenagers talk about their favorite card games in a diner across the street from a convention. The passions created during a youth spent in nerdery were meant to build this, human platforms for change, people with impossibly large appetites for the specifics of what it would take to do something never been done before.

"That's crazy."

"It's a big deal," Reina interjected.

I clarified. "In eight years?"

"Yes." They both nodded enthusiastically.

"I hope you get it. I do." I made a point to follow the news about all this, moving forward.

"Well. It's tough," Jamie whispered.

I leaned in, "What do you mean?"

Jamie looked around. "This is off the record? Not public?"

I shook my head. "No public parts of this."

She took a breath. "I don't know where the country is going to be in eight years."

Reina agreed. "You said it."

"You're worried about the politics?" My eye was drawn out the window to a woman across the street facing us. She seemed to be walking against traffic.

Reina continued. "It's extended beyond politics."

"Who knows if this country will even be here in eight years." Jamie stacked her plate up. You could tell she was one of those "clean my area up to make it easier to bus" people and I liked that.

Reina made a box-like motion with her hands. "Closed up, isolated. It's getting worse."

Jamie shook her head. "We're lucky. NASA is like an oasis, but how long can that last?"

I looked out the window again. The woman walking toward the street had crossed and was making her way slowly toward the restaurant. It looked like she was coming right this way. Her pace was steady, not rushed, and she had a blank look on her face. As she got closer I could see her shirt was ripped and sliding off of her shoulder. She wore what looked like a number of skirts over each other. I was reminded of the homeless people I'd seen who often wore everything they owned at the same time.

Part of me was listening to Reina's concerns about the country while part of me was staring, focused, trying to figure out what this woman was doing.

She kept moving toward the window to my right without stopping. She was five feet away and it was clear she wouldn't stop.

"Guys…"

She put her head down and slammed into the window. The first time, a five-foot crack appeared running upward, with a tiny circular space where the top of her head had met the glass. She put her hands on the window, widely apart, and slammed her head into it again.

The third time, it shattered, sending shards the size of business cards flying into the diner, forcing us from our seats in the booth as we pulled away amidst the chaos.

She hammered her head into the broken glass at the base of the window and used her forehead as a claw, slamming into the brick below the broken pane, pulling it out one piece at a time as the occupants of the diner screamed.

I realized that there was no blood, no marks, no abating of the intensity of the violence.

She was Salvada.

A scream came from her – wild, primal, animal. I tried to train my ears to understand what she was saying. Until almost as if ungarbled via a translator, my brain heard it.

"DEAD PEOPLE. DEAD PEOPLE. DEAD PEOPLE."

I reached down to call 911 but my phone slipped from my hand and under the table behind me.

"DEAD PEOPLE. DEAD PEOPLE. DEAD PEOPLE."

She twitched and flopped like a reptile, crawling into the diner through the newly opened window, cracking and breaking everything in her path with her flailing head. The illusion that she was a snake was fostered by her arms, still plastered to her side as she swung her head like a wrecking ball.

She was chasing us. Shrieking. Slamming her head against the floor.

She screamed more loudly, flopping on the ground, crawling toward us, using her head like some kind of weapon, like a tool. Her face slammed into the ground over and over as she propelled herself forward.

"DEAD PEOPLE. DEAD PEOPLE. DEAD PEOPLE."

Someone from the diner must have called the police, because a large black truck made a u-turn and pulled up right outside the window. And three men with strange-looking rifles came rolling out the back. I tried to position myself in front of Jamie and Reina, but as I looked back at them I saw that both of them had picked up weapons, silverware, to fight back.

I wondered why I hadn't.

Rope netting came out from the front of the rifles as the three men wrapped the woman up tightly and began to carry her to the truck. It all happened so quickly, I barely caught any of it. The back of the truck closed up and I saw the symbol as it drove away. It was an official looking silhouette of a bird, in shades of red and orange, on the dark navy black-blue of the truck.

And this was the first time I saw what the government's response to us was.

***

I tried to find her. I discovered that this woman who had attacked the diner was a local homeless person named Florida. No one seemed to know her last name. But she had disappeared for ten years or so after the Savior Event and only recently returned, causing havoc everywhere, across Houston. I went down to the local precinct and they didn't know anything. And when I asked them where she might have been taken, no one was interested in answering. All I did know is that this woman, this homeless Salvada, knew what Jamie and I were, even through the glass.

Even from across the street.

I returned back home to catalogue the stories. I'd been detached from a lot of what was happening in the streets, in America. I flicked through the news and found a man with short black hair in a bright blue suit orating animatedly.

He waved his arms around as he told his own version of what had happened in front of the diner. In front of a graphic that said "Shellshocked!" He called her a "shell," alluding to the idea that she had died and come back "empty" as just an invulnerable shell. This was the first time I'd heard this pejorative for us and it gave me a chill.

It seemed so inhuman.

And it propagated the story that we had died. In this narrative, the people who all tried to commit suicide on Savior Day had succeeded. And then returned to live as empty husks. Suddenly the bird on the van made more sense. It was a phoenix. Returning from the dead. Alive, but empty.

Soulless.

It would be hundreds of years before I saw Jamie again. But what happened next with her could be found in the news.

***

The Illiad landed in 2065 after a perfectly executed mission. Nica lost her voice from cheering, amazed at the feather-soft landing that they had managed directly on the target. The landing demonstrated a fluid vertical take off and landing for a spacebound vehicle and the ship was nearly ready to launch again even as it set down. This was a huge win and everyone watching knew it.

Not long afterward, Jamie and Reina discovered they would lead the crew of the Sargasso. Jamie was appointed captain and Reina would be the XO. For this test flight, there would be a complement of 10 people, including the two women. The job was to go out for two years and return. After this, similar ships would leave the solar system, bringing much larger crews to unexplored planets.

The Sargasso was impressive on paper, but in real life, standing on a platform at NASA, it was bigger than life.

It was made for the imagination of dreamers and poets immersed in the lore of science fiction for generations, mindful of their own visions of what the future looked like – massive, sleek, and shiny. It was the size of a university campus, and equally erudite, eschewing traditional ideas of aerodynamics in favor of a giant brooding comfort, an anomaly in the history of the space program – a ship designed not to maximize space at the cluttered expense of the claustrophobic occupant, but to exercise the expansive whimsy of a generational occupant, one who would raise children in its holds and plot futures in its galleys.

The largest part, the core body of it, was barrel-like, with a couple of rotating cylinders that would provide a consistent artificial 1G of gravity across the expanse of it. It was large enough that, for most purposes, down would be a near-perfect-looking vertical for any regular sized human observer, even in the larger areas. Outside of that core, It was a ship composed of many smaller modules, capable of detaching once it landed on a planet, with some pieces remaining stationary to house families and other pieces capable of roving, flight, or even long-term living elsewhere. And its surface reflected that functionality through its scored and ribbed external appearance. Someone in the know could draw lines on the outside of the ship, determining where it might open up and split, allowing this piece to travel independently to some nearby destination while the whole remained stationary, providing shelter to the occupants building homes, colonies, entire timelines on some alien planet. It was one-of-a-kind and so was this outing, intended to prove that generational ships were possible.

And Jamie would lead this mission.

The suspicions she had garnered when she joined the space program, due to her status as a Salvada, had mostly disappeared as she rose through the ranks and more and more people had the chance to work with her. They realized that she hadn't gotten to this place because of her invulnerability. It was because of her ability to lead, her resourcefulness, her quick mind.

It was her human gifts that had gotten her here.

Most of the team had gone through the core training, either with Jamie or under her. Beyond that, they were chosen specifically to be able to spend two years in space together, congenially. So, as you might imagine, they bonded pretty quickly.

There was Lee and her husband Rama, both doctors, who had been close since high school. Getting them to do karaoke without dueting was difficult. But the minute they were on a ship, they were professional and capable on their own. Jason, an engineer with reddish hair and an easy laugh. Mig, a navigator, smart, sarcastic, always in on the joke. Sarah and Xila, the newest on the team, botanists and foodies. Zandra, a mechanic. and Elo, in communication.

They were all so handsome, something the media focused on relentlessly in its coverage. The progressively more and more nationalized American news channels trumpeted the idea of America's supremacy in space, despite the fact that Japan had put generation ships into space 10 years ago. But, as Jamie had recounted, being inside NASA, they were insulated a bit from the political grandstanding.

They had enough to do.

The mission plan for the Sargasso was a little different in the front end than any mission Jamie had been on, so far. A week before launch they were all meant to board, living together until the ship was propelled into space. This was the final flight test to see if they had forgotten anything they might need out there – something that they couldn't stop and load. No one knew what that might be, but, you can't plan for the unknowable.

The ten of them brought every single item onboard that was loaded. This was specifically so that they would know where they stowed it. No one wanted to be searching for something that some member of the ground crew had stored in a location that seemed reasonable to them, yet inscrutable to everyone else.

Jamie and Reina felt like old hands by this time. At 38, each of them had three live missions under their belts and more pilot hours in planes and shuttles than they could count.

They focused on bringing things onto the ship they wished they'd had in previous outings. Even though the supplement packs were packed with vitamin K, D, A, and E, they still missed, more than anything, real fruit. The onboard rehydrators were the highest quality ones they had ever used, which meant that the little square dehydrated oranges they carried in boxes could be turned into actual real-tasting fruit pretty easily. In fact, the only fruit it couldn't manage was bananas, and they had other ways to get potassium.

Jason brought the media server on board. Once he set it up, they were amazed at how easy it was to stream movies and music all across the massive ship. Jamie asked him how much content was on it during dinner the first night. He laughed.

"Infinite, Captain. It's huge." He winked. "Try to stump it."

Xila yelled out, "No way! It has A Christmas Story!"

Sara was reading from her phone, connected to the server. "And Elf, and Scrooged, Mary Xmas, and Killer Elves."

Reina laughed and grabbed a chicken leg from the table. "Well, Christmas is covered."

Jason looked up and waved his hands. "We're gonna be up there for two Christmases. So I got surprises, people."

"Satan at the North Pole. Damn. You're probably a secret genius." Mig patted him on the back as he got up to grab a drink.

This is what Jamie was hoping would happen. Bonding over silly things was far superior to bonding over crisis. And Jamie had the same functional joy watching people bond and connect as every captain has since the beginning of time. She was literally watching her team coalesce this week. She stood up.

"Okay, you guys know why I've brought you here today. Let's launch this dinner."

All around the table, the team pulled out tiny boxes and containers. Except for Mig's, they seemed classy and well-packaged.

Lee looked around, grabbing her husband's hand. "It's not until…"

Reina jumped up with a glass in her hand. "Tomorrow, ladies and gentlemen. Is, as we all know, Lee and Rama's 10th anniversary. We give them gifts today because we are sneaky fucks."

Jamie yelled out along with the rest of the crew, "yeah, little bitch."

Reina bowed.

Rama was shaking his head as he reached for Mig's gift. "I want to see what this is. It looks wrong."

"It's so wrong." Mig was relatively short and swarthy. His rough beard, olive skin, and black hair made his teeth shine like pearls, bright and illuminated white, when he smiled. Which was often.

Rama and Lee pulled the wrapping from the large, human sized package to find a pillow, plush and comfy looking, shaped like a naked woman.

"It's a threesome pillow." Mig announced.

Lee put her head in her hands, laughing. "She looks so soft. And fertile."

Rama was ordinarily shy and this would have been the kind of thing that caused him to go beet-red. But not in this group. He was home here. He set the pillow in between him and Lee as she reached for its breasts and pumped them.

"I think we're just going to stay in our room for a bit, sorry guys."

Jason raised his glass. "To no HR department!"

Everyone toasted.

They passed their gifts, each one a little siller than the one before. Except Jamie's gift, a tiny, perfectly to scale metal model of the Sargasso.

"Wow. This is amazing. I bet there's a little me in there." Lee was awed.

Jamie nodded, "Well, it wouldn't be the lil Sargasso if there weren't a lil you in there."

The first day turned into the first night. They ran diagnostics and tried to act as they would if they were in space, every once in a while asking Jason's database on ship for a song they thought might stump it.

The next week went by without any trouble, and Jamie got to watch 10 people become a family with a purpose.

With a goal.

They prepared for launch day

The launch was late at night. Being able to visualize the stars cleanly and escape the glare of the sun was a big win. The goal was to make it to low Earth orbit and then use the ship's complement of thrusters to leave for space. They'd follow the sunrise around the world. The Sargasso was designed to operate in atmospheres as well as in space, and for that, it was unique in NASA's arsenal.

The launch was easy, and there were cheers as the massive thing lumbered upward, toward the outer atmosphere. After one near-complete orbit of the planet it would be in position to move upward, toward its destination in the outer solar system.

This trip to the edge of the solar system and back would then be 28 months. And the initial launch was the only time that the crew would have to be seated and protected from gravitic effects.

Within the hour, the red lights around the main control area of the ship blinked off and the remaining lights glowed a steady green. The drums around the main section of the ship began to spin, ensuring that gravity on board would be consistent while in orbit. The crew began to move around, staying mostly within the 1G gravity zone provided by the spinning drums.

Except Jason and Zan, whose jobs had brought them to the outer aft ring to fix what seemed like a faulty coupling. Reina insisted on going with them to speed the job with an extra hand and Jamie nodded, not overjoyed with the prospect of them being so far away. The ship was huge and the internal shuttle would take 15 minutes to get there.

Jamie had settled into the control mod with Mig and was going over the navigation plan, when her phone's communicator rang out with Reina's voice.

"Captain, we still have an hour until this next stage launch and we'll be back in about half that."

"Ah, well, don't make promises you can't keep."

"Ai, Captain." Jamie could hear the wink in Reina's voice when she called her "Captain." It made her smile.

She went over the launch protocols over and over again until her brain nearly hurt. Then, she leaned back and stared at the holographic map in front of her.

"It's a free trip around the world." Mig smiled at her.

"Kind of a bonus, right?" Jamie searched the live updated map for any anomalies.

Mig caught it first. "Hey, Captain. What's that?"

Jamie squinted. The map showed movement in front of them coming up from the planet. It looked like a series of small projectiles. Then, an explosion. Jamie called down to control.

"Blue One, This is Sargasso Actual. We have an event in low-level orbit in front of us, are you seeing this?"

"We are, Sargasso Actual. It looks like an explosive event of some sort, maybe low-yield nuclear. It shouldn't affect you, but we have eyes on it."

"Well, I don't like it, Blue One. Can you run some scenarios?"

"Running now, Sargasso Actual. We'll have more information for you in a minute or two."

"Thank you, Blue One." Jamie switched gears. Even if this was nothing, she needed to control it.

"Reina, I need you to get your people back to the Drum. We're seeing some kind of event up ahead."

"What kind of event, Captain? We just got here and started."

"I know, Commander, but we're safer under the drum. Confirm?"

There was a pause as she interacted with her team. "Confirmed, Captain, we are on our way back."

Mig was shaking his head. "I don't like it, Captain. It's over an area with a ton of satellites and lower-orbit mechanics."

"What are you worried about?" Jamie turned the map around.

"I know these. They're communication networks. Literally hundreds of them."

"Right?"

Mig shook his head. "Look." He pointed to one of them, closest to the explosion. It shifted in orbit and exploded. "It's a chain reaction."

Jamie looked down and saw the red dot that marked the spot where Reina, Jason, and Zandra were on the internal shuttle coming back. They were at least ten minutes away,.

"Blue One, this is Sargasso Actual. Do you have my situation?" Jamie began to panic a little.

"Sargasso Actual, this is Blue One. We do. This is not good news. We have a chain reaction with a series of satellites. You can see it beginning."

"I do see it, Blue One. How much damage are we going to take?"

"Everything in the main cylinder, under the drums, will be fine. We're looking at significant damage to the lower rings and sparse damage to the second level rings."

"Fuck." Mig pointed to the red dot. They were just entering the second-level rings.

Jamie ran out of the command mod toward the shuttle area. Along the way, she grabbed three thinsuits from a side closet. If she could get them to the shuttle pod, the team could handle the decompression that would happen if the module they were in was impacted. She tried to think as calmly as she could. There were no suits in the pods themselves.

The pods needed to be light and empty. These internal shuttles were egg-shaped shells that moved from section to section, module to module, speeding across the ship. She reached the door for the shuttle that Reina and the rest were on and opened the control panel for the doorway. It hissed open to the wide space of the shuttle shaft.

The interior shafts of the shuttle weren't affected by the gravity generated by the drums, intentionally, so that there would be less drag on the shuttle pods. That didn't mean she couldn't turn it on. That seemed like the fastest way to get to the pod. She held onto a rung jutting out from the wall and used her phone device to log into the internal control. Suddenly, she felt one full gravity pull her down toward the shuttle. She held tight to the suits and let go of the rung.

She started to fall. At first, at a reasonable speed. Then, faster and faster. She was approaching terminal velocity. The shaft was a blur, fading into a grey rush as she held her arm out to slow her fall, her invulnerable skin cracking and shattering the rungs and handles next to her as she slowed. She opened communication.

"Reina, I'm in the shuttle shaft, just about 300 meters in front of you. I need you to slow the pod so I can enter. I have thinsuits for your team."

"Got it, Captain, I see you. We'll slow to you."

Jamie saw the pod approaching, silently giving thanks.

A door opened at what, to her, was the top. She slid in and landed hard on the floor of the pod.

Jason helped her up, grabbing a suit and slipping it on. "Thanks, Captain. That was amazing."

Zandra and Reina slid into their suits. Thinsuits weren't really made to be worn in space, but they were light and easy to put on, and they would protect, you for a short time, from explosive decompression and the impacts of a hull breach.

"Jam, how much time do we have?" Reina was dressed now and forgetting protocol.

Jamie called up to the navigator, "Mig, how much time do we have? I have the team here. Can you see us?"

"I see you, Captain. We're looking at impact from the larger of the satellites in less than a minute. There isn't time for you to get back. Move as far away from the hull as you can."

Zandra stopped the shuttle and they spilled out, running toward the center modules of the ship. Jamie was overwhelmed, again, by the sheer size of the Sargasso, built to nurture and protect a crew of 3,000. She felt so small, her people so vulnerable.

Rumbles from lower-level impacts shook the ship. They could see walls buckling as they moved forward, closing and sealing doors behind them. Jamie took the back, aware that it left her closest to the hull, as she pushed her people forward. They were only about 100 meters away from the thicker hull of the interior farm area. If they could make it there, they could be safe.

That was the last thing that Jamie thought before the wall behind her disappeared, dissolving to open space. She felt the pull of the blackness behind her as she pulled herself toward the team. Zandra dove into the module ahead of them and Reina shut the door behind her.

"What are you doing?" Jamie yelled out at Reina, the thin air barely able to carry the sound.

But she knew what she was doing. She was trying to keep Jason and Zan safe, letting them move further inward toward the center area of the ship. Jamie reached out and grabbed her, pulling her in closely. The thinsuit was holding up so far, keeping her safe and breathing as the room was exposed to space. The Captain wrapped herself around the smaller woman to protect her, crawling toward the next module, hoping that this was it. Hoping the impacts were over.

A piece of a satellite tore through the open space next to her and slammed into the walls in front of them. Jamie saw the ravaged bodies of Jason and Zan float into space, surrounded by pieces of the ship. She held onto Reina even tighter, trying to grab onto something, anything, that would keep her anchored in the ship. Another impact created an explosion in front of them, throwing them backward, out of the Sargasso entirely. Jamie spun, Reina still curled up in her arms, falling away from the massive ship.

She tried to feel for signs of life in the woman in her arms but she was afraid to look, to let go, to open up for a second. Maybe she could protect her from what was coming next with her own body. She thought about Clyde for a moment -- what he had endeavored to do -- and tried to take what was in her, the thing keeping her alive in space, and transfer it to Reina. Her eyes squeezed shut and when she finally opened them she saw the ship getting smaller, moving out toward open space. Command was right. The drum area was intact. But all the modules below it were gone.

Jamie felt the fragile, frozen body in her arms snap and crack under the pressure of her embrace, but she couldn't let go. As they fell, she could feel her friend melting while she struggled to hold on to her. They fell downward, with an eastward speed of 7 kps from the inertia of low Earth orbit, hitting the atmosphere like a bomb and then impacting Earth with the force of 50 grams of TNT, leaving a crater in the South Khorassan province of Iran,

She stood up, holding what was left of her best friend's bones in her arms.

***

Rama had died, as well, from an errant impact. The rest continued the mission without her, with only half the compliment of crew. Mig became captain.

That was her last mission for a long time. The idea of surviving while her crew was picked off, one by one, by tragedies, while her best friend dissolved in her arms – all this followed her.

It took Jamie six months to learn the full story of the nuclear explosion that had killed half of her crew, and even then it was heavily redacted. The U.S. government used it as an excuse to ramp up its own weapons program, but that was something anyone could have seen coming. She learned about the plain black suitcase at a weight station in an airport in the Middle East, something no one on the ship could have prepared for. She recalled her mother's injunctions against plain black suitcases and watched her world dissolve into bizarre coincidences that made no sense.

It would take her years to realize what we all saw, eventually. When you live so long, there are patterns that form in the space you live in, thick and black, like recurring lines in the sidewalk in front of you. The lines marked off suitcases, and nuclear explosions, and the shapes of spaceships, metal wires, the events that built our remarkable lives, recycled over and over to fill in thousands of years, flashing in front of the eyes of people who had learned young to identify patterns. She remembered something that she had heard in Ms. Carvin's class, in a speech given by a classmate.

In that speech, he had talked about "superstitious pigeons" – how their brains were optimized to identify patterns so effectively that every time they were fed, they considered the conditions of that feeding and tried to replicate them. Were they hopping on one leg? Were they bucking forward? They repeated those random actions over and over.

And you could see them spastically moving on the cement walkways of the park, each performing some elaborate dance of half-remembered superstitious motions, hoping for some eventual payoff.

In 2090, Monica Symone passed away in her sleep, a few months from her 89th birthday, holding hands with a daughter who had camped in her bedroom since she had gotten sick the year before. Jamie had never let her mother forget how she had changed her life, moved, uprooted everything, just to make that daughter happy one day, just to keep her in the world. Her death created a kind of "detachment moment," a point where everyone from your previous life is gone. Or it would have, if Monica hadn't worked so hard to stay alive, in her heart. Over the course of the last 40 years, she had recorded hundreds of holographic videos, talking to Jamie, telling her secrets, lifting her up, reminding her that she was brought into this universe in love and that's how she had been simmered and cooked and served to the world.

Eventually, Jamie would watch them all.

And eventually, NASA folded. After two full lifetimes of research, teaching, and study, she stepped away. It was her biggest passion, but her greatest heartache at the same time. She knew she would have never left on her own. Closing was a brutal mercy, but a mercy nonetheless.

In 2146, Jamie tried to meet up with Clyde. She made her way to Atlanta and sat in the broken down restaurant that had long since replaced the convenience store across from the hotel. America had closed up to anyone from the outside world decades ago and there was a desperation in the eyes of the other people in the restaurant. She was there because Clyde would remember Reina, and Jamie's library of her needed something – anything. One more book, one more paragraph. She couldn't even remember Reina's last words. She wanted something.

Something.

Three masked police officers entered through the glass door and marched their way to the back, not even stopping at the counter.

They laughed and pointed to the display area that showcased two different flavors of pie. But that would be for later. People had developed a blind spot for the police, wandering through the streets, looking for people that didn't belong like ghosts while we all pretended that we were in control – that they weren't there.

Jamie paid and stood up. She was tired and she figured she'd wait outside. She remembered the flowery suitcase her mom had bought for her 200 years ago when she was here. Her arms were empty now. She was traveling with just what was in her pockets. She wondered if she could convince Clyde to go with her to Mexico.

If he showed.

In 2246, she returned to the area to try again. It was empty now, and it took her a while to find the exact spot. 31 years earlier, this was the site of a series of nuclear explosions that represented the world's response to the 20-Minute War in 2215.

She wandered through the remaining rubble and wondered how Clyde was. After his failure to appear 100 years ago, she really didn't harbor much hope he'd be here now. But a part of her, the same part that runs tongues over painful exposed nerves in teeth, wanted to see this again. As impossible as it was to believe, there were still people here. Jamie had heard stories about a Salvado by the name of Luke Tiatehui who was working to organize these few states into a functioning country again. He claimed he had support from Mexico and South America and traveled with a few other Salvado, the only people who could move around freely in this radiation and decay.

She wished him luck. But Clyde never appeared.

In 2346, she made her way up from Mexico to try again. Much of what was once Atlanta was now a wide open area called Acxotlan and it was being shaped by many of the local tribes that had lived in the area, survived, and thrived. After America fell into rubble, following the war, many of these tribes had assembled and acted quickly to help manage the resultant fallout.

Native tribes across North America had a head start in dealing with the apocalypse. To them, in modern America, it was already the apocalypse. This was just no surprise.

Greenish-gold signs all around her reminded her that the area was nearly free of radiation, after hundreds of years. And, while she believed the science behind those signs, it was hard to manage any kind of environmental hopefulness about Acxotlan today. The insects had returned, but no animals yet. No people, as far as she could see.

And no Clyde.

She returned again in 2446.

As she moved through what used to be Atlanta, she looked for signs of life. The Aztecana Government was busy rebuilding here, just as the Canadian government was, thousands of miles North. America was gone, but the land was here. A sign in Mvskoke, the Muscogee language, set a timeline for new construction. It seemed a bit far away. She tried to remember that this was Nuevamarietta now. But she couldn't help it. In her head, this was Atlanta. It was Mastodon and Roxor, great bands. Coca-Cola. Peach festivals. Trees.

A shadow near the sign drew her attention. A person not too much bigger than her, in a red hoodie and jeans, was peeking out from behind it. Jamie hadn't seen a single person in kilometers. This one didn't seem dangerous. If anything, they looked lost. Jamie waved and yelled out.

"What are you doing here?"

"I'm sorry. I'm trying to. I'm sorry. I can go..."

Something about her seemed off. And why was she here? Why now? No one was around? This was a weird coincidence. Or not. Jamie moved forward and grabbed her hand. She didn't pull away. She was small, with smooth light-brown skin. She looked like she might have been from deeper in Mexico. Except Mexico was now Aztecana.

Jamie tried to let go of the past a little, but it followed her around like a little sister might at a family reunion, always in the corner of her vision, no matter what she did.

"Who are you?"

"My name is Leah. Leah Santos."

"You don't have a mask? Are you one of us? Are you Salvada?"

"Us? Yes, in a way. In a kind of way. Can we talk?" Leah looked around.

"I was supposed to meet someone here. Three hundred years ago. I come back…"

"I know. He's a friend of mine. Was." Leah closed her eyes.

Jamie's stomach dropped. "What do you mean was?"

"That's what I wanted to tell you." Leah ran her fingers over her scalp, pulling her hood down. She was very nearly bald.

"Clyde can't be… he's one of us."

"I was in a hospital. Almost 150 years ago. Here. Actually, a bit north of here. Clyde was my nurse. He was so sweet."

"How did you end up in a hospital. If you're one of us?" Jamie let go of her hand and ran it over her hair. She looked up into the eerie empty of the sky. No planes, no birds.

Nothing.

"Cancer. I had cervical cancer. Clyde came into my room one night and told me he wanted to give me something. He put his hand on my head. And I felt it."

"Wait, he gave it to you?"

"I felt this breeze through me. And I could stand up. I could walk. And the needles…"

"They couldn't pierce your skin anymore?"

Leah shook her head. Jamie could see it hurt her to tell Jamie her friend was gone. Leah's face was so pretty, so wide open, and with the thin patina of black hair barely visible on her scalp, she looked vulnerable, even kindly. Accessible.

"And Clyde?"

She shook her head again. "He stuck himself and the needle went right through his skin. He didn't have it anymore."

"Because he gave it to you?"

Leah started to cry as she nodded her head. She looked like she was desperately trying to find a place to put her hands.

Jamie breathed out and tried to be precise. "What happened to him?"

"He left to do medical work. He sent me. That was a long time ago. The last time I saw him he was...older. He looked older than us. He was helping people. He loved being a nurse."

Jamie looked down. Her feet pulled at the layer of dust on the street. How was this a city once? What would happen to it now? What was time doing? More than ever it was clear there was no plan. Time had no plan.

It just tore things apart.

Leah was talking when she finally looked up.

"Clyde gave me a kiss to give you. He said it was the best kiss of his life, because of... well. Reasons. He had reasons. I was supposed to give it back to you. "

"He's gone?"

"I'm sorry."

Was there a glitch in her programming that she expected to see Clyde, after all this time? But he was long gone. Dead for maybe a hundred years.

Did that even matter? Or was it some kind of interruption in the way that the world was supposed to work? After hundreds of years, she had finally snapped back into something resembling her normal shape from Reina's death. But at night she could still feel her best friend's body unravelling, bleeding out, freezing, falling to pieces in her arms. Clyde had managed to do something she couldn't.

He gave it away. He stepped away and let someone else live.

She looked at Leah. He did it. Leah was his gift to the world, his way of following through and being true to himself. Why couldn't she have done that for Reina? All of this was confusing.

"Are you okay?" Leah asked her. This was what Clyde had asked her. His first question.

She could feel the thing inside Leah. This was the first time she felt like she could feel it. And she could feel parts of Clyde in it, parts of all of them. None of this was her fault. In the middle of this desolation, Leah could just walk away from her and none of it would be her fault. She didn't even have to have come if she didn't want to. None of this was her obligation.

All she had to do was live.

Jamie grabbed her hand. "I think you have something of mine."

She pulled her in slowly and kissed her. They stayed that way for what seemed like years – decades. Jamie opened her mouth and imagined. She wasn't sure what she would feel in that kiss. Would she feel Clyde? Would she feel death, anger, the pointlessness of all of it. The freedom that Clyde found? Or was it purpose he found? What was there to feel?

It turned out, she felt everything.

6 - Touching Fingers
New Manchester, Albion - 2650

If you live long enough, you will see some similarities in the offices and homes of Salvado. And Lelei Mwangi's outer office was no different. It was large and felt wide-open, uncluttered, but that was mostly an illusion created by the fact that it had nooks and crannies, enough to accommodate the material consequences of a long life spent in eras that could be broken down if you paid attention.

For example, that far wall seemed to carry the pieces of teaching in distant inaccessible areas of Nairobi, working with young people who had rarely seen the inside of schoolhouses. A picture of her first graduating class of 14 students sat next to a document of excellence, petitioned from the Kenyan government, that mounted next to a piece of her first desk, names drawn on it and a phrase carved in it, drawn from The Prophet by Kahil Gibran, something meant to remind her that the preciousness of childhood was meant to be sustained joyfully through everything we do, not shattered by the oblique function of the teacher. Barely perceptible now, some 600 years after it was etched into the desk by a student given license by a committed teacher, it read, "Strive to be like them..."

Seek not to make them like you.

From there, the language shifted, the imagery and locations became endemic to Tambacounda, in Senegal, a school that protected and educated members of the albino minority. eople who might have fallen behind, been lost underfoot without the drive of a teacher who could uplift and shelter them.

A row of images played across the wall, unapologetic, including a mounted class paper, title written overly largely in marker at top, "I choose to live."

Stepping back from the wall, this was the phrase that possibly caught your eye first, a phrase that she had turned into a mantra.

These weren't walls, they were stories, but as each one had possibly been written in a different place, in a language unique unto itself, with characters and dynamics that didn't propagate across the rest, maybe I can take the lead in translating these walls – in telling this story as a whole.

For Lelei Mwangi, the story didn't begin in 2045, 605 years ago, but nearly one year earlier. And it was linked to a terrorist group named al-Shabaab. When she first spoke out against them.

The Harakat Shabaab al-Mujahidin—more often known as al-Shabaab— was the militant wing of the Somali Council of Islamic Courts that took over most of southern Somalia in the second half of 2006. They were initially defeated but returned over and over, expanding their operations outside of Somalia to neighboring countries, including Ethiopia and Kenya. They struck on a number of occasions over the next 40 years, throughout that area, bombing, causing rampant destruction. Lelei had lost a distant relative to a café bombing by the organization in Mogadishu and her family had spent time mourning.

Their attention turned to her. And after the Savior Event, they convinced the towns that she taught in that she was evil -- some evil undying thing. And so she wandered.

From place to place. Because she was.

Not evil.

But an undying thing.

***

Kuras Singh sat in that room, looking around, translating what he saw. In another life, he prided himself on knowing how to read people from the rooms they lived in. There was something unusual about this one, though. And looking over at the girl sitting behind the desk, he could see it now.

She had a pretty face, for sure. A short blonde bob. A mouth that looked ready to erupt into a massive glassy grin at a moment's notice. And a simple, easy facility with her wheelchair -- enough to make Kuras think she'd been in it for a long time, despite the fact that she herself couldn't have been more than 30. It explained the room, though -- filled with pretty reminders of the past, each arranged on the walls, none higher than five feet or so from the ground. She had taken the artifacts of her boss's life and used them to build a room that her patients could feel comfortable in.

And it worked

She looked up and said, quietly, "can I see it?"

Kuras smiled. "What?"

And there was that smile. Her name was Tia. And she asked to see it every time.

"You know. Come on."

Kuras stepped over and lifted his pants leg, showing her the high tech bracelet around his ankle. She smiled.

"Does it blow up if you go somewhere you're not supposed to?"

Kuras shook his head. His hair was black and wild and it flowed like a wave around his head whenever he shook it. "Nope. It just silently alerts the police."

"Boring." Tia rolled her eyes at him and slid some paperwork in the drawer.

"I wish I could just explode for you."

"If you cared, you would." Tia pulled her wheelchair back and grabbed a file from a cabinet behind her, winking.

Kuras was still smiling when the door opened and Lelei stepped out, handing a pile of paperwork to Tia. The use of actual paper seemed to fit the carved wooden nostalgia of the room. It was oddly comforting.

Lelei crossed her arms. "Ok, what do you make of him?"

Tia looked Kuras up and down. "My professional opinion?"

Lelei was a thin woman, with almost blue-black skin. After nearly half a millennium living in Albion, her accent had been ground smooth, leaving her sounding silky and professional and vaguely exotic. Her relationship with her assistant seemed relaxed and playful.

"I like him. But he refuses to blow up for my amusement." Tia ignored Kuras and spoke directly to her boss.

Lelei shook her head. "Shame. Well. Come on, convict." She motioned him to follow her back into her office.

Kuras stuck his tongue out at Tia and followed. "Yes, Ma'am."

They stepped into her office and Kuras looked around. This was a much more modern space. Clean and nondescript. The walls were dark and there were plants everywhere. If anything, it made him more curious about her.

He slid into the couch as Lelei sat at her desk. Kuras crossed his legs. "I need to hear your story at some point."

She cocked her head at him. "I'll tell you what, Mr. Singh, if this goes well, I promise to tell you all about me."

"Deal." Kuras breathed in. He was a handsome man, made rugged by a rough shadow of a beard and wild black hair. He didn't wear socks under his linen pants or a coat over his black turtleneck but his wrists and ankles sported leather bands, each with mystical symbols that seemed to beg someone to ask, to touch them, to start a conversation. Everything about Kuras was meant to do that. Every part of him invited attention – to give him an in to talk to someone.

"After this, two more sessions." Lelei said matter-of-factly as she stood, leaning in front of her desk.

"That's crazy."

"What do you think about that?" She looked at him closely. Everything was a test.

"I think my life is in your hands. But I'm also anxious to hear what you have to say."

"Well, I appreciate you following the protocol here. It's important." Lelei waved her hand and the wall came to life, filled with notes, words. She looked without turning away from him.

"I've been writing every night. I'm trying to make sense of this." Kuras said sincerely. "I do want you to know me, you know?"

"That's the job, right." She smiled.

"You are much kinder to me than you need to be. I wonder why?" Kuras unfolded his legs and leaned forward. It's true. She really tried to see him. As himself.

Not the monster.

To the rest of the world, the ones who hadn't forgotten, Kuras was the beast. And this beast had spent the last 600 years as the guest of a penal system that had broken men in far less time than that. This was a fraction of his sentence, though.

150 life sentences. To be served back-to-back.

Kuras Singh had led a group of penitents. A cult, one that had followed him, listened to him, in Gujarat, India. It was called Bhavishy Kee Aasha, or "Hope for the Future," and on March 29 in the year 2045, 150 of his people, had each drunk a small vial of botulinum toxin intentionally at his command, as a symbol of their commitment to their leader. To the Beast.

To Kuras Singh.

Every one of them had died. And on the next day, on Savior Day, as the police swarmed his compound, Kuras put a gun to his temple during an interview and tried to follow them. He survived. And joined the ranks of everyone else who had attempted suicide that day. He became invulnerable to harm.

He was convicted and sentenced. He spent nearly 160 years in prison in India, until the fallout of the 20-inute war that forced India to outsource its prisons, sending many of their most deadly convicts to England. Kuras sat there as Great Britain dissolved into the democratic republic that was Albion.

And now, after 600 years of his sentence served, he was approaching parole. The anklet let him spend short periods of time with Lelei Mwangi, the psychiatrist meant to evaluate him, before he made his way back, inevitably, to prison each night.

Kuras understood why he was where he was. He didn't know why she treated him so well. Could it just have been curiosity? That was something he could understand.

She waved at the wall again and the writing flickered.

"I see here in the notes, you say it talks to you?"

Kuears shifted in his seat. "I knew you'd focus on that. But, yes."

"You can hear it in your head?"

"I can. But I'm not insane." It was important for him to clarify.

"I never suggested that, Mr. Singh."

"I think you need to call me Kuras." He crossed his legs and considered how he wanted to sit. How awkward would this conversation be?

LeLei nodded, "Okay, Kuras. It talks to you?"

He pursed his lips. "Yes. Sometimes it does."

"Do you have a name for it? What do you call it?"

He took a breath and let his arms fall into his lap. "Well, it says it has different names all over the universe. Originally I called it Aavashyak."

The doctor turned the page flickering on the wall. "What does that mean?"

Kuras's eyes slipped to the little red light behind her that alerted him to the fact that the room was recording him. He spoke clearly. "The essential. The thing that is needed. But now it asks me to call it the Gorukai."

She repeated. "Gorukai? And what does that mean to you?"

Kuras felt his hair swim around him again as he shook his head. Over the last 600 years he had often wished he could shave or cut his hair. His hair would forever be at that "unkempt madman" stage that he had let it grow to intentionally, imagining how that might play on television as he sent that bullet through his head. "Absolutely nothing. I've never heard the word. Or anything like it."

She stepped over to sit on the couch next to him, smoothing down her black pencil skirt. "Are you sure?"

He turned to her. Kuras loved seeing an "in." Those moments where he could pick out the intent of a question. He faked seriousness. "I know what you're doing. You're trying to suggest this is all in my head. It's not."

She shook her head, carefully. "I'm not. I'm just digging."

He nodded and looked at her. This was an uncommonly handsome woman. She looked only a year or two older than her assistant. But her movements were attenuated, elegant. Not one motion was wasted. Kuras recognized that instinct in him, as well. The ability to extend the least amount of effort for maximum effect. It created a kind of stillness that acted like a physical whisper, pulling people in.

"Can you hear it in all of us? In me, for example?"

He leaned in. "In other Punarjanm?"

"Is that what we're called in India?" She tried to trigger his storyteller gene. This is part of what she did.

This is what made her so successful as a teacher and as a therapist. She was what her friends liked to call a "story victim." She sank into stories, making it easy for the storyteller to go on. In Kenya, people like her would stand transfixed, on the corner, repeating "Yabo" at the manic teller of stories. Go on, continue. I'm listening. Good job.

"Yes."

"Here we're called Salvado. And the…" she motioned to him.

"The essential thing?"

Lelei smiled. "Yes. People call it 'the radiance.'"

Kuras' face lit up. "That's beautiful. So much better."

She whispered conspiratorially, "better than 'shells.'"

That surprised him. "Or Kathaputaliyon. The pejorative name. It means 'puppets'"

The doctor cocked her head. "That seems awkward."

"It is. For sure."

She pulled herself up, sitting up straight. "So what does it say?"

"I can almost feel it from you, speaking. Like when you see two people reaching out, fingers almost touching, you feel that phantom sensation. You can imagine the fingers connecting."

"And it speaks."

Kuras rubbed his nose. This is where he maybe didn't sound as sane as he'd like. "That's it. I mostly don't understand. But it's forceful. It wants to communicate, maybe more than my brain wants to understand."

"What do you think it's saying?"

He laughed. "It says to send me back to jail for another hundred years"

That was surprising. "It does?"

For a moment, he looked wistful. "At least."

She slapped her legs and stood up, seemingly shaking off the conversation entirely. "C'mon." Moving to the door, she motioned to him with a flip of her head.

"Let's go for a walk."

***

It was warm outside with a breeze that felt almost alive. Manchester was beautiful this time of the year. It was spring and it felt like the whole city was complicit in the desire to grow new life. The last of the world-spanning conflict triggered by the 20-Minute War was over a hundred years ago but to Leilei it seemed, finally, that the planet was willing to forgive them. The papers waxed on about the possibility that the worst was behind them. Today it felt true.

Kuras walked next to her, breathing it all in. His voice held a wink. "You're just trying to get me outside."

She laughed, pulling open the thin coat she'd thrown on before leaving the office. "Am I?"

"It's nice out here. Things are starting to... bounce back."

"They really are. We have a world again, Mr. Singh."

He stopped and held out his hand to shake. "Kuras."

She looked down and took his hand with an exaggerated shaking motion. "Kuras, we have a lot to look forward to."

He shook his head. "If you say so."

"So, why do you think this Gorukai wants you in jail?" She put her hands in her coat pocket and continued forward.

"Maybe, after 600 years, it sees who I am. Maybe it's not taken in by my, you know…natural charisma." He said the last with a smile, almost trying to downplay it. Kuras had always felt silly talking about this. But it was the elephant in the room, really. How do you convince 150 people to take their own lives?

"And you think I am?" For a moment, Lelei was a woman, not a professional. Was it possible she was being taken in by this man? He tried to read her.

"Maybe. I'm having some trouble figuring you out."

She smiled, easily. "Is that frustrating to you?"

Kuras thought for a moment. "Honestly, it's calming, It's relaxing." And it was. Not knowing where she was at lifted this burden of responsibility from him. He could just talk.

She shrugged. "Maybe there's not much to me to figure out."

The dark-haired man let out a long sigh. "It says that I'm still a danger and I'm just here, trying to convince you I'm not. But it wants to protect people."

"From you?"

"From me." Kuras looked up. "I think. It's very hard to tell, but I think it wants to help people be safe from me."

She turned down a smaller street, lined by trees under the clear canopy of brilliant solar glass. It had begun to trickle down and the clear panels had extended from the elegant rails on the sides of the walkway that housed them. Everything above them glittered. "Do you have another cult in the wings?"

She realized that the interplay of machinery, glass, and foliage above them, meant to be beautiful in execution, was all new to Kuras.

It had only been a few weeks that he'd been furloughed for treatment, in preparation for a parole. All of this was fresh, novel.

He tore himself from his fascination with what was happening above them. "I know you're joking about that. But I've always been able to sort of sway people to my opinion."

"And yet, you never sold cars."

He laughed. "That's funny. That's very funny. Not a bad idea, either. That might be safer."

She ran through a list in her head. "Or a lawyer. Have you thought about that?"

"I have."

As he was, thinking of himself as a gun pointed at the world, would he make it out here? There was so much beauty. The people who made it were the ones who felt worthy of it. So often, she walked her patients down this way, trying to make them feel the heirship of it all. This is the beauty that you are the beneficiary of. This is your inheritance.

"Why do you think people went to you?" she asked him.

"What do you mean?"

"Not just why you were able to convert them, sell them, take over their will. Why do you think they showed up at your door? These people came to you?"

He nodded. "They did."

"Well, it seems like you are looking for what about you has been perfected. What is the thing that has been made...more." It wasn't always easy talking about the changes they had all gone through. But they had had over half a millennium to think about all that. How they had been changed against their wills.

"Certainly my charisma."

She shook that off. "But what else did they see? Why did they gravitate to you?"

He squinted. "You think there's something else."

She tipped her head to one side. "You seem to think you're a shallow thing, a well-dressed charlatan who knows how to sell."

That certainly didn't seem wrong. "What if that's it – that's all I am?"

"Well that's nothing you can work with – to build a life." And it wasn't. As a therapist, Lelei knew what kind of mindset was needed to survive after prison. That wasn't it.

"No, it's not," he conceded.

"So, what if there's more?"

Kuras laughed. "You think there is more to me."

Talking about specifics would be hard. This would be a hurdle, she thought.

"Give me a name. Someone who came to you. Someone who joined you. And tell me why they did."

The rain was coming down harder now, but the solar panels above them had kept them both dry. The rainbow interplay of light from the solar microcoating on the glass, propagated across the streams of water, made it hard not to look up constantly as they walked. The world was a light show.

"Seriously?"

She lifted a finger. "One name."

Kuras thought for a moment and then offered one. "Kashvi Das."

Lelei nodded. "So tell me, what did Kashvi Das need? Why did she come to you?"

His steps slowed as he thought. "She had a miscarriage, It was her second. Her husband, the mealy little... her husband left her. He blamed her and left her. But not before he put his hands on her."

"I'm sorry."

He continued, "Yeah. It wasn't my... I wanted to help her. He was a monster."

Kuras stopped and looked upward. He needed to flip a switch. "But, at the end of the day, he didn't kill her did he?"

He looked over at Lelei.

She shook her head. "No."

Kuras closed his eyes in the rain, wishing he could feel it. "I did."

Lelei moved closer. "Why did she come to you?"

His eyes pressed shut, kept the tears from pouring down his face. Each sat behind a well of liquid. "Not for that. Not to die. None of them did. I am the beast."

From this distance, you could see only an inch or two of difference in their heights. She inclined her head slightly and looked up at him. "Yet you can feel compassion for Kashvi Das?"

Kuras's shoulders moved slightly. "Can we not say her name anymore?"

"Why did she come?" she pressed.

His breathing seemed labored now. "I don't know. I don't know. She seemed broken." He opened his eyes.

Lelei whispered. "So what did she want?"

His arm lit kindly on her upper arm. She could see him pulling himself together. "Can we stop? This is me. I can take this back. To the prison."

She turned to see the Elegance station.

It would take him back to prison for the night. "Okay. Tomorrow. Two more?"

Kuras smiled broadly. "Two more."

***

"Does it vibrate?" Tia laughed as she looked at his thin ankle monitor.

Kuras pulled the leg of his linen pants down and counted off. "No. It doesn't. It doesn't hurt. It doesn't shock me in the bath."

She shrugged it off. "So it's no big deal?"

"How about you? You haven't told me how you ended up in that wheelchair."

She looked around, facetiously. "What wheelchair?"

Kuras laughed. "Fair enough."

She reached for his hand. "No, I'm kidding. I know I get to sit and relax all the time and that must frustrate you standy-walky people."

He leaned back, hands out. "Exactly. Why do you get to be the princess?"

Tia corrected him. "It's mermaid, actually. I used to put a blanket over my lap and pretend."

The dark-haired man nodded approvingly. "You were a mermaid?"

"Yup. I can still swim, you know. Like a dolphin, I wave my legs using my hips. Tie them together." She wiggled her hips. Kuras could see that her paralysis seemed to begin right at the root of her waist.

He smiled, "That must be something."

Tia leaned in, as if to tell a secret. "I dove into the shallow end. In fifth grade. At a pool around the corner from the school. My head hit the bottom and snapped back. I heard it crack. My neck."

"I'm sorry."

She looked slightly sad, for the first time. "Before the war, there were all these advances…"

He put his hand on hers. "And there will be again."

Lelei stepped out of her inner office. "Oh my god, Is she telling you her story?"

Kuras nodded, "It's fascinating."

Lelei made her way to the coffee pot and poured two cups. "It's all a lie. She can walk, she's just lazy."

Tia looked apologetic. "I really am." As if to punctuate the point, Lelei handed her a cup of coffee. The blonde girl winked at her boss.

Kuras took it all in. It would have been very hard not to like her. "I think there will be an advance. You'll walk again."

The doctor took a sip from her cup. "Is that what the voice says?"

"So, no doctor-patient privilege?" Kuras stood up in mock concern.

Tia looked over. "Ooh, Is he hearing voices?"

Lelie nodded. "A lot. But we have one more session after this, I can fix him."

Tia waved them into the inner office. "Good luck. Earn that paycheck."

Kuras stepped into the inner room. "You're going to get her hopes up, you know?"

"I could say the same to you." The doctor slipped into her chair.

Kuras let himself down into the couch. "I do think there will be an advance. I mean, maybe I am. Getting her hopes up."

"It's okay. I try to be positive." Lelei smiled.

"She's a sweet girl."

She took another sip. "Her mother was a patient. She came in to pick her up and never left."

"And you don't teach anymore?" Kuras was digging, hoping to get to know her better.

"Aah. You see all the pictures. Yes, I was a teacher."

He pressed. "Now you're a therapist. An agent of the courts."

"I'm not supposed to tell you this, but the rest of them have signed off on you. No one seems to think you're a threat except your voice."

"The Gorukai, yes."

"But…" Lelei stood up and legislated it. "How do you know for sure? You say you don't really understand."

"We understand each other in different ways."

The doctor considered what she'd seen. "Tia really opened up to you out there."

This surprised Kuras. "She isn't usually like that?"

Lelei laughed. "No. She hates talking about it. She wants to be the playful, silly hot girl."

He put his hands up. "No pushback from me on that."

"Is that your charisma?"

Kuras ran his hands through his hair and leaned back. "I don't turn it on or off. It just is."

Lelei turned off the wall monitor and made a point to press the button on her desk. The recording light switched from red to green. She tended not to record this question with patients. It would be easy to misread it or misunderstand it.

"What will you do if you are paroled? Where will you go? When they say your debt is paid?"

Kuras saw the light flicker from red to green. "Honestly?"

She nodded. "Of course."

He stood up. "Away from people. I thought hard about what you said yesterday. About Kashvi Das."

"You can say her name today."

He started pacing the room. "I owe her that, at least, don't I? But, about why she was there."

She looked at him as he paced, traversing the room. "Did you figure it out?"

"Not yet. But I want to. I want to get in her head. And figure it out."

"Away from people?" She offered up.

"I've heard that some Salvado -- some of us – have gone underwater. To live down there. " She could tell he hadn't said this out loud yet.

Her eyes followed him around the room. She asked, "and that's something you want to do?"

He stepped more quickly. "It's not about want, it's about safety. We don't need to breathe. Or even eat if we don't want to."

She tried to imagine it in her head. "Alone, underwater. That's something."

"It may be good. It could be." It seemed like he was trying to convince himself. He waved his hands.

"You did that like someone would motion about death." She felt bad calling him out, but this was obvious.

Kuras stopped. "Did I?"

Her eyes burrowed their way into his chest. "Are you up for another field trip?"

He smiled. "Where do you want to go?"

She stood up and grabbed his arm, pulling him along with her. "Take me where you go. In the city. You've been out and about for a couple weeks now during the day. When you aren't here. Where do you go?"

"You want to see?"

"I do."

***

It only took about 20 minutes to get to the Manchester Wind Tower. This building, built almost a hundred years ago, was a massive celebration of modern architecture. The ridges along its sides were designed to generate power from the Manchester winds that buffeted the building night and day, Driven by the heatsink of Ireland and Wales, still suffering from the nuclear fallout of the war. The Atlantic had cooled and the cooling water breeze, hitting the warm fronts over these areas, often attacked Manchester with a uniquely powerful suite of winds. And the wide platform at top was home to cafés and gardens, as well as at least one movie theater. It was a beautiful building and the top was a magnificent testament to how the human race was committed to bouncing back.

"This is impressive." Lelei felt the thin air around her. As Salvado, she didn't explicitly need to breathe. But she'd never spent time in places where she couldn't.

Kuras looked alive up here. "Have you ever jumped from something like this?"

She shook her head. "I have not."

They stepped over toward the side. "We'd survive it."

She stared incomprehensibly over the edge. There was a wall of glass preventing anyone from falling off. They were nearly 2,000 meters above the ground. Lelei felt small in comparison. "Oh, I know. I've seen footage of some of us doing it. We'd just stand up and walk away."

"But you won't do it?"

She shook her head. "I have no need for that. That would give me nightmares."

"It's different standing up here knowing I wouldn't die if I fell." He was hypnotized by the edge. Lelei had to admit it held power. She wondered for a moment if that power were stronger for people like them – people who would survive it. She turned to look at him.

"But you still sort of want to."

He nodded. "You see it, don't you?"

"I do. Part of you still wants to die. That's what going underwater is. You know who you are?"

Kuras smiled. "Who am i?"

The doctor pointed to the café. Pulling him by the arm. "You are Orpheus. With your lyre. Playing such beautiful music that people would part for you, follow you, fall in love with you. And all you want is to descend into Hell. But why?"

They stepped into the open air cafe. "Why did Orpheus do it?"

She looked at him. He knew. "Well, he had Eurydice, didn't he? He had his love."

Kuras sat and looked through the menu. "That didn't end so well, did it?"

She shook her head. "No, it did not."

He looked through the drinks. "It did not."

It all felt a bit surreal to her. Talking about Greek mythology with an immortal while she selected from an array of fancy foreign sodas. She pointed to a triple citrus cream cooler as she handed the menu to the waitress. Kuras lifted up two fingers and joined her. She realized he had barely looked at the menu.

Lelei turned to him. "So, pretend I'm not your therapist. Tell me. Like I'm your journal."

He looked around and then at her. "My journal. Huh. Dear Diary. Here's the thing. What if you don't understand? What if I'm a bomb? I'm a weapon. Every day I look around and I see people like they're food, like they're placed next to me in some cage. Triggers. And some part of me asking If I can pull them towards me with this? Charisma. Strength that I have. The only thing that makes me who I am?"

"I feel them moving towards me. Like I feel you moving towards me. I feel that one finally. And it feels good. And all I want to do is to have them – and to die. All I want to do with that is to take it somewhere dark. Somewhere final. And I want to. I want to build a fire of some sort. I want to light up the world. A little part of me, though, always wants that. It's not all of me. Not even most of me. I fight that."

"Yes. I hate prison. I hate those gates. I hate those doors. Not being able to see the sun, what I want. "

"But what if I'm just a weapon? What if that's all? " He took a breath. "What if, huh?"

Lelei considered him. She took the glass from the dark-haired waitress who wandered by with the orange colored opaque drinks. "Have you jumped from here?"

He paused. "No."

She leaned in and whispered, "and why not?"

"I would make a crater at the bottom. Maybe hurt some people. Disrupt everything. Wreck people's day. A hailstorm. A shitshow."

Lelei agreed. "Definitely that."

Kuras's smile slowly disappeared. He looked thoughtful. "I see what you're saying. The people here. They all hold me back. I really don't want to hurt anyone, do I?"

LeLei pointed to the right at the massive interactive wall. It was covered in pictures, shifting across its surface. "This is it, isn't it?"

"The messages? What do you mean?"

She ran her finger over the payment port on the table and stood up, bringing her drink with. The message wall was huge. It spanned nearly the length of the common area of the platform. Pictures, coupled with messages, of various sizes, swam across its surface. Kuras followed her.

She lifted her head toward the message wall. "That draws you up here. It's not the height -- the danger. It's the connection."

He stared. "It's pretty amazing."

"It's from all over the city, isn't it?"

Kuras nodded. "When I first saw this it seemed like the place where secret agents would leave obscure messages for each other, during the resistance. And they'd return here and... I don't know. It's a big stupid fantasy."

"It's not that big a stretch" she wandered down the wall, zooming in on a few of the messages.

He followed her. "What do you mean?"

She opened her arms wide. "The space."

The wind had picked up. Kuras tried to speak over it. "I'm not following."

"The space between wanting people to die for you and wanting them to *want* to die for you."

He pulled his hair back as it waved in the wind. "I see that. You think maybe I just wanted to be loved?"

She stepped over, apologetically. "That's pretty facile, I know."

He gave up finally and left his hair to the wind. "I don't think you are wrong."

***

For the last session, she met him in the courtyard of the Maryfield minimum security prison. There were only one or two inmates wandering around. They were all wearing white jumpsuits, just as Kuras was, in an airy, breathable fabric. The prisons across Albion had become very human-centric, very focused on creating humanity out of despair, hope in cases that might have seemed desperate and without merit in the past. The prison was more of an academy, clean, filled with educational and rehabilitative rooms. It had entire sections dedicated to art and liberal arts, to compassion, to integration.

A few of the other inmates were playing with dogs across the courtyard, throwing frisbees and running with them. Sprinklers shot off at odd intervals, giving the game intrigue for the dogs.

The inmates laughed as they cheered every catch. Kuras smiled and cheered along as she walked up to him.

"Complex rules to that game?"

He shook her hand. "Oh, yes. Catch the plate, don't dodge the water. Repeat."

"I can see why you want to stay."

"Well, pizza night is pretty amazing. But so is freedom, I suppose."

"You never hurt anyone in here. Surrounded by hundreds of people who lost their way, looking for something. You never hurt anyone."

"I didn't, did I?" Kuras looked across the yard to where the protests were. "Maybe I should tell them that."

"Looks like they found out." She put her hand up to shield her eyes. There were about 20 people gathered with signs.

"Before I did. But I guess I'm leaving here today."

"Yes. It was unanimous. The warden, my office. In an hour or so, you will be a free man."

"Kind of free. They'll be watching me." He opened his eyes wide to humorously describe how that might look.

"Ha. Well. As free as any of us are." Lelei started walking around the courtyard. In her mind, she imagined this would be the last time she'd see him.

"I looked up what happened. To you."

She nodded. "You did, huh?"

"I mean, not a ton of information. But there are stories about you." He shoved his hands into his pockets and followed her. This was how he wanted to spend his last day here.

With the person who had no human reason to believe in him.

But did anyway.

"If you really want to hear my story, you should hear it from me. You know how al-Shabaab forced me to run, place to place, to abandon students? Well, even before that, they changed my life. al-Shabaab was there on Savior Day."

He nodded and let her continue.

"In Kenya...Nairobi... I was a teacher. I woke up every day and I walked to class. I lived near the school so walking was easy. Every single day."

"Something else I did. When it was time for us to go play, outside – the class. I'd line them up by height. And there was a message to the taller students, the 16, the 17-year-olds. These are the 12-year-olds. These are the 10-year-olds. These are the ones smaller than you. You look out for them. On the playground you're looking out for them. You make sure that they don't fall."

"And to the younger ones. Watch how fast you grow? See how fast you move up this line. And that responsibility falls to you. And they laughed. It was just a little moment. Lining up to go play games. Soccer, kick the can. Anything. But it meant something."

"The kids, though. They were so smart. They had that light, you know, looking at them, answering questions, hands shooting up in the air. They were funny. They were so... alive. You look in these faces. Thank you, God. You know. Thanks for being able to walk to school every day to see this. Thank you for this." She looked up, as if speaking to something, in prayer.

"At one point – the teachers in the school earned the notice of al Shabbab. The teachers had spoken out against the way they had kidnapped children, spoken about it. The cruelty – the inhumanity. We thought it mattered. That we could say something and it would matter. We were so full of ourselves. You teach a classroom and you feel like you have some kind of authority."

"Then one day, they're gathered in front of the school, right? And they marched in. And they took the children – brought them from every room, and they brought them outside, and they brought them away from us. They blindfolded us."

"And we heard the shots ring out over and over again. We heard. Every child. First, we heard the raw, skeletal sharp bang of the shot and then, the dull sound of them falling to the ground. And the noise was impossible to escape. It was a bang and then a thud. And that's the first lesson of cruelty. You can't get away from it. You can't. Escape it.

You can't close your ears to it." She stopped and looked at him. "Cruelty is liquid. It seeps into everything."

Lelei continued, "and then, when they were done, they lifted me by the arms and dragged me out. And they pulled off the blindfold. I remember they ripped off an earring. It felt so superficial. I saw the blood on the white rag they used as a blindfold. My eyes were trying to adjust to the red-orange sky, the sun. At first, I couldn't see anything. I saw the whims of cruelty in front of me. Because they lined up those children. They lined them up by height. On the ground. In a pit in front of us. I recognized each of them. And the ones they'd shot in the face, I recognized them by the order. By the student at their shoulder. The same order. They had lined them up like we did."

"My eyes snapped shut again and I heard them laughing. And I couldn't close them tight enough. There was nothing I could do. My knees just gave out. When I fell into that pit. I let them cover me in dirt while I screamed. I felt the dirt press against my face and no more noise would come. The dirt filled my mouth. It pressed me down, it crushed my head."

"Until it blotted out the light battering against my eyelids. The red-orange lines in the sky. And I laid there. I tried to die. I thought I was dead. I felt the earth clumped in my throat. I didn't crawl out of that pit until the next morning. The ground was wet with dew. My face was covered in red mud. I sat on the side of the pit and threw up. Over and over again."

She stopped walking. Kuras's eyes had welled up. He didn't know what to do with his hands as she went on.

"And that's what I'm here for. I think. To teach. And that's what I do. That's what happened. What I'm perfected to do is to teach. I can teach you about cruelty. About what cruelty does. And if you're truly fighting it – if you're really fighting to eliminate that from your heart – if you really don't want that? I can teach. Because cruelty doesn't make anything or invent anything. It steals from you and it mocks you and then it falls into death There's just the bang and the thud, Kuras. That's all there is."

She smacked her fist into her hand.

"The bang. And then the thud."

"And then it's all lined up for you to see."

For a moment, Kuras believed he could see it. He could see the bodies of the children, lined up by height, in a pit in front of him, piles of dirt being shoveled onto them.

His head dropped as he let out a sob.

"I'm that, aren't I? That's why you took this? My case?"

Lelei looked at him with tears in her eyes, too. "Yes. You are the gang, the cult, the cruel thing. Maybe not the exact cruel thing, maybe not al-Shabaab. But that is what you've been."

"I'm sorry." Kuras slid to the ground. He wanted to crawl into it. The doctor dropped to her knees in front of him.

She held his face and lifted it to her. "But you won't be, again. Ever again. That's what you tell that thing inside you, inside us. You tell it that you won't be the cruel thing. You're going to choose to live. And the smaller ones? You're going to choose to keep them from falling, too."

"Yes, ma'am." he nodded through the tears. He put his hands on hers and breathed slowly.

"You figure out who you are, now that you know for sure what you are not, Kuras Singh." For a moment, Kuras could hear her Kenyan accent. She was a schoolteacher in Nairobi holding a student who had fallen down in the dirt. She saw the fall. She saw the marks on his knees, the tears, the rip in his pants, the artifacts of the fall. She saw it all.

And now she was helping him up.

***

He looked straight ahead as he went back to his cell and cleaned up. He threw on the black turtleneck and lifted his single bag. The paperwork was mostly done. And walking through the last of the few stragglers protesting was uneventful.

He just kept looking straight ahead.

He made his way to the train platform as her words ran through his head. This would take time to process, but he had every possible tool he needed to do it.

Including time.

He dropped the bag in a rubbish receptacle outside the train and ran his thumb over the payment port. No one on the train even noticed him as he rode east toward Old Sheffield. He stopped into the lunch car for a sandwich before stepping off an hour later. The trains were so fast now, it was only a few kilometers to Tiene. In his research, he had learned that it was, once, a place called Mablethorpe Beach. It was a common place for families to go, to bring their children, to play.

To vacation near the water.

He pulled his shirt off on the beach and looked down where the ankle bracelet once was. There was no sign of it. No marks on his skin.

Nothing.

In front of him was Denmark. Maybe he would walk there, He might try swimming like a mermaid, like Tia did. That thought made him smile as he stepped into the North Sea. It was warmer than he expected, he thought, as the waters swirled over his head.

***

Lelei felt her phone buzz in her pocket.

It was Tia.

She lifted it up and saw the blond girl's pretty face. She was animated

Excited.

"Is he there? With you?"

"Who? Kuras. No. Are you ok?"

"Did he do it? Did he go into the water?"

Lelei had been trying not to think about it. "I don't know."

"I have to send you something. Can you get it to him?"

"I don't know." Lelei looked down at her phone as Tia sent the image through.

Her eyes widened as she turned around. She ran.

It took 20 minutes to reach the top of the Manchester Wind. LeLei stepped out of the lift and took a deep breath. The air still felt so thin up here, but in a way that registered as healthy. As if it only had what you most needed to survive in it.

Stepping over to the message wall, She reached into her pocket and pulled out the phone. She looked up for room on the busy wall, pressing her phone against it. The picture appeared on the reactive wall. She moved it with her finger, opening up a comment area below. The picture was taken in her own outer office.

It was a clear shot of Tia standing next to her desk, unassisted. Standing.

She looked over at the café, slowly filling up, and she used her finger to write on the white comment area.

The earth was mostly water. There was no way to know what current Kuras had caught -- no way to find him below the oceans.

But if he came back, he might stop by here. And if he did, he might look at the board. And if he looked at the board, at all, he might see the picture. And he'd read what she'd written just for him. He'd remember putting his hand on her arm and telling her she'd walk one day.

Lelei had written with her finger: "She came to be healed. They all did."

Lelei Mwangi stepped back and looked at the rest of the notes left for people. They blurred into a collage of hopefulness, stretching across the active wall. Maybe he'd never see it. But if he did, maybe he'd know. Maybe he'd know what he'd been perfected to do. And it wasn't to sit underwater, wasting his days endlessly in liquid solitude, afraid of what he was capable of.

She closed her eyes, and her desire to teach reached out to the part of the Gorukai that desired to heal.

She could almost feel the fingers touch.

7 - The Saints of Boats and Cities
Heilongjiang, China - 2825

I'm in a unique position to talk about what happens when you are in a near-direct nuclear hit.

As we huddled, tied together in Akana's basement, we thought that the nearest major center to be hit might be Sapporo. But, either intentionally or by accident, there were a number of hits between here and there, with at least one nearly directly to the east of us. We were far away from the windows, but the first thing we noticed was the light permeating the walls, almost as though there were an array of spotlights set up outside, shining into every crack.

The heat that immediately followed was insane. It felt like a hand directly in a camp fire, but not localized. It was everywhere. It was in the air, in your bones, everywhere. I never imagined that air could get that hot. It was dark heat, arid, devoid of moisture, like right inside the coiled space of a hairdryer.

Next, the massive crack as the sound reached us, louder than anything I'd ever heard. It sounded like a white noise generator turned all the way up and amplified through several concurrent PA systems. We felt it in our ears as the sound attempted to rip open our eardrums. Then, immediately afterward, the atmosphere effects as all the air around us was sucked away, pulling parts of the grey rocky box down on top of us. We felt the force of the blast last, slamming into us like a massive baseball bat connecting full on, pushing us to the west where the cement came crushing down in wave after wave. It was space turned into a hammer.

It felt endless, as though the initial boom wasn't an event, but a thing, a noun, an object that was built to stand the test of time. I nearly lost consciousness until I realized I was fine. I thought for a minute about the fine layer of oily soot all over everything around me, infused in the air, and realized that it was the fat and oils from every living thing within a mile radius, deer, people, insects. All of that was turned into a sludge the consistency of dust mixed with coconut oil.

I stopped breathing intentionally, just to keep that gunk out of my mouth, and realized that I didn't need the air anyway. As my eyes got used to the black, I reached my right hand out to touch Akana. She held it tightly and squeezed. Yazmin grabbed my other hand and affirmed that we were good. We were together. We were all right. Somehow, our hurried efforts to tie ourselves together had actually worked.

I was trapped laying nearly completely flat. We heard other explosions, from far away, but for us, the 20-inute War was really only the first five minutes or so. We listened until there was nothing left to listen to.

The quiet afterward was debilitating. I'd never heard anything like it before. A lot of people who survive nuclear attacks claim there is a screeching silence that happens afterward. Yazmin's voice was the first thing to pierce the space around us. It was calm but assertive. I came to learn that there was a tone that Yazmin used – one that she was completely fluent in. Since then I've tried it a few times myself but it never works as well as when she does it. She sounds like, no matter what the situation is, she's done it before, enough to know what works and what doesn't. She never says it, but that's the impression.

That's the impression she gives.

It took us nearly seven months to dig our way out. There were days when we made progress, and that was a few inches, possibly. The job was to move debris on top of us to somewhere below us. To shift it behind our backs and to push upward. We tried to find better ways, but there were none. Some days we made no progress at all. And the days where we slid backward, falling down, invalidating weeks of progress.

Those were bad days.

The three of us talked. We joked, planned. We tried not to express our fears that we were working, every day, to return to a world that we knew nothing about.

One that could be completely dead.

So there was no real urgency digging our way out. Somewhere around the second month, we were able to kneel, then stand a month later,, hunched over. Akana talked to us about instances of other ones, nearby ones, other Salvado that we might interact with once we dug out. She could feel them, still, all over the world. And while the room-sized map we had built was gone, there was another one -- just as accurate -- inside her head.

They had all survived. All 1936 of them.

This was impossible for me to wrap my head around. I knew, from having looked at the map that many of them were in the epicenter of an explosion. They were right where you might reasonably expect a bomb to drop.

Did some of us survive a ground zero explosion?

***

During the very first nuclear bomb test in New Mexico, the Trinity test, the intense heat melted the silica in the desert sand and fused it, along with local chemicals and impurities, into a series of smooth green, glass-like stones scattered all over. This was called Trinitite. Something similar happened during the explosion at Hiroshima with the substance created named Hiroshimaite. Some of these were rich in copper and came out reddish, while others were almost pure silica, clear, almost diamond-like, even with the ability to separate light into rainbows.

Some people said it was even beautiful.

The region where Akana's house had been built \ was rich in quartz and feldspar, though, ensuring that the crystals scattered all over would be richly bright green, filtering that hue into the air around them.

And that's how the second map of us became a 30-meter-long mosaic of greenish glass across the damaged and smoothed-out rocky floor of the space that was once my friend's home.

One of the things I had become quite good at in my travels was logging and identifying the map of the world. By that time I had traveled everywhere, mostly on Xenovera's corporate dime, seeking out and meeting others like us, learning their stories. I like to think I was a bit of a geography wiz to start with so I was helpful in establishing just what the world map looked like while Akana filled it in with bright green representations of where we were, all over the world.

The anomalies we had found remained, but there were a few more to find. Including another water-bound one.

"Ok, this is in the sea of Japan, right," Akana stood over the tiny piece of green glass and pointed.

I nodded. "Yes, it's just west of us." I walked from Oketo to the spot.

She picked it up and moved it. "And now it's here." She moved it toward the west coast of Japan, closer to us.

I looked up and thought. The little knob looked familiar. "I think that's Shakotan. It's a port."

She nodded and picked the stone back up, moving it about a meter away. "And three days ago it was here."

"That's definitely Russia. A port city. It's that sliver of Russia right above where Korea is." I tried to think about the name of the ports there.

She crossed her arms. "It's moving too fast to be walking underwater. Back and forth." For a second I was amazed again at what our bodies could do. Why not run fast underwater? Until Yazmin walked over.

"It's a boat. It's one of us on a boat."

I nodded. That made more sense. Yazmin looked sad. I reached over to put my arm around her. She dug her face into me and then stepped away. "That's the closest one of us. We should reach out. Go there."

Akana looked concerned. I could tell she wasn't happy about leaving the area.

Yazmin had been walking around for hours every day while Akana and I had worked on the map. Now that it was finished, she seemed to not know what to do next. She ran her hand through her hair. "I can't find anyone. I've been looking. No one. If we're going to find out what happened and what is going on, we need to find more of us."

I had almost finished sketching the map, too. I figured no matter what came next we couldn't carry it with us. The biggest anomaly, though, was still one that made no sense to any of us. It gnawed at me like a woodpecker against tree bark. Akana had done the best she could to show it on the map. A giant stone right in the middle of Heilongjiang, China.

The size of a city.

We rested for a few days before we got on the road. A year ago, we would have driven the four hours to Shakotan. It wasn't far by car.

But that was a problem.

We'd been walking for a full day before we found our first car. The electric engine wouldn't start. Radiation levels were still high and they were damaging all the electrical functions around us. We had no radiation detector, but Yazmin had discovered an interesting substitute.

"Look at this." She stepped around the car to the back tire. She lifted her foot and kicked it. The rubber was hard and brittle, shattering under her foot.

I shook my head. "Radiation does that?"

"It will make all the rubber brittle. At least we can tell how high the levels are." She sighed.

The air was a little chill as the thick layer of soot and dust blocked the sun. I could still feel the fatty oil all around me, mixed with dust, and there weren't enough baths in various creeks and water holes to clean it off. If we walked for five hours steadily every day, we could make it in a little over 2 weeks.

It turned out we were a lot slower than we thought. It took us almost a month to reach Shakotan. And every kilometer on the way there was its own horror film. Broken and ripped apart buildings peppered the landscape, with bones and human relics dropped around them like crumbs from giant cakes, disorganized, with no discernible order. No one seemed to have any real awareness that this conflagration was coming. Nobody seemed to have been trying to save themselves or really do anything but die on the spot, in the places they stood.

The terrain was soul-crushing. As we passed Sapporo, I remembered the thousands of people that gathered there for festivals every year, laughing, drinking...

Living.

There was no flesh on any bone that I could see. I remember a hate pundit from my youth who used to rail about how transgender people were an abomination because long after you were dead, they could tell if you were a man or a woman or whatever.

From your skeleton.

But these skeletons had no gender information to deliver. They had no race, they had no demographics. Poor, rich, fat, skinny, they were all hot-air-stripped pale architecture on the glassy ground, mingled, shattered, broken, mute testament to the stupidity of hate punditry. When you are surrounded by death like this the first thing your body – even these bodies of ours -- recognizes is the loss of possibility. Every minute these people had left was an opportunity for a great idea, for an innovation, a piece of art, a joke, a great song.

In the flesh they carried was possibility, in every cell because they were alive. They were different. They were unique events in a universe that used uniqueness as a driver to create.

But like this, they were all the same. Chalky, brittle, broken bone.

Just things to walk over.

Akana tried to keep her eyes forward. Yazmin had grown up on death, and I was, well... I was me. But Akana was just gentle. She had devoted her life to a kind of gentleness that was one part forgiveness and one part vision. She saw people. And it made her love them. I couldn't even imagine how moving through this museum of death was killing her soul. I didn't want to think about it – what she saw.

I tried to keep her mind off of it. I tried to tell the stories of the places we passed, even stories she didn't know. I tried to tell stories of the Salvado I had met and interviewed. I tried everything I could to keep her moving forward during that month it took us to move through what could have been some toxic Grecian underworld.

It was night when we arrived at Shakotan. It looked no different than any other place on the way except there were a few large boats, dark, and fallen into disrepair – each looking too dead to even be haunted, as though the world had left them behind.

Except for one with lights arrayed around the main deck.

It was a huge boat, one of the largest. It looked like it might have been the yacht of a prince or a duke, regal, with at least four floors. The captain's deck rose up toward the front, seemingly with room for a big crew. It was opulent looking, yet seedy, as though the royalty it belonged to had fallen out of favor and this was the last of their possessions they were permitted to take as they left in disgrace.

And there was a rope-lined walkway leading up to it.

I called out, but no one answered.

As we walked up the bridge, we saw that the door was open.

I turned my head to Yazmin and she nodded. The main floor inside looked like a modern condo, sleek and comfortable. Unlike the exterior, it seemed barely lived in. I called out again, wondering where the owner was. This boat was still running.

They were here somewhere.

We went down the stairs to the next level below. They resolved into a lounge which I presumed opened up in the back to a series of bedrooms. A deep and well-stuffed modern grey modular sofa filled up the out fringe of the lounge, framing an area that looked like it could seat 20 people comfortably.

I suppose none of this was surprising, until we descended into the hold. This space was wide, without breaks, walls or partitions. It was the gunmetal grey of the lower boat hull, unpainted, unfinished even. And all around were thick metal tables filled with pillow-like bags of white powder, guns, and what looked to be millions of dollars in currency from various countries.

I looked at Akana. She motioned me forward. What we were looking for was here. She reached the bottom of the stairs and nodded at me. I called out again. No answer.

I sighed. "Sonofabitch."

From the corner of the hold I heard a voice. It belonged to a young man, one with a slight, almost imperceptible Russian accent.

"It is the cocaine, right?" He stepped out from the shadows. He was a young-looking man, early 30s maybe, with long brownish-blond hair and a wide face, smiling as he ate a sandwich.

I jumped.. "Holy shit."

Yazmin moved forward towards Akana and me, protectively. "I admit, I was looking at the guns."

He reached out to shake her hand, eagerly. "Those I kind of want to get rid of."

I leaned in. "I'm Anjo, by the way. Is this your place? Or boat?"

"In a way." He looked down, then wiped his hands on his black shirt and shook ours. "I'm assuming you are all saved. I have never seen three traveling together."

Akana stepped forward. "We were looking for you."

I nodded at the man. "She can sense Salvado -- what you are. We saw you traveling back and forth. We need to get to China."

He laughed and put the sandwich down, moving through the hold. "I thought you were here because of my fun-loving exterior."

I laughed and looked over at Yazmin. She shrugged and replied, "I mean. That's a plus."

He sized us up and decided, laughing. "Well, I think I've got the room. I can get you to Kamenka. Then you can get into China. That's all you. Kamenka is where the party is, though." He danced a little.

"If that's something you can do?" I tried to be polite. We had just barged onto his boat. I wasn't expecting anything. But he looked as anxious to talk to people as we were.

He moved toward the table full of guns in front of us. "I can. But first, I really meant it."

Yazmin looked around. "What?"

"The guns." He pointed. "I have no need to be self-defended. And most people we might come across will likely be bullet-proof." He reached down and grabbed an armful of weapons and moved toward the stairs. "Are you coming?"

We made our way up the stairs to the bridge level, each of us with an armful of guns. I looked at him as he tossed the first group over the side, to drop into the water.

He smiled in satisfaction. "Boom."

"Where did these all come from?"

He inhaled. "Well...they were here when I acquired the boat."

Yazmin cocked her head and tried to figure him out. "Acquired."

He grinned at her and put up a finger. "I know who you are. I've seen you on tv." He motioned to her and she dumped her load of guns over the edge. I'm Ponimaniye Kuretzov. My friends call me Poni."

Yazmin made a show of brushing off her hands. She was no fan of guns. "It's nice to meet you, Poni."

"So...I float around, trading up when I find a boat." He spread his arms. "This one is the biggest yet. There were a few people on it, dead of radiation poisoning. It is creepy but that is why God made Lysol." He grimaced at me.

Akana nodded. "These ships were all out to sea when the bombs dropped."

He turned to her as she dumped her armful of guns over the hull. "Yes. They were far from population centers, but the radiation waves were not kind. Before the 20-Minute War, I had an old fishing boat I won in a card game."

My ears perked up. "Is that what it's called?" I finally dumped my guns over the edge. One more trip and we'd have gotten rid of them all.

Poni seemed almost alarmed at how little we knew. "It's been a year, almost. Nine-and-a-half months No one talked to you about the war?"

I shook my head, "You are literally the first person we've seen."

We started moving back downstairs. "How far did you go to get here?"

Yazmin followed. "We came from Oketo."

Poni scrunched up his face, imagining the trip. And the absence of people. "I'm sorry."

Akana looked back at him on the stairwell. "We're a bit in the dark. Can you tell us what happened?"

He reached the bottom and started collecting more guns. Many of them were foreign and some looked expensive. For a moment, I tried to imagine what the people who originally had owned this boat were like. I decided it was better I didn't know.

"I can tell you what everyone thinks happened. When America closed up, no one really knew what was happening there. No information was going in or out. All the treaties they had built with Russia were void. From what I understand, the whole country got more and more suspicious."

Yazmin nodded. "That much we saw."

Making our last trip, Poni stepped cautiously up the stairs. "What we found out afterward is that America was one of the countries that had automated their nuclear response systems. And at one point, the automation just decided this was the correct response."

Yazmin asked first. "Where did they fire?"

"That's just it." We heard more splashes in the cool night as the guns hit the water. " Because the nation had closed up, they no longer had documented allies." Poni seemed lighter, more comfortable, now that the guns were gone.

I cut in. "So, everywhere?"

"Yes, and America had built their nuclear arsenal back up. And more."

"How many?" Yazmin looked visibly upset.

Poni mirrored her, making an uncomfortable face. "Over 50,000 high-yield bombs. Many more smaller ones."

Akana was anxious to know more about everywhere else. She had already seen too much of Japan. "And the rest of the world?"

We followed him into the lounge. Poni motioned to us to sit down. "Some of their automated systems retaliated."

I flopped down on the couch. "So what's left?"

Poni began pouring drinks. It occurred to me that we hadn't eaten or drunk anything in days. We didn't need to eat or sleep, really, but it felt wrong to stop. For me, I realized I felt less human, less civilized, if I ate nothing. It felt comfortable sinking into Poni's hospitality.

"Large areas of Africa are untouched. Big areas in South America. Some Russian coastline. Australia and New Zealand suffered minimal damage."

Akana asked without wanting to look too hopeful. "The rest of Japan?"

I added, "Brazil?"

He brought us out some lemonades. There were raspberries floating in them and they looked amazing. Poni tried to funnel everything he knew into something sensible. "Some places there survived. Europe is a wasteland. There are areas north of Denmark that survived."

I let out a long breath. "Jesus."

"The Middle East?" Yazmin asked.

He shook his head and slid into the couch next to us.

I felt the paper in my pocket, our portable version of the map. Suddenly, it occurred to me to pull it out. I had filled in the large area that Akana had seen in China. I pointed to it and asked Poni, "Hey, do you know anything about this area?"

"I don't. It looks like it is in Heilongjiang, China, right?. Maybe Yichun?"

That seemed right to me. And familiar. "Do you know of anything strange here?"

He looked around the room, back and forth. "No, but it's important to you. It's filled in. What are these dots?"

"Well," I responded, pointing, "those are Salvado. That's you."

"No shit. I look better big." He lifted the map and looked. "So this area has a lot of our kind in it?"

Akana shook her head, "Actually, it's one big one."

"Shit," he mused. "Like a giant?"

Yazmin laughed. Something about Poni seemed to be making her more comfortable. As though his relaxed demeanor were contagious. "Why not. I'm a little one. Why not a giant? This was great, by the way." She motioned to her empty glass.

"Yeah, frozen raspberries. Instead of ice cubes. A good amount of food on this ship."

"So you know my story," Yazmin continued, "I'm sure Anjo wants to hear yours."

His eyes darted toward me. "So, you are the keeper of the stories?" He smiled at that idea. He wasn't wrong.

"I am. And I haven't heard yours."

He laughed. "Mine is easy. In English, it's only ten words." He put his drink down and held up all ten fingers, dropping one with each word. "Terminal disease. I tried to end it. I got better." He leaned back and grabbed his drink again.

I thought about the thousands of words I'd written on Salvado from all across the world. This seemed almost like some kind of strange but familiar haiku.

It worked. "I may need to shorten mine."

"Well, we'll have time." Poni got up and bowed. "We can start out tonight if you are all ready. We can be in Kamenka in a few days. "If you go that way, you can all find rooms that you like. I'll point us and get underway."

We were crossing the Sea of Japan. It would not take long, but there was no reason we couldn't pretend we were on a cruise and enjoy it. We dug through the closets full of clothes on the ship and found a few nondescript items to wear. Our clothes had been mangled in the initial blast and everything we found along the way was brittle and stiff as well. I found myself longing for one good solid wearable t-shirt. But for all my clothing problems, Yazmin's were worse. As a permanently 12-year-old girl, her choices were often annoyingly cutesy or, a product of the demented times leading up to this conflagration, overly sexualized. She tended to wear baggy adult sweaters a lot. Yazmin was eternally hiding under a mass of ill-fitting clothing.

The original owners of this boat had been out to sea, apparently, for long stretches and were terrified of scurvy, clearly. There were pounds and pounds of frozen fruit. At one point Poni showed us the massive walk-in freezer, filled with supplies. An entire room-sized area was dedicated to frozen fruit. Oranges dominated, but the fruit was of all kinds and it seemed to go on forever.

"Holy shit. They really were afraid of scurvy." I picked up a frozen orange and juggled it.

"Oh, yeah. Scurvy is real. Pirates had to deal with it."

"Cocaine and fruit. It's a full-on pirate party in here."

Poni shrugged. "Except the cocaine won't work for us."

"Really." How did I not know that?

"Yup. Your monoamine reuptake transporters cannot be blocked. No Dopamine buildup -- no high."

I thought about that. "Huh. Crazy."

Poni squinted at me. "Wait, have you not tried cocaine in the last 200 years?"

"I'm not much of a partier." I started warming the orange up in my hands. I figured I'd bring it upstairs.

He laughed as we went up.

Once the ship was set on course, there wasn't much it needed, so, after we had rustled up some clothes and done our part to clean up, we really had nothing to do but relax and talk. We sat on the deck and drank lemonade made from a large stockpile of frozen lemons and oranges.

The air out here was fresher, less acrid than in Japan. And the oily detritus of stolen organic life didn't hang so oppressively. It was almost clear. And once the sight of land slipped away it was almost easy to look around and make that pretense -- that we were on some happy springtime cruise, in a world that was fresh and new all around us.

Except for the fish.

We saw few signs of marine life, but no large fish or anything. And we had no expectations we'd see any.

Which is why, after two days, it was so surprising when we first saw the Glorious.

At first, it looked like a whale in the distance, slowly moving toward us. Poni showed us through a pair of binoculars he had found in the engine room.

"It looks like it's not moving."

I looked. It just looked like a kind of gray lump. "Hey, would a dead whale float?"

Poni looked at me in a mild disgust. "I don't think so. That would be horrific. Thousands of floating dead whales."

Suddenly, I missed Devilboy. My phone had been incinerated. He was still out there somewhere, in the cloud, assuming any servers were left standing. I could get him back. But surely this was a question for him.

Yazmin walked up and grabbed the binoculars. "A dead whale might float depending on the state it was in when it died. As it decomposes, though, the gasses would build up and it would float until they escape. And then it sinks."

I was having one of those days when everyone seemed smarter than me. I looked over to see Akana sleeping in the sun on one of the deck chairs. This was no reason to wake her. The three of us could figure it out.

Until it got closer.

I was the first one to call it out. "That is not a whale. It's some kind of a vessel. A ship or something."

"Well, I'm sure it's not bigger than this one." Poni took the binoculars back. He smiled at me.

"It's not a pissing contest." I stuck my tongue out.

"Yes, but if it were, I win, Angel-boy. I could piss all over that thing. I could probably do it from here."

"Is it just floating?" Yazmin was the first to really be alarmed.

Poni tried to walk back and forth on the deck, triangulating the distance of the object. "I can't tell. It's not leaving a wake, I see that."

"So, it could be moving slowly?" She looked up at both of us.

Poni nodded. "You know, I have a little boat we could drop and a couple of us could go get closer."

Yazmin shook her head. "No, uh-uhn. We don't split up for any reason." I thought back to Akana's house, how Yazmin had made it so we wouldn't lose each other. It was smart then and it was now.

"Okay, no little boat."

It was at that moment that the ship buckled under us, pushing backward and sending us flying aftward. It was like the water dropped out from under us at the back end of the entire boat. I grabbed Akana and saw Yazmin grab Poni as we slid down backwards, holding onto the light-filled ropes surrounding the deck. We were clearly sinking, but we hadn't hit anything. But we had heard the explosion. Compared to the nuclear one, it was small. But it was enough

Yazmin sighed. "Okay, we'll get the little boat."

Poni looked around. "Probably a good call."

I looked down. The water was approaching quickly. We didn't have time to grab anything. But we could make our way portside where the rowboat was hanging off the hull. It was a white plastic looking shell that could have fit 4 more of us, too. The lower fin of the rowboat was almost at water level now.

We slid down the ladder into the rowboat and began to paddle away. The ship was large and it seemed to be sucking us down with it until we cleared the space around. We made it about 200 meters from its inevitable suction and stopped rowing.

Poni stood up and sighed, watching the ship sink below the surface. "Damn. I really liked that one."

Yazmin still had the binoculars around her neck. She stared at the object. "Well, no surprise, but that's a submarine. And it is moving this way."

Poni stepped over and pointed himself at the approaching sub. He unzipped his pants and pulled his member out, aiming for the sub as he started peeing.

I shook my head. "I really don't think that'll reach."

He kept peeing. "It's making me feel better." He raised his voice and continued to piss in their direction. "You suck, dickheads."

At that point, Akana summed up what we were all thinking. "I'm really getting tired of being blown up."

I was, as well. But my bigger concern, watching the submarine approach, was that these things tended to happen in threes.

I just didn't want to say that out loud.

We watched the sub get closer. We tried paddling in the other direction, but it was advancing faster than we could paddle. As it began to rise from the water we could see more of the hull. It was huge. And across the front it read "SS Glorious SSGN 1734." I was the only American in the rowboat – the only one who could know what bad news that was.

"It's a nuclear sub. Guided warheads." Poni looked back at me. "You can tell by the hull designation."

"American." Yazmin shook her head.

It seemed to take 30 minutes for the sub to rise. Eventually we were staring at a large round airlock. It hissed as it swung open and men in opaque black suits poured out.

"We stay together," was the last thing I heard Yazmin say before the blanket was wrapped over my head and it went dark.

***

The lights were bright as the black-suited men pulled the blankets off and stripped the four of us. I heard the clicking of radiation counters while they scrubbed and hosed us down. We ourselves weren't radioactive, but probably everything we were wearing was dangerously high in ambient radioactivity. They kept scrubbing until the special lead drains filled up and the clicking sound faded.

The four of us stood there naked. Poni tried his best to stand in front of us. A preoperative trans man, a woman with the body of a 12-year-old girl, and a very shy Japanese woman who had lived most of her life in solitude lined up behind him.

Here's the thing, though, about being hundreds of years old. You stop caring so much about some things. Yazmin stood there unphased, looking at the man closest.

"You like looking, huh? You like naked kid bodies?"

The men looked back and forth and tried to turn away as a larger white-haired man in a maroon uniform walked in. The men in radiation suits opened a path in the middle as he spoke.

"My name is Captain Barelli, and for the foreseeable future, you are our guests…"

Yazmin broke in. "No."

The captain looked confused.

She continued. "No, there is no foreseeable future, and what you mean is that we are your prisoners. We are not. We could sink this ship and walk to Russia underwater if we needed to. The only thing that's up to you, Captain, is how much we need to."

The captain stared. Suddenly his face opened up into a smile. "I have seen your speeches on television. I've listened. That one was not your best, Ms. Gazzawi."

We moved in closer to her to show support.

"It's also not my last. Note this moment. Your ability to negotiate decreases from here."

The captain considered for what seemed like a full minute. "Get them some clothing. The non-radioactive kind."

Two of the men left as the rest took off their helmets. They looked terrible. They looked like men who had been in a submarine underwater for nine months. Poni pointed to a man with a rash on his face. "That guy's fucking got scurvy. You know where there was a freezer with a shitload of oranges? Idiots."

The captain raised his hand. "We can talk more in my ready room." Then he looked down. I heard the splatter before I saw it. It felt oddly satisfying to see Poni pissing all over his boots.

We were given blue jumpsuits and the men all glanced away as we put them on. I peered over at Poni. "I'm transgender. As you can see."

He smiled and pulled his hair back. "Dude. I have an irritably small bladder, as you can see."

Yazmin pushed him aside playfully, having slid into her jumpsuit. "Resist any move to separate us." She looked around and we all nodded. "Don't eat or drink anything. They can't poison us, but they can put a tracker in it, or some other kind of device."

I stared at her with a renewed respect. I literally never would have thought of that.

She turned to Akana. "Can you tell how close we are?"

She nodded. "We're moving closer, actually. They are headed our way. It feels like we should be at the coast by the morning."

"Why would they blow up my fucking boat and then just take us where we were going?"

Yazmin nodded. It didn't make sense. "Well, we can go ask him in his cosplay ready room. Ready?"

The men all looked tired, too. I tried to imagine what the last nine months had been like for them. The outside world was wildly radioactive. This area was toxic to them. Down here, surrounded by the lead in the hull, was the only place safe for them. The sub was large, huge by submarine standards. But I could see that some of the taller men still had to crouch a little stepping through its corridors.

We followed them to a larger room, one with maps and devices all over. In the center of it was a table. The captain stood at the head of the table. "I'd appreciate you not peeing in here."

Poni sat down at the head of the table on the other side, "Yeah, well, I'd appreciate you going back in time and not blowing up my fucking boat." Poni's slight Ukrainian accent seemed to make everything sound bouncier.

I sat down. "Yeah, what was that about?"

The captain looked at Yazmin. He had already codified her in his mind as the leader of our group.

She sat to his right and pointed at me. "He asked you a question, Captain." She said the word "captain" as though it were a prod – an incentive for him to come clean and act like one.

He sighed, looking us over. "Maybe the rest of you can tell me who you are, we can exchange that much."

"We will, when you answer the question. You just cost this man a very important boat. And you need to explain why." Yazmin crossed her arms.

Suddenly, I could see that the captain himself looked tired, as well. "The truth, I swear, is that we didn't know there was anyone on board. We hadn't considered that there might be shells aboard."

Yazmin jumped in. "We don't respond to that. It's Salvado. The word."

He looked down. "Of course, Ms. Gazzawi. Salvado. We were just following protocol."

Poni tried not to look agitated. "It's protocol to blow up my boat?"

The captain continued, "Yes, it is, actually. These ships out here are filled with dead bodies, rotting. But they are also filled with organic radioactive matter. And they are just floating all over, headed in different directions. They are a huge risk to anything that might be alive anywhere.

Akana spoke up. "So you thought it was just an empty radioactive thing floating around, a danger?"

Barelli nodded. "Yes. I'm truly sorry. If I still had a government, they would reimburse you."

"Yeah, well, if I still had a boat, I could buy you a new government." Poni leaned back, deflated.

The captain looked confused. "I don't get that."

Yazmin turned to him, "It's not important. So, once you saw it was inhabited, you rescued us and had to detox us."

"Yes. You were steeped in it. I'm sorry." Captain Barelli motioned to one of the men. They brought a couple of cups of coffee and set them in front of us. We ignored them.

I spoke up. "So now you're going exactly where it is we wanted to go?"

The captain looked pained. "I didn't know that, honestly. We're heading toward the ports in Russia, hoping to find somewhere to go."

Yazmin leaned back. "You need to find somewhere to live?"

Captain Barelli stood up and waved his men away. They turned and left. "Yes. Here is where things kind of get awkward. We need your help. We've been in this ship since the war, we are nearly out of food, we've already lost men from disease and lack of sunlight and just last week, one of our men hanged himself in hopelessness." He looked at us plaintively. "We're dying. And unless we find a safe place, we can't survive."

Yazmin was looking at me. I could tell she was thinking the same thing I was. "First. Before we talk about that, this is a nuclear submarine. You had a compliment of warheads. Where are they?"

The captain's breathing was shallow. "We were part of an automated system that – "

Yazmin leaned in. "How many do you have left?"

The captain's eyes passed between us. I reached for Akana's hand and held it. I could feel her trembling as a tiny moan came from her.

"None. We have none left."

Suddenly Yazmin seemed hundreds of years old. Older than this giant of a captain, this decorated puffed up thing. Older than the ship, than anything I could think of. She was powerful. And Captain Barelli sunk into himself as she spoke one word to him.

"Where?"

His face was wet and his eyes were glassy with tears. He dropped his head.

"Sapporo."

Akana began crying. She pushed away from the table as though she couldn't bear to touch anything on this ship. I thought about the bodies we had stepped over to get here. I thought about Akana's blue list, the map of descendents she lovingly watched over.

All gone. The map. The people. All of it.

Poni stood up. "This sonofabitch wasn't going to tell us."

The Captain sat back down. "I'm so sorry. I wish... I wish I could go back in time. I truly do."

Poni continued. "Say it. You were just following orders. Go ahead. Here are your orders." he spit as far as he could across the table. It landed toward the center as he sat back down and reached for Akana, too.

The room was silent for a minute until Yazmin spoke up. "Poni, what was the port we were going to?"

Poni breathed in. "Kamenka"

"Kamenka. We're going to huddle and think about this. We'll tell you what we decide once we get to Kamenka."

The captain stood up. "Of course. Thank you. I will have the men get rooms together for you."

"No. One room. A big one. One that locks from the inside. Four beds. We can wait. We don't need sleep."

That last I could tell was to remind him of our otherness, of our otherworldly abilities. It was meant to make him afraid. It was the first time I had heard Yazmin do that, use what we were to frighten people.

I didn't love it, but I understood it.

The captain nodded and within minutes, men pulled beds into the ready room. This may have been the largest room on the ship, besides the hold. I was glad not to be separated. As they left, Poni pushed the door closed and locked it.

I checked the door and moved over near Yazmin, addressing the room. "Do you think they're listening to us in here?"

Poni shrugged. "I don't know, man. We didn't give them much time to set it up, so maybe no."

They had taken the smaller map I had drawn. So I grabbed a marker and drew it on the table. The area of importance. "I have a hunch and I need to tell you guys before we make any decisions."

Yazmin stared at the table as I drew. "A hunch?"

"Yeah. It didn't really register until Poni said something back on the boat. The area in Heilongjiang. Yichun."

He nodded. "Yes, I think that's there. The city." He pointed to the area on the table.

"There is one of us in Yichun. And she's not a giant. I think I know what's going on." I turned to Akana. "Are you ok to hear this?"

She nodded. She had stopped crying but we were all taking turns holding her hands. Right now, Poni was sitting next to her on a bed, holding her left hand tightly.

I took a deep breath and started. "I think this is Lian Chen. She was a nurse here before the Savior Event. She quit her job about five years earlier, though, to take care of her mother. Her mom came down with a congenital disease that caused fatty buildups in the brain. "

I kept drawing, outlining the area as if to make a point. "It was causing her to lose her personality, lose milestones, language, everything. She was basically reverting to a baby. Since her father had died years earlier, Lian was all she had, except for an older brother who was very busy as a policeman. So for five years, she watched her mother sort of become something else."

Yazmin spoke up. "So, sort of like adult onset Tay-Sachs disease?"

"Exactly like that. Doctors couldn't do anything. It began with a tremor and ended, well, it ended in death. And after five years of that, her mother died, unable to speak, to hold her head up, to focus her eyes."

"That sucks." Poni had put his arm around Akana. I looked at her to see if I should continue.

"Well, Lian wanted to go back to nursing. All she wanted to do was to take care of people. And then her older brother, the police officer, had to retire. His arm began to shake. The tremor. A year later, he couldn't walk. Lian was tested for the disease and she didn't have it. But she did have to care for her family as they died off one by one. Before he lost the ability to talk completely, her brother agreed that she should kill him. At that point, Lian was empty, she had spent herself completely trying to take care of her family. Her plan was to kill herself right after euthanizing her brother. So she did."

Yazmin added, "on March 30th, 2045."

I nodded. "She hid away for a long time, but this is who she is. She's a caretaker. She's a protector, a nurturer."

Poni pointed to the map on the table. "So you think that's her?"

I waved over the table. "I think the whole effect is her. I think she's keeping the people in that whole city alive somehow. And this is how that looks to us."

Yazmin ran her fingers over the map. It was a huge area. "That's... wow."

Akana's voice was small as she asked, "how many people?"

I looked over at Poni. He was more familiar with the area now, but I was more familiar with geography in general. He shrugged. "It looks like it's not the entire city. Maybe an area defined some other way. But 250,000 people, easily."

"So we go there." Yazmin was definitive. "But do we bring them? It has to be a unanimous decision." Her eyes darted to Akana. "Ok, sweetheart?"

Akana nodded. Yazmin raised her hand. "I say we do it. Getting revenge on these people does nothing. Saving them saves lives."

Poni dropped his head and grunted. "Fine. I agree. I will piss on them again, though."

I tried not to focus only on Akana as I raised my hand. "I don't know. I guess yes. They can't all be assholes, right?"

I held my breath waiting as Akana raised her hand.

Yazmin put her hands together. "Ok. It's settled. We take these assholes to Yichun."

Poni interjected, "I mean, it's over 3,000 kilometers. We can't walk it."

Yazmin shrugged. "Okay. Then they take us."

***

In the morning, Yazmin stood on the helm to address the Americans. There were about 80 of them on the ship. Captain Barelli handed her the microphone.

"What is your first name?"

"My... oh, Veren. Veren Berelli." he reached out his hand and she shook it.

"Okay, Veren Berelli. It's nice to meet you. This is Anjo Killean, Akana Tanaka and Poni Kuretzov. I need to get your signoff on this. I'm not bringing a cadre of soldiers anywhere. I will help bring people. Are you okay with that?"

He nodded. She lifted the microphone and continued. "Hello everyone. This is Yazmin Gazzawi. I'm standing here with my friends and with Veren Berelli. We are making plans right now for our journey to Yichun. To make this journey, you must leave behind ranks and military symbols. No weapons, no guns, no explosives. Please dress in clothing that is as civilian as possible. We will be taking every vehicle in the ship's complement, but it will be barely enough for all of us people. So only take what you absolutely need. Food and medical supplies take priority. And now, here is Veren Berelli to organize the timing."

She handed the mic back to Berelli. He picked it up and continued, "Thank you, Yazmin. Please pay close attention to what she says. Once we are underway, we will not be able to leave the vehicles. We don't have enough rad suits. Please make sure that every vehicle has a medical professional in it. We are trying to get somewhere better, somewhere we can live. Please, hang in there."

I could tell that he was lost without his military presence. He seemed deflated. I tried not to feel sorry for him. This unbound militarism had brought the world one thing and it would take centuries to fix it.

The entire ship shook as we made ground in Kamenka. Moving down to the hold we saw the row of wide military looking vehicles, black and ominous. Men were pouring out from the stairwells, filling the vehicles. The two large ones could each fit 20 men while the five smaller ones sat 10 each. The four of us would ride in a smaller one that led the caravan. I could tell as we made our way to the truck that these people around us were afraid of us. Part of me was sad about that. But I also recognized the power in it. It made it easier for me to stand among the 80 strangers that had bombed my friend's home.

The plan was to drive for about two days straight. Drivers would change out regularly in four hour shifts.

We sat on padded benches against the inside walls of the trucks. I had always hated riding in a bus or anything sideways. I wish I could have faced forward.

The trip was mostly uneventful until later in the second day. One of the people sitting next to us had lifted his arms up to place a bag in a rack above him and Poni nudged me.

"A gun." I could see it, too

"He's got a gun."

Yazmin stood up and walked over to him. He comically towered over her as she demanded he give her the gun.

"No way. I don't know where we're going. I have a right to bring a gun."

She stood up taller. "We're going somewhere where you can possibly live. If you want to stay right here, out there, on the radioactive glass, you can have the right to a gun."

I stood next to her in support. I wasn't sure if that was making things any better.

For a moment, he looked like he was going to hand her the gun. Instead he pulled it out and pointed it at her. "Sit down, little girl."

"I was a little girl hundreds of years before you were born. And I'm bulletproof. Shoot me and one of your friends will get hurt. Is that what you want?"

He looked unsure. "Bullshit."

She shook her head. "What's your name?"

"Edwards." He kept the gun trained on her.

"What's your first name?" She stepped closer, toward the gun. If she was close enough, maybe it wouldn't ricochet.

"Jaxon," He barked out.

"Jaxon, when we get to where we are going, we're going to have to prove to those people that we aren't going to ruin what they have. What would they think if they saw you holding a gun on a little girl?"

"You said you weren't a little girl."

"Jaxon, I love that you're listening. Can you give the gun to Poni so he can store it for you? If they turn us away and you have to live for your last few days in the radioactive wasteland you can have it back, ok?"

"I'll fucking tag it." Poni held his hand out.

I feltl like this could have gone a bunch of different ways. Looking at Yazmin, it was clear she expected it to go the way it did, as Jaxon handed the gun to Poni. She had stood up to tanks and presidents.

One gun was nothing.

It was morning when we started driving through the dense defoliated trees that surrounded Yichun. With every kilometer, though, they seemed to grow richer, more green. The sun was high in the sky when we drove through the leafy living forest front of the city. Right away, we saw it.

There were people. Everywhere you looked, people were walking, driving, alive.

A few people came over to see us as we opened the doors of the trucks and stepped out. The radiation meters registered nothing.

No radiation

Akana and I stepped over to a woman in a bright yellow dress. Her Mandarin was better than mine. "Lián chén zài nǎlǐ?"

Where is Lian Chen?

The woman shielded her eyes from the sun and smiled. She pulled a piece of paper from her purse and drew us a little map. At the top, she wrote, "Chéngshì shèngrén."

I handed the paper to Yazmin. Berelli had come to stand next to her.

She showed him the map.

"What does this mean? At top? Chéngshì shèngrén?"

Yazmin smiled at Akana. She translated.

"It means 'Saint of cities.'"

***

You probably know the rest. Most of the medical knowledge that survived on Earth came from Yichun. Technology, Literature. Yichin wasn't just salvation for 250,000 people, it was a home for information that the earth desperately needed.

Lian remembered me with a big hug. She was surprisingly cheerful for someone who hadn't slept in nearly a year. She had used the power inside her to shield the entire city, as we suspected. But she really had no idea how she had done it. All she knew was that she could keep the radiation away through constant vigilance.

It was no surprise to me that Akana chose to stay behind to help her -- to learn so that she could sleep one day. But when Poni told me he was staying, too, I was taken aback. It turns out that he had been floating around looking for purpose. And keeping a quarter of a million people safe seemed like an irresistible purpose for him.

Yazmin and I stayed for a year or so before she left to rebuild the World Council and I left to rebuild a company that I thought could help people, too. It felt strange going in a different direction than her. Walking away from her.

Of all the stories I have to tell, I feel like I needed to tell you this one. I needed you to know why I would jump up and follow Yazmin Gazzawi anywhere. If you don't understand this, there is a question she will ask me later, one i say yes to, and it will feel unrealistic to you. Why would I?

You had to know her. You had to be around her.

As for the rest, It would be hundreds of years before I heard from them again. In fact, it would be almost half a millennium.

In 2825, we had returned Brazil to what it had been before the war, and, in many places, it was even better. Nearly 20 generations of Brazilians had grown up without the spectre of war or chaos over their heads. We traveled, we ate...

We lived.

And I had turned Xenovera into a company that used its resources to invent and make life better for people. I was proud of it. In fact, I was on a tour, showing some kids around when Poni showed up with the note from Akana.

I hugged him tightly. He was dressed playfully, almost like a pirate, reminding me of his pirate past. The kids on the tour wanted to know his name. I introduced him and they laughed.

And so did he.

It wasn't until they had left that I had the chance to sit down to dinner with him and read the note. I pressed him for more information, but he had none. The note itself was self-explanatory. Akana would have come herself, but she was invested in the people around her.

Unsurprisingly.

My mind conjured up a number of scenarios while I considered how I might find Yazmin again to share it with her. Penciled on a bit of parchment in a sealed envelope, it said:

"Anjo – There is another one on Mars now. And it's not one of us."

8 - The Silence of Water
Forte de Greta - 3060

"His name was Nazar Musayev. And he was a prisoner in Owadandepe, a state prison in Turkmenistan. He had been a reporter before that. He wrote about families, about animals, zoos, pets, human interest pieces. He wasn't really political. That's what he told me. Until a woman came to him with a story about her husband, who had been abducted."

"I think this is how it goes."

"Anyway, he wrote the article. And a follow-up. And testified, implicating certain people in the government. For a while, he thought that they would do the right thing. That they would let the man go."

"But they didn't."

"Instead, they arrested him. He went to prison –"

Leah interrupted. "That was the Owadandepe prison?"

"Yes. I looked it up. It's closed now. Actually, I think it was nuked out of existence." Martine looked thoughtful.

Leah lifted her drink. "To nuking prisons."

Martine laughed and clinked glasses, "absolutely."

"Woot."

"Anyway, he went to prison. And he was there for two years. He realized how bad the situation was for the prisoners. How some of them were beaten, disappeared. Tortured. So, he helped lead this rebellion. It didn't go that well. And some people died. He kept coming back and then, at one moment, he stood up in front of the other men and basically sacrificed himself."

"Ouch."

"Yeah, I guess that counted as a suicide. It was on Savior Day. He didn't realize until he crawled out of the trash where they threw his body."

"That is pretty shitty."

Martine laughed in her little French laugh. The one Leah had to admit she loved.

"It is. Very much. He lived for another 600 years after that until one day he was in Paris and he saw me."

"The pretty girl."

"Thank you. I didn't look that pretty. I was just run over by a bus. I was laying in the street, dying."

Leah leaned in. "And he passed it on to you?"

Martine shrugged. "He didn't know how he did it. But he did."

"So, now, 400 years later, here you are."

"And here I am."

Martine was dark-skinned and smooth, with a wide, beautiful smile and open, inviting features. Her hair was cut nearly as short as Leah's, but, as they sat in the hotel bar, both women wore wigs – Leah's a sandy-brown long one and Martine's a short black pixie cut. She put her hand over Leah's.

"We're both sort of second generation. I've never met another one."

Leah nodded. "I've met two other ones. But we're definitely rare. More and more, though, I think, people are learning how to pass it on."

"I'm glad we decided to meet." Martin took a drink. "I'm especially glad we decided to meet here."

"Here" was Forte de Greta. Originally, it was a fort along the promontory of Santa Catarina, on the western edge of the Bay of Mós, in the civil parish of Vila de São Sebastião, in the municipality of Angra do Heroísmo, on the Portuguese archipelago of the Azores.

But that's a lot to remember. Now it was just one of nine volcanic islands in the Macaronesia region of the North Atlantic Ocean, in between what was once the USA and Europe.

And today it was beautiful.

"On a map, this place is terrifying. It's just a tiny island in the middle of a massive big body of water." Leah looked around. "But once you're here, it's not scary at all."

"Well, all the TesouroEterno places are like that. I think Fiji is worse. So much water."

It might make sense to stop here for a minute and explain what this TesoroEterno that Martine Shorat was referring to really was.

But to really do that, it might be necessary to give a bit more backstory.

By 3060, when Leah Santos and Martine Shorat sat facing the Atlantic Ocean, it had been a little over a thousand years since the Savior Day, the day that created the 1936 Salvado that lived, all over the planet, undying, invulnerable to harm. For 23 hours on that day, as the Savior Event, a reddish-orange artifact, sailed through thee sky, every person who tried to commit suicide survived and became Salvado.

This was long before either of these women were born, though. They received their Salvado status when an existing one passed it on to them, becoming a normal baseline human in the process.

For Leah, it was Clyde Morrison, a conflicted and troubled nurse in the country now known as Aztecana. For Martine, it was Nazar Musayev, a normally soft-spoken reporter from Turkmenistan, an area now known, 1000 years later, as Aljanat.

For the next few hundred years, people all over the world struggled to figure out what to do about these people, the survivors. It was easy enough to see them as broken, as people who had tried to hurt themselves, as people with potential psychological issues. And, certainly, some were. Hundreds of them became cyphers, disappearing, unable to come to terms with the fact that they were still, against all reason, here. But twice that number became servants, leaders, people who changed cultures and even, after a worldwide near-complete nuclear conflagration, preserved them.

The world went from seeing them as troubled and enduring artifacts of poor mental health to recognizing them as real survivors, people who, more often than not, meant survival for the people around them. Books, stories, movies and plays that had once depicted them as exclusively villains and madmen began portraying them as the magical continuity for mankind that they could be. Countries that had passed laws preventing them from serving as elected officials now welcomed their input as the nations of the world began to pull together, more and more, creating a stable world oversight that ensured that the kinds of earth-sweeping wars we had experienced in the past stayed there -- in the past.

And one of the drivers in that shift, if I say so myself, was a company called XenoVera. XenoVera had begun, nearly 50 years before the Savior Event, as an opportunistic and ethically-challenged biotech firm, dedicated to leeching cash out of new discoveries around biology to line its shareholders' pockets. It looked like any one of 20 other biotech companies at the tim, scrambling for market dominance on drugs and new advances, each one another dollar in the till.

Before Savior Day, they had successfully lobbied to change the rules of ethical organ donation, enabling them to pay people facing poverty for their organs, giving the wealthy a way to maintain health and live, according to the brochures, nearly forever.

This is probably why it was so ironic that the very first Salvado that they had brought in to study would eventually outlive the bad-faith founders and owners of the company to become the CEO, moving the company into a more benevolent and service-focused direction.

XenoVera still made money, but not at the expense of the poor. And what it learned it used to ensure that people had what they needed to survive. Its subsidiaries that provided services to people who were poor were all free, operating vigorously until the number of people who needed free services dwindled and disappeared and the concept of paying for things needed to survive, well...

It died.

XenoVera became devoted to increasing the level of human happiness, to supporting art, adventure, ideas. When holographic technology became viable, they built holographic parks that let people play and have fun while the surfaces around them generated energy needed to keep the holograms alive and vibrant. When teleportation became possible, they helped build the worldwide goods networks that ensured that people could get what they needed anywhere in the world. And when food replication technology got close, they picked up the ball and ensured that no mother or father on Earth had to go more than a few meters to feed their child.

These advances gave humanity more happiness than it had experienced before. But more than anything, they gave human beings the one thing that they realized they had been most impoverished of.

Time.

Some people used that time to raise their children joyfully, and that helped everyone. Some people used it to invent. Some to write, to make art. The equation became clear, though, regardless. Given enough time, people would do something of value. Often they just needed a model. Sometimes they just needed a finger, pointing in the right direction.

And that's how XenoVera's subsidiary TesouroEterno was born.

The idea was simple. Identify things that need to be found, discovered, located, or done, and help people do them. For some, it meant adventure. For some it meant purpose. And for some it was about bucket lists, doing things they had always wanted to do.

They had a worldnet presence where people could meet and engage in some of these adventures together. Along with a special section for Salvado, people who might be able to go places few could.

And that's how Leah and Martine met and ended up on a secluded island in the Atlantic ocean, preparing to look for sunken treasure.

Sort of.

"So, tell me about your wife?" Martine reached over to hold Leah's hand.

"My primary. My wife. She is cool. We've been together for over six hundred years, on and off, which is an insane thing to say."

"It really is."

"Her name is Jamie. She's young-looking. She was in high school when she was saved. She's beautiful, dark like you. She's very focused and sometimes a little...haunted." She flashed a picture on the table using her bracelet.

"I bet." Martine kissed her hand. "She's so pretty."

"She'll be here soon, but all of this is more my thing, the exploring, the adventure. She has projects to finish. She should be here tomorrow night."

Martine looked confused. "But she's an astronaut? But not an explorer?"

"Oh, yeah, but she's more about being a pilot, the mission, the objectives."

"Got it." Martine smiled. "I wish she were here already."

"Me, too. I have a feeling we're going to get along. A third would be nice."

Martine looked down, a little afraid of overstepping. "Would she be ok if we started without her?"

Leah flashed a grin. "I'm sure she'll be just fine with it."

They drank for a while and then made their way up to the suite that they had booked with Xenovera at El Tiovivo. Like nearly everything here, it overlooked the water, facing east. The room was wide open and bright, with a kitchen they would probably not use. The bed was built for at least three people and the large hot tub would fit three more, at least. Recessed behind it was an open shower area that fell onto a stone floor with a square center drain. It was a beautiful space and Leah and Martine made the most of it for the rest of the night, letting the water fall down on them as they kissed and got to know each other, each treating the other like something to be explored before the larger exploration began.

Before she went to bed that night, Leah sat near the white wall and used her bracelet to call her wife.

"Hi, baby. Is this time ok?" Leah tried not to wake up Martine, who had fallen asleep in the bed still half-covered in her white hotel bath sheet.

Jamie answered, smiling at her, the bright Aztecana sun to one side. "Yeah, sweety. It's like four hours earlier here. How are things in the future? How is she?"

"The future is good. She's hot. And funny. You're going to like her. We just spent a few hours in the shower, which you will also like."

"Nice. Is she excited about the thing?" Jamie's voice was like a wink. You could tell that this was a vacation that she was looking forward to.

"She is. We both think you should be here now. We need a grown-up."

Jamie laughed. "Oh, is that what I am?"

"Oh, you know you're in charge of this expedition, and I better see you take charge bigly."

"You know I will, wench." Jamie squinted at her. "It looks so dark there."

"It gets so dark. I told her you actually know the guy from XenoVera and she has questions."

"Well," said Jamie. "Answers are on the way. I miss you."

Leah sighed. "I miss you so much, sir." Leah only called Jamie that when they were alone. It was a playful way for them to connect. In reality, Leah looked up to Jamie so much. Her experiences were legendary. And in the course of the last few hundred years, she'd become the only reliable thing in the world to her. Even during those times when they had been broken up, it was Jamie who Leah wanted to reach out to, to vent to, to just talk to. Sometimes Leah felt like a bird, capable of incredible flight, but she only really rested on her perch, and Jamie was that perch.

Leah touched the wall. "Hurry up, okay?"

Jamie nodded and signed off. Leah slipped into bed next to Martine and moved closer. In her mind, she was leaving room for Jamie, room that even if she didn't come take right now, would always be there for her. In every bed Leah had ever slept in for the last 600 years, that space had been left open, intentionally, available to the one person who would fill it the right way.

And even empty, that room was comforting.

***

"So we don't have a map." Martine was looking over the mission at breakfast, trying to make sense of it in her head.

"No. We have these." Leah pulled out the pulseometers. They were small, just a few centimeters long. But when you pressed the button at the bottom, they let out a loud series of bells, sharp sounds they could hear underwater. All three of them glowed a rich bright red color.

"And they start red?" Martine grabbed one to look at it.

"No, they started black. They just turned on when I got to the island to meet you."

Martine grabbed an orange. She usually didn't eat, except to be social. But she was thinking that she wanted to taste like something good when she kissed. "I can't wait to meet Jamie."

"I talked to her last night and told her you were hot. And excited about this."

"Hold on, wheel back to the hot part. Did you send her an updated picture of me." Martine winked.

"No. Should I?"

"If it gets her here faster." Martine pulled her shirt off. She really was beautiful. Leah laughed and pointed her bracelet at her. If she were a normal human, she would have an implant to do all this, but her skin couldn't accommodate one. She loved the bracelet, though. She took a few pictures of Martine and sent them through to Jamie.

Leah smiled. "Maybe that will speed this up."

"Good. Does she know anything more about what we're looking for?" Martine seemed uninterested in putting her shirt back on. The rest of the open air restaurant didn't seem to care, so Leah shrugged. Probably better this way.

"Nope. We have no idea what we are looking for, just that it will look like it doesn't belong down there.

Martine scrunched up her face. "That could describe so many things. I think a giant panda would not belong."

"No arguments from me. To giant pandas." And the two toasted. Thousands of miles away, two giant pandas in an Aztecanan zoo looked around, their ears itching. And soon, Jamie would be getting on an air shuttle not far from there.

"We have to be at the beach in a half-hour." Martine lifted the mission to show her. "For training."

"I'm in. This should be fun." Leah finished her drink and they started toward the beach, holding hands.

Over the last few hundred years, there had been a movement among Salvado to figure themselves out. What were they? They had discovered that not only did this energy, that some people called the radiance, keep you safe from harm, but it also worked to sort of "perfect" you over time. It took the thing about you that you were most good at, the thing you loved, and it made that part grow, expand. It made your strengths stronger, if that made sense.

This caused a lot of people to stop and ask, "who am I? - what, exactly, are my strengths?" Ironically, this was a question that was often relevant for people experiencing the kinds of challenges that led to them looking at suicide in the first place. There were so many things about this that were unknown, and that caused a lot of people to start a journey into themselves.

Who am I? What are my strengths?

Leah had discovered that she was an explorer. She was a xenophile. She loved the newness of ideas, things, experiences, places. She was driven to explore in ways that the average person would be afraid to do. And her enthusiasm for the unknown dovetailed perfectly with Jamie's own desire to explore --- to fly to places that no one had been, to experience things. Jamie was a natural astronaut. Leah was a natural ethnologist, with a passion for newness.

And Martine? She was the youngest of them and hadn't really finished her journey yet. She was smart and good at so many things. But her strength? Maybe she'd find out in the water.

There was a floating table at the beach that had everything they needed. As Salvado, they wouldn't need to breathe, but as ones inexperienced with that, they might need to start with respies. These were small clear devices that attached to your face that prevented you from breathing in water. They blocked your mouth and nose comfortably.

At the same time, they let you speak normally and have it transmitted to the earpieces in your group. Ironically, most baseline humans had earpieces and implants surgically installed by the age of five. So these items had been designed exclusively for the use of the 1936 people on the planet who could use them. It was no accident that they hadn't seen them before.

Most people hadn't

Leah and Martine had left their wigs back in the suite. Leah's hair was tightly cropped, leaving just the faint impression of the dark Latin mop of hair she used to sport before she was diagnosed with cancer -- before her nurse had saved her. When you become Salvado, your hair and nails stop growing. Which is for the best, because razors and scissors were ineffective after that.

Martine's hair was cut short, as well, fashionably tight to her head, just a shade or two darker than her skin. Martine's face was heart-shaped, neatly complimenting her wide nose and thick lips, while Leah's was rounder. They stripped down to black one-piece bathing suits. Even at the depths they'd be visiting, their bodies would be fine.

And each took a water ballast pack with a light. This attached to their backs and allowed them to control how buoyant they were and how fast they could move, using water pressure around them. These were designed to operate all the way to the ocean floor here. And the light would illuminate far into the darkness of the depths.

They listened to the instructor and tried talking back and forth to each other. The sound was nearly perfect. There was no way to test the water ballast pack, though, except to just get in the water.

So they did.

Sliding into the water, they walked along the shelf. It went out surprisingly far before it began to drop. As their heads dipped below the water, they were nearly a full soccer pitch out from the land. They kept walking as the angle got steeper, until they reached a plateau of about ten meters.

As they walked, Leah couldn't help but feel like there was an illusion of a glass rooftop above them, with only sky above that. The water was clear and warmer than they imagined it would be.

This shelf went on for another 50 meters until they reached another decline. This one carried them down to another shelf at about 40 meters underwater. At this point, the waters began to fill with life. Fish, plants, creatures swam all around them. The light was dimmer, giving way to a brilliant kind of cerulean blue that could have been alcohol ink, clear, colorful, swirling around everything they saw.

The final drop was the big one. Leah looked down at her pulsometer. It was glowing orange.

They were closer. And this was as far as they would walk for the moment. Martine looked over at Leah. "Do you want to take these off for the way back?"

Leah shrugged. They could always put them back on to talk. She unstrapped her respie and wrapped the cord around her hand. She had been practicing not breathing on the way out. It didn't seem that hard, once you got out of the habit. Martine pulled hers off, too. For a moment, she looked like she might be in distress, but that passed quickly.

Leah reached over and kissed her. She grabbed her hand and they started walking.

There is a feeling, as a Salvado, walking underwater, unassisted, casually. You look around, you take it all in. And some people say, you feel like a survivor. You feel like you belong in the world. When you aren't at immediate risk of dying, it's easy to think that it's the world around you -- that's the thing that's changed. It no longer has any interest in killing you. This world that has predated you your whole life, stalked you, with fire and flame and cold and sharp objects, with cancer and buses, and weapons on every corner. This is what's different.

You feel like the whole world has given up on its plan, concocted on the day you were born, and updated with every minute you live, to kill you.

Leah hoped that Martine felt that. She hoped that Jamie felt that. It was a feeling she would wish on the people she loved.

At the top of the shelf, returning, they stopped. Leah turned to Martine and slid the top of her bathing suit down. Martine stepped out of it and tied it around her arm. This felt like freedom. This felt like belonging. Leah let Martine strip her as she kissed her hard on the lips. Martine grabbed her suit and tied it on her other arm as Leah slid down her to kiss her all over. She pulled her down to the shelf and swallowed her, making love to her under the glassy roof that rose above them until it faded to night.

They put their suits on before stepping out of the water. It wasn't quite dark yet, not as dark as it got on the island at night, but it was hard to make out the shapes on the shore. But as they got closer, Leah grabbed Martine's hand and pulled her as she ran across the shallow shelf.

On the beach, in a red bikini, was Jamie, waving wildly. Leah jumped up on the sand and tackled her.

Jamie kissed Leah deeply and then looked up to see Martine standing above them.

"You're so tall. Maybe you need to get down here."

Martin let out a hoot and then dove onto them. And the three of them laid there on the beach talking until it was too dark to see.

***

They sat in the hot tub flanking Jamie, while Martine peppered her with questions.

"So astronauts train underwater, anyway?"

Leah laughed. "Yes, she does this all the time."

"Whole teams of you do it together?"

Jamie sank down a little and tried to turn the jets up with her feet. "I don't really fly with other people any more."

"So you're out there all alone? In space?"

"Sometimes." The jets fired up higher. They were quiet for as many bubbles as they were producing.

"That is so cool." Martine leaned in and kissed her. Jamie was so different from Leah. She was so strong and confident, but still silly. She was about the same height as Leah, but she seemed taller. It was easy to like both of them, though. Just for different reasons. Jamie took her time kissing her back, letting her tongue dart in and out of the French woman's mouth. They were close to the same color, but that's where the resemblance ended. Jamie's face was long and elegant and her hair, sleek and shiny, laid down past her shoulders. Martine, in comparison, seemed like an imp, an elf with nearly pointed ears framing her wide face, opened up by her resonant smile.

Leah snuggled in under Jamie's open arm and let out a sigh. She wondered, for a moment, how hot the water was and if it was in a range that baseline humans could tolerate. The longer she lived, this would become the most unusual thing for Leah, trying to figure out if the environment she was in was safe for regular people. Being here, with Jamie and Martine, she could put that out of her mind.

"Your story is sad. But I'm really glad you're here. Your mom sounds pretty awesome." Martine had come up for air and was speaking very close to Jamie's lips.

Jamie gave out a tiny laugh. "My mom was amazing. She made a lot of things better. Did you ever see this?" Jamie lifted her bracelet out of the water and flashed a hologram in the air. It was a painting of a woman on a cloud.

Martine nodded, "Yes, everyone has. That's Nouissant. It's "Femme dans les Nuages." I saw that when I was a kid."

Leah smiled, "It's her mom."

Martine looked confused. "I don't understand. It was painted by a French painter. It's in the new Louvre."

Jaime made the hologram bigger. "I commissioned Edward Nouissant to paint a picture of my mom, hundreds of years after she died. I had these holos that she left me. And I gave him pictures. But he nailed it. That's her."

If Jamie had been looking for a way to shock a French woman, she found it. Martine put her hand out. "Oh my god. This is one of… Oh my god. I touched that painting when I was in high school. It was on the cover of my History of Modern Art book."

Leah laughed, "ta-da."

Martine was overwhelmed. "What a beautiful…"

Jamie pet Martine's hair. "I made sure it sat there. Where people would see it. So people could know her."

"She looks like you."

"I was kind of the doll version of her." She flipped off the hologram. "But maybe my mom shouldn't be hanging out in the hot tub with my naked bitches."

Martine was impressed, but that was just a part of it. This whole trip for her had been nothing but fun. The idea that they might be looking for something that could potentially help people was bizarre.

This was helping people?

"So, fishes, you know the direction?"

Leah nodded and splashed a bit, "yeah, almost accidentally. We made it to orange. After that is yellow…"

"And then green." Jamie was interested. "Okay, so we go back out tomorrow, the three of us and do what you did. Then keep going."

Leah winked at Martine. "But we have to do the exact same thing."

Jamie understood. "Oh, yeah. Okay, you two will have to show me."

Martine kissed her neck and sunk into the couple. "You know. Since we don't need to sleep, we can just stay up and leave at 6. That gives us the whole day."

Leah kissed Jamie. "Which gives us time to show you."

Later that night, they laughed as she called them her fish bitches.

***

They all wore respies setting out this time. Leah and Martine were in their black bathing suits while Jamie had picked up a yellow bikini to wear. She had figured it would make it easier to see her down there.

They started out forward again. The respies made it easy to talk and navigate. They walked casually until they reached the larger drop. Jamie took the lead.

"You ladies good for this?"

"This is so cool." Martine was excited. This was alien. And she could feed off of Leah's excitement.

Leah nodded. "Let's do it."

They stepped over the edge and let themselves fall. The ballast packs let them sink at a fairly even speed. Jamie looked down at her bracelet gauging their descent. As they fell, she marked what the pressure was.

"You fishies feeling okay?"

"Yes, sir." Leah shot back.

Martine nodded and laughed. This was like slow skydiving.

"We're past six atmospheres. So we've already reached a place regular people can't go.

Martine flipped on her light. "Can you see the bottom?"

Jamie shook her head. "I think it's 150 meters. That's going to be…" She did a quick calculation in her head. "Sixteen atmospheres. 15 water ones, one air. Lot of pressure. If anyone starts to feel weird…"

Leah spun a little as she dropped. It was easy to feel elegant and graceful in the water. "I feel good. You guys okay?"

Martine was giddy with wonder, but feeling good. "I'm great."

They slowly sunk to the ocean bed. It was nearly flat.

Jamie showed Martine the bracelet. "155 meters. Not too shabby."

They started walking forward. Leah showed off her pulsometer. The orange was fading to yellow, indicating they were going the right way.

The mission was accurate so far.

They swam forward, under the strength of the packs on their backs. Compressed water pushed them forward at a speed slightly faster than walking. Jamie looked down at her pulsometer, not wanting to miss it. "So what do you think this is?"

Leah chimed in, "I've been thinking about that. They don't know what it is. They just know what it's made of."

"Why do you think that?" asked Martine.

"Well, think about it. From far away they can't tell what shape it is or anything. They just know it doesn't belong. These things are attuned to it. So I think it's some kind of material we need to find."

Jamie looked out in front of her. "That sounds about right." The pulseometer had begun to move toward red again. "Okay, guys. We stop here. We have to backtrack a bit and pick a direction. We seem to have passed something."

They dropped to the bottom again. Jamie was surprised at how firm the ocean bed was.

Leah whispered, "guys. Look." She pointed to their right. Breaking out of the blue all around them was a shape. It was huge, so large it blotted out all light coming from that direction.

Martine breathed in and whispered, "what if what we're looking for is in a whale?"

Leah whispered back, "what if we're about to be in a whale?"

Jamie laughed. "Whale mouths don't work that way. But damn, that's big."

They stopped and stared. Jamie was reminded of the trains slowly passing in front of the road when she was a kid. Car after car obstructing traffic, seemingly endlessly, until finally the last moved by and cars could pass. This was like some bizarre organic train, majestic and alien. She remembered before the war how much smaller the whales were, before the irradiated water caused them to thicken and grow, and survive the challenges of their environment by expanding four to five times their previous size.

The fit ones survived.

And they were magnificent.

They turned and began walking back the other way. Jamie watched the light color on the pulsometer and waited until it showed a steady orange again. "Ok, guys, right or left? I say right." That would take them away from the direction the whale had come from.

Leah's voice rang out, "I say left, to be controversial."

"Ok, Martine. You break the tie."

Martine thought for a second. "Okay. Right."

Jamie turned to the right and kept walking. Leah and Martine followed.

They alternated walking and swimming until the pulseometers glowed greenish yellow and then, finally green. The device in Jamie's hands began to beep.

Leah called out, "is that you?"

"Yeah. it's mine. I must be closer than you. Stay there."

"What do you want me to do?" Martine asked.

"Okay, you move forward, slightly to the right."

Martine moved forward to her right and hers began buzzing as well. "Mine went off."

"Okay, move more right until it stops." Jamie pointed.

Martine moved right two steps. On the second one, it stopped.

"Ok, now back one." Her pulseometer went off again.

"Now, Leah, you move forward to the left."

She did. Her device went off. She moved left until it stopped and then stepped back one step.

Jamie did the same moving forward. They were in a triangle about a meter wide. .

They turned off their devices. Jamie turned to them. "Okay, fishies. What we're looking for is in this triangle. Let's search while holding our position."

They sunk to the ground and started sifting through the sand. Martine saw it first. It was a tiny piece of metal, about a centimeter wide and three centimeters long. She reached over gingerly and picked it up.

Something that had no business being down here.

She handed it to Jamie. She rolled it over in her hand. "Holy shit."

Leah looked over and shivered. "Damn."

"What is it?" Martine hadn't seen the engraving on the back of it. Or was it the front. Etched into it, in block letters, was one word.

"EVIL"

**

They made their way back to the beach as the sun was going down. Somewhere along the way they realized how caught up they'd been in the superstition of it all. A tiny piece of metal with the word "EVIL" on it made this beautiful ocean into something imposing, something terrifyingly massive and unknowable. They walked up onto the beach and breathed in. Jamie remembered how much she loved that feeling of a breathful of air after not breathing for so long. It was remarkable. She turned the metal fragment over in her hand.

"EVIL"

Suddenly it popped into her head. This didn't seem right. She pulled out her pulseometer and turned it on. It glowed red.

"This isn't it." She shook her head.

Leah reached for hers. It said the same thing. "No fucking way. It's a weird ass chunk of metal with a mysterious inscription. And it's not it."

Jamie laughed. The fact that it wasn't the mystery object seemed to suck all of the grave energy from it. If it wasn't alien and mysterious, it didn't mean anything.

But that wasn't what she saw in Martine's face.

That night they talked about a lot at dinner. And back in the room, they talked about even more. And when Leah flopped into bed, almost forcing Martine onto the floor, Jamie tried to lighten the mood. She grabbed her wig and tossed it aside.

"That's it, you little imp. You lose clothing privileges for the night." She looked over at Martine who smiled, feeling like she was in on the game.

And when Leah stripped for them both that night, she took her time.

***

Martine was sitting on the floor in the dark when Jamie came into the front of the suite from the bedroom.

Jamie stepped over to her. "I wondered where you were, floor girl."

As she moved closer, in the dim light, she could tell the other woman had been crying. Jamie reached out and touched her cheek. "Hey, do you want to talk?"

Martine opened her hand. In it was the tiny piece of metal.

Evil.

Jamie put her own hand over the woman's and closed it, sitting next to her. "It's just a piece of metal. It doesn't mean anything."

"What if my thing is bad?"

She turned to Martine and cocked her head. "What do you mean?"

"I mean, everybody finds their thing. All of us. What if my thing isn't good. What if my strength is just destroying things?"

Jamie rubbed her arm. "Sweety, you aren't destroying anything. And you aren't evil."

"The sea thinks I am. I found this."

Jamie laughed, holding up the tiny piece of metal. "Well, first of all it's an ocean and they lie all the time."

"He was a good man." Martine whispered. "Nazar Musayev."

"The one who saved you? Yes, he sounds like he was a good man."

"He was really quiet and kind. It's crazy to think he would lead a bunch of prisoners. He was just a sweet man who couldn't ignore evil."

Jamie nodded. "He was. It sounds like he was. And he paid for it. It wasn't fair. But then he had hundreds of years to just be his own damn glorious self."

"He outlived them."

Jamie nodded. "By a fuckton."

"He made me."

"Well, he didn't... He found you and he was there to help. And I bet he didn't regret it for a second."

"He saw me." Martine closed her eyes.

Jamie put her arm around her. "He did. He saw you and he helped."

"I mean he saw me intentionally step in front of that bus."

"Oh." Jamie pulled her closer.

"And he still gave up everything for me."

"And I'm sure he never regretted it. You had a moment of weakness. Like me."

"It wasn't a... I don't know. My whole life, I just saw it. I knew it would end like that. My life was good. I had no reason. I just don't know why. Why?"

Jamie pulled her closer and lifted her chin. "You just stepped out in front of that bus. It was a whim. It just happened."

Martine nodded, sobbing. "And now he's gone."

"And you're here."

"What if I shouldn't be?" Martine sank into her.

"I've known you for two days and I'm thinking that it's a good thing you're here."

"I'm not here to be a drain -- to make you take care of me. I wanted to just add some fun. You have a pretty relationship." When Martine was worked up, her French accent came out, light and bouncy. It made Jamie think of old movie sirens, bombshells who didn't know how beautiful they were. She thought she'd try a different tactic.

"Martine. Have you ever heard of Margaret Mead's femur?"

The other woman shook her head. Her eyes were filled with tears. Jamie took her hands and shifted on the floor facing her. "When I was young, I remember reading that the famous anthropologist Margaret Mead was asked a really important question during an interview. She had just come back from digging up the bones of people all over the world to find out what we all had in common. And they asked her, 'In your opinion, what is the first sign of civilization?'"

Martine nodded. "And what did she say?"

Jamie pulled up her shirt and wiped Martine's face dry, carefully. "Well, she said that the very first sign of civilization, she believed, and it was only her opinion, was a skeleton with a healed broken femur."

"What does that mean? Why is that important?"

"I'm glad you asked, student." Jamie winked at her and Martine smiled, despite herself. "A broken femur takes a long time to heal and it hobbles you. You can't walk. You can't get away from predators. In order to one day die with a healed broken femur, someone had to nurse you back to health. Someone had to take care of you. You had to have people."

Martine nodded, her face falling into tears.

Jamie continued. "That's civilization. Having people. So that you can live long enough to heal."

Martine let out a long breath. "That's really beautiful."

"And it's true. You have people, Martine. That's how you heal."

"People…"

"You have us."

"Thank you." Martine hugged her, digging her face into Jamie's neck. "Thank you."

At that moment, Leah stepped out from the other room in her nightgown, still half asleep, still wigless. She looked at the two women hugging.

"Are we doing sexy stuff? Because I say we move it to the hot tub."

***

They took the next day to explore Forte de Greta. Nearly every part of it was beautiful. And nearly every building, balcony, and platform seemed to face the ocean. Jamie had heard that there were some Salvado who had gone into the water to live and she could sort of understand that. If she were alone, she might be inspired to do that. It was welcoming and there was a kind of solitude down there that couldn't be found anywhere else.

But she had Leah. Jamie watched Leah dancing erratically at brunch with Martine to some bizarre tribal music. They were both beautiful. She remembered that year when she traveled with her friends, escaping school at her mom's bequest and just drove away with Reina and Fancie. She could have been gone. She could have been dead a year before that. And her mother would have sunk into despondency, her friends would have forgotten her.

There would be no great painting hanging in the new Louvre.

Today, it seemed like there was no chance or circumstance at all.

There was just the will of the universe that she could manipulate, in tiny ways, to spend time with the people who mattered.

And they mattered. And it was time to get up and go dance with them.

They explored the dry land all around them. And then, again, after one more sleepless night, walked into the water at 6 AM, aiming straight ahead.

"All right, fish bitches. There is a chunk of metal out there that says 'good' and we're going to find it." Jamie took point, walking ahead of them.

Martine giggled. "That would be really stupid and cool."

Leah jokingly moved forward ahead of Jamie. "That's my nickname. Stupid and cool."

They took turns racing and taking point. The water swirled around them and Leah and Martine found that they were feeling more and more comfortable down there. Jamie had logged, literally, thousands of hours underwater training for deep space, but the other two women were just learning all about the freedom that being below the surface could provide.

They swam more this time, trying out different strokes and making up a few of their own. And near a beautiful coral reef, Jamie grabbed Martine and pressed her down, pulling her suit off and leisurely fucking her as Leah sat and watched.

Until she joined in.

Jamie insisted that you weren't really an underwater creature until you had sex underwater. And then, slept underwater. And then built your own home underwater. They rolled around on the ocean bed laughing, playing house and pretending to be underwater things, alien and at home.

And they moved closer to the triangle they had found before. There was no urgency in their mission today, though. Taking the day off yesterday had reminded them that there was no timeline, no day that this must be done -- only a playful mission handed down to create a sense of adventure.

This was a great race, a game of people. This was a roleplay mystery.

It was nearly dark down there when they found the spot again. Jamie turned on her light and set it on a nearby piece of coral. "I think we're going to have to dig. It's not on the surface, but it's here."

They kneeled down and began pulling away at the ocean floor. It was surprisingly malleable and soft. For all the walking they had done, the floor gave way with any real pressure applied. So they dug.

A half-hour later, it became clear that the shifting water would make it hard to get rid of the silt and sand they were uncovering. Once they stopped, the ocean began to automatically fill in its crevasses, its cracks. Jamie took off her bathing suit and made a rope tie from it, anchoring herself to the floor-mounted coral. Then she took off her ballast device and held it near the hole as the other two dug, letting compressed water carry the sediment away. This way, they were able to make a remarkable amount of progress.

They dug for about another hour, and then Martine saw it. It looked to be a piece of metal, almost like a floor of metal a few meters below the actual ocean floor. Until they dug out the edges, there was no way to know how big it was.

As they pried it out it became clear that it was nearly square, almost as though it was built as a panel of flooring. It was thick metal, scarred and rough to their fingers. Martine lifted it out of the pit and she and Leah tried to clear the silt from it as Jamie put her backpack and suit back on.

It was dark now, too dark to see much detail of the artifact. But as they walked back, they turned the pulseometers on over and over again.

This was it. This was what they were sent to find.

The artifact sat in their room until the hotel staff boxed it up to send it to XenoVera. Before they did, though, the next morning, Jamie, Leah, and Martine had the chance to look it over.

Once they turned it over, Martine laughed. Of all the things they thought they might find, this was not even on the list.

Martine changed her flight to return home with Leah and Jamie. She would have her stuff sent a week later, selling her apartment in Paris over the phone. Martine moving in was the incentive for Jamie to have a hot tub installed, something that she and Leah had talked about a lot. They chose one that was not too dissimilar to the one in their suite in Forte de Greta.

Over the next couple of hundred years, the three of them had a lot of conversations about the artifact. They went on other adventures but none had a mystery like this at the end. They came up with their own explanations for it, but none really held up.

At the time, I couldn't explain it, either. We opened the case at XenoVera and tested it with pulseometers. Sure enough, it registered perfectly. It was large for a fragment like this - the largest one we had. It was pockmarked and scratched all over one side. The other side was slightly smoother, but still discolored. There was really no way to determine how long it had been there, underwater, but it was at least 600-800 years.

It was tightly machined, clearly not natural – a manmade artifact.

And it was made from a metal that didn't exist on earth anywhere. In fact, this metal only existed in one other place that we knew of. And I needed to know more before I talked to anyone about it. For the moment, I had all the mysteries I could want on my hands. Because as strange as this artifact was, as otherworldly and bizarre as it was, it was nothing compared to what was carved into the metal on the other side.

Jamie had assured me that they didn't do it. That it was there when they found it. It was nearly impossible to believe, but I'd known Jamie for almost 900 years. And why would she lie? Why would they have carved this? Why would they have done any of this?

The metal flashed slightly incandescent orange as we turned it over. This was a native characteristic of the material, we discovered. In a way, it was really beautiful.

The other side of the piece was smoother, except for the carving. It didn't make sense. And trying to make it make sense was laughable. But if you looked closely, you could read it. In English:

Leah loves Jamie & Martine.

.

9- Our Goddess of Mirth

Bahia Trinidad, Aztecana - 3220

Yazmin was already in the room when I let myself in. I hadn't seen her in person in a few years, but I loved how easy it was to just pick her up and hug her. I wasn't that much bigger, but this felt good. She fussed a bit waiting for people to show up. I moved chairs around the room. Busy work, really.

"Anjo, that's a lot of chairs."

"I know. It's like a giant poker game." It was a big room. A massive conference room with a large oval table in the center.

"You know. This is a lot for me to ask you." She stepped over to the far side of the table.

I tried to find a way to be glib. But this felt important. "Remember when I told you I'd think about it and then called you back in ten minutes?"

"I know that wasn't very much time."

"I didn't need ten minutes. I didn't need one minute. This is what we're doing. Now we just have to convince them."

"Thank you." She put her head down. She wasn't really used to asking for help. And I didn't want to make her ask. Sometimes all you can do for your friends is to make sure the right people are in the right chairs and that they all know why they're there.

So I did.

We sat at the table and talked. I fiddled with my bracelet. It was comforting to know that Devilboy was back. And even though I couldn't carry him around in an implant, I had this. Yazmin flicked her bracelet and the hologram lit up the room. It was deep and red and beautiful. I felt like it should have a soundtrack.

"Now that's a fucking planet." Poni stepped through the whirring black glass door and moved toward the table. He was dressed in a thick white shirt and a pair of brownish black pants that could have been some kind of velvet. He looked good. Yazmin jumped up to hug him.

I smiled. "I love your outfit."

He swung around and gave me a big bear hug. "This is how all the Martians are going to be dressing soon."

Yazmin shot me a panicked look. Poni pulled up the chair at the head of the table. "Yes, he told me. We're going to Mars."

"There's a lot you need to know…" Yazmin looked flustered. That didn't much work for Poni.

"I know enough. I've been practicing my Martian."

"There are no people on Mars speaking Martian," I laughed.

He leaned in to Yazmin. "I'll translate for all of you."

Despite herself, she smiled. And she was still smiling when Akana walked in the room. The two women's faces lit up to see each other as they embraced. I walked over and inserted myself.

Poni gave her a kiss on the forehead. "How are you, kiddo?"

Akana smiled and rocked back and forth a little. "I'm going to Mars, how about you?"

"Did you tell everyone?" Yazmin was trying to figure out whether to be mad at me or not.

"Jamie already knew. They're on their way now. So is the doctor." I tried to stand up a little taller. The fact that everyone had already said yes should make this easier.

Jamie arrived just a few moments later, along with Leah and Martine. I had seen them at the main teleport platform, so I knew what they were going to say. The doctor was still a bit of a mystery.

Jamie hugged me and then gave Yazmin a kiss on the cheek. At this point, they had worked together in four separate space programs in four different countries. I said hello to Leah and Martine and we hugged.

"Okay, I think we've got the hugs mostly out of the way." Yazmin stepped over toward the chair opposite Poni. the head of our longish table. "We have one more person we're waiting for and then I'll start.

Poni clapped. Yazmin shook her head and grinned. "Someone tell the pirate he doesn't need to applaud."

"I don't need to applaud alone."

Jamie and Leah applauded, too. Then I did.

It was then that the doctor walked in.

His hair was slicked back and he wore a thin-rimmed pair of glasses, an anachronism in this time. Also totally unnecessary. But I could see how they made his face look more serious. He closed the door behind him, smiling.

"Was that for me? I haven't done anything yet." He put his hand on my shoulder as he leaned against the sidetable behind me.

We were all here.

I pointed to the man behind me. "Folks, this is Dr. Kuras Singh. He is one of us."

Martine interjected. "You're a doctor? Do we need one?"

Kuras laughed and took off his glasses, slipping them into his coat pocket. "I'm a doctor who cheats. And, no, you seem perfectly healthy, young lady."

Yazmin spoke up. "If you guys give me a sec, I'll go over this all."

She waved her arms and the hologram of Mars rose up and grew, spinning slowly until a highlighted area was visible. "Okay, ladies and gentlemen, this is Mars. Named for the god of war a long time ago. The Romans called him Aries. Which is the astrological sign you would have if you were born on March 30th, 2045."

I looked up. This wasn't going where I thought it would. She continued.

"Now, none of that matters. But it demonstrates something interesting. Given a long enough timeline, coincidences are inevitable, sometimes absurdly improbable ones."

Kuras interjected, "and our brains recognize patterns. We want to connect them."

She nodded. "Yes, exactly. Right now, we need to put these aside, because they will just nag at us. We have to focus on what we know."

She waved again and the area highlighted zoomed in more. "This is the Rise of Tharsis. A large equatorial bulge home to the solar system's largest volcanoes, including Olympus Mons, Ascraeus Mons, and Arsia Mons. It's also home to something we've begun calling Mons Mosaica. It's an area right about here…" A smaller area became highlighted near the center.

"Where our spectroscopy has identified a bunch of elements and isotopes that don't belong in our solar system. They seem to come from somewhere else."

Leah raised her hand. "So is it an alien colony or something?"

Yazmin shook her head. "We don't know what it is. All we know is that it's there. It's part of the bigger mystery but, right now, only because it seems to interfere with our objective."

Martine spoke up. "And what is that?"

Jamie stood up. "About 20 years after the Savior Event, a man, a Salvado, working for the World Council way back when it was the United Nations was, well... ejected from Earth's atmosphere. We think he landed on Mars. And we think he's up there still alive."

Leah shook her head. "For 1200 years? Jesus."

Yazmin walked around the hologram, pointing. "He is a friend of mine. Years ago, Akana, who is able to sense other Salvado, saw him up on Mars in this general area. I don't know how much of a coincidence that is. Then, later, she identified another Salvado, this one not one of ours. When we're up there, she can help us find him."

Kuras tilted his head. "Wait, what do you mean, not one of ours?"

"I mean not one of the 1936 Salvado that were on Earth after the event. Maybe not from Earth." She looked over at him.

He nodded. It was hard to read him. I couldn't tell what he was thinking. I interjected, "since then, we've also found pieces of wreckage, here on earth, most recently one found by Jamie's team -- Leah and Martine -- that match the composition of the Mosaica."

Kuras let out a sigh. "I see where you are coming from. We can get fixated on these coincidences that make no sense right now..."

"Or we can go get our guy." Yazmin waved and the planet disappeared. "And Dr. Singh, I barely know you. But I also don't know what shape he'll be in, after living isolated for over a millenium. You can heal. But I can't ask you –"

He nodded. "Oh, you're not asking. I'm coming. We get your man and I'll make sure he's ok."

Yazmin looked tired, but hopeful. "Thank you, Doctor. Here is my dilemma. I've been to Mars six times. Jamie's been there seven, to this specific area. And we were unable to find him. So we have no choice, if we want to find him, than to bring Akana. Honestly, I can't do this without any of you. And if you say no, it's no.

Akana looked up and slowly raised her hand. It took a moment to understand what she was doing. Until Poni raised his hand, then Kuras. Jamie, Leah and Martine raised theirs as did I.

Kuras stood up. "So. we should get ready."

But first, Yazmin and I needed to talk to Poni.

***

"There's more than ten words." I leaned against the desk in the smaller room behind the main conference room and tried not to act imposing. It felt odd to me that I could be. But Poni always looked about two degrees more relaxed than everyone around him. Right now, he was sprawled out over two chairs with his arms folded.

He smiled. "Ha. I knew that wouldn't be good enough."

"It's not that it's not good enough. It's just for me. I want to know." I smiled back.

"For us. And, again, you don't have to." Yazmin pulled a chair up next to him and intentionally sat in it in reverse. I'd never seen her do that before.

He ran his hand through his hair and breathed in. We'd been friends for hundreds of years. Why was this so difficult? "I literally know nothing about you."

"Angel-boy, you know everything about me. I'm an open book."

Yazmin laughed. "You are a wonderful book, but not open."

"You don't have to tell me if you don't want. The gig is yours regardless." I tried a new angle.

For a moment, he looked like he was searching for a place to spit. He laughed. "What gig? This space thing? I'm in. Don't cut me out."

'I have a feeling about this. I feel like we don't come back."

He looked at Yazmin."You think this, too?"

She nodded. We had no idea what we'd find, but something was nagging at me. And I think Yazmin felt it as well.

He shook his head. "You will if I'm going. I'll get your asses back here."

Yazmin took his hand and kissed it. "I know. I know. But we need you here."

I dropped it on him. "You need to run this operation from down here."

His face got red.

He shook his head vigorously. "No. No fucking way. You go up and I stay? Not happening."

Yazmin held onto his hand calmly. "Poni. Look at me. There are 134 people on this base, running it. And you and Akana are the only ones who know how to keep them safe if something goes wrong with the launch."

"And she needs to be with us to find what we're looking for." I could see he understood. He didn't like it.

"Bullshit. Fuck that. I can't believe you're okay with this."

"There's more." Yazmin glanced at me.

"I need you to take over this company from me. We do important work and I don't trust anyone else."

"But you trust me?" Poni shook his head.

I laughed. "I do."

"Yeah, well, then, you're an idiot. I don't even own a tie." He spread his arms. Yes, I had to admit that the white shirt he was wearing was slightly puffy, giving him the illusion, as usual, of being a pirate. I knew he did this on purpose.

I moved closer and pulled up a chair. "You don't need a tie. Just a vision. Understanding."

"How long have you been preparing thatT?" He pressed his forehead against mine, holding my head. In Russian, his name, Ponimaniye, meant "understanding."

Or "insight." Vision.

I put my hands over his. "It's good, right?"

"I'll do a terrible job."

Yazmin slapped him in the head. "No, you won't. And you know it."

"Ow. That's abuse. You people are crazy. I want my lawyer."

Yazmin sat back down. "So, spill it. What's your story?"

"You won't like it." he leaned back.

"It doesn't matter. One way or the other, you know what you have to do. So, let's hear it."

He let out a long breath. "Okay. Sit down. Here it is. The Ponimaniye Kuretzov story. I was born in Ukraine. Okay, I was born in what was left of Ukraine. We lost a lot of people. I lost parents. We all lose things. I grew up in one of the Kosciuszko orphanages. They had a bunch of them, all over. Different age groups. So, you get older, you move. It's not a very consistent operation. So, I didn't have many friends. Some of these orphanages were good. I don't know too much about those ones. The ones I saw had angry people in them, running them, telling you what to do. I don't like too much being told what to do."

"No. Really?" Yazmin interjected.

"You are funny. You make fun of me. But still, look, I continue. So, I moved around a lot. Then I get to a really bad one. This one is big and clean and modern looking. A lot of money. But the rooms are small. They're dirty. It's all for show, you know. And you see what the show is about."

He continued, "I'm about thirteen at this point. And I'm big. Bigger than some other kids. So they bring me into this room. Now, if I want to eat, I have to fight other kids."

I dropped my head. "Jesus."

"I know. That's what I said. One of the boys they brought in with me is someone I remember from, like, two orphanages ago. Dimitri. We call him Dimi. All the boys. He's kind of big, too, like me. He whispers to me that he has some kind of plan. I need to volunteer to fight him. I'm confused, so I do that."

Yazmin cut in, "so you fight him?"

"Yes. About a week after that, we're in a big white room. People are watching. It's all clean and tidy. And he tells me to hit him and keep hitting him. So I do. I hit him. And he comes back, pushing me. He doesn't even hit me. He just pushes me, you know. Now it feels strange. He doesn't fight back. He actually leans into my punches, right, like he's making me do it. Then the blood. Blood everywhere. He spits blood at me and smiles and I go crazy. I hit him again. Why won't he fight back?"

Yazmin held his hand, intertwining her fingers with his. She rubbed his arm.

"He falls down and pulls at me. There is blood all over now. In my eyes, in my mouth all over my skin. I throw up. Finally he lays down and he's breathing hard. They want me to keep fighting but I'm crying. I can't see because of all the blood. They call the fight. I didn't win. I wouldn't keep going. I'm back in my room. This is my life."

"I'm so sorry." I pulled my chair closer to him.

"It's a long time ago. But. You know. It's a long time ago. So, a week later, Dimi is sick. Or he starts showing he is sick. He was hiding it. They test everyone. And I'm sick, too. It's that Hepatitis Z, the new one that came up. There's no cure, only treatment. I can't fight anymore. That's what Dimi was trying to do. Make it so we couldn't fight."

"He knew he was sick?" Yazmin asked.

Poni nodded. "He did. And now I did. They start giving me medication for it, you know. No cure. Treatment. And I take it. Dimi doesn't. After two months, he's gone. He wastes away and dies. Now, when we turn 16, we're allowed to leave sometime. Furlough. So I do. And I don't go back. I think they're happy they don't have to pay for medication for me anymore."

I nodded. "Now you're on your own?"

"Right. So I get a job with a mechanic. At a garage. I take my first paycheck and I make sure I have enough for medicine. I learn how to fix cars, engines. All kinds of motors. Buses, everything. But I mostly work so I can get medication. It's not cheap. The garage shuts down, I move to a new one. This one I fix motorcycles. This one boats. Engines are all alike, right. I get a paycheck, I take my medicine. Times are not good, though. Medicine seems to get more expensive, while every new job I get seems to pay less. Twelve years of this. So, on my 28th birthday, Instead of medicine, I buy a gun. And it sits on my table for two days. Two days, I don't touch it. On the third day, I felt it. I felt the sickness start. I walk outside on my front lawn and look up in the sky. There's like a lightshow. It's all beautiful and cars are honking, people are making noise like it's a big holiday. And I put the gun in my mouth. Boom."

"And here you are." Yazmin looked over at me.

Poni lifted his arms up. "And here I am. I bet you're thinking twice about that offer."

I laughed. "Nope. You're not getting off that easy."

Yazmin stood up. "Wait, so you fix stuff. That's your thing. The thing that was perfected. You're like a mechanic."

"I can't fix everything."

Yazmin cocked her head. "None of those ships really worked when you found them, did they?"

He laughed, "oh, way back then? No. Not really. But an engine is an engine."

She looked thoughtful. "Everything's an engine."

***

From that moment on, the eight of us were mostly inseparable. We lived, ate and slept there in the building. And when Jamie showed us around, she was so proud of it. This place was built on the original NASA site in Houston, Texas. Leah and Martine wouldn't know what that meant, but the rest of us did. The city was now called Bahia Trinidad after Trinity Bay, a town near Houston that had survived the war a little better than most. The was the largest space facility in Aztecana.

And it was impressive. But it was nowhere near as impressive as it should have been. Since rebuilding, the world had experienced a bit of a renaissance. And cleaning up this planet was part of it. So much had gone into making life better here, on Earth, that some of the passion for leaving earth had dwindled. Space was something people imagined they would conquer at some point.

But there was no real urgency.

You would have thought that journeys to the closer planets would have been casual by now. But only a few flights to Mars every year fed a small colony, the size of a small city, called Choristos, in Arcadia Planitia. But it was 2,000-plus kilometers from the Tharsis Rise and was no help at all. To do this, we were going to basically have to take a giant shell of a rocket, filled with minimal life support, some land vehicles and gear, and shoot ourselves like a bullet to Mars. We couldn't rely on any real return mechanisms.

If we wanted to return home, we would need to drive or walk to the colony and wait for a return ship.

Reasonable walk time to the colony for all eight of us in low gravity would be about four months. I don't want to figure it with the ATVs.

Who knows if they would make it.

Something was drawing me to this. I was beginning to feel like we might miss out on answering every question we had if we didn't go. We'd been all over the Earth.

Let's see what Mars had to say.

***

Kuras was sitting at a long table in the tea shop on the first floor of the building when the long distance teleport bands in the corner glowed green. He put the book aside and stood up, smiling. He adjusted his shirt as he watched her walk to his table. Her eyes lit up when she saw him.

Lelei was well-tailored, with a pencil skirt and a black sweater that rose up just below the nape of her blue-black neck. Her voice was as silky as ever when she greeted him.

"Dr. Singh. It's good to see you."

He wrapped his arms around her and whispered in her ear.

"Dr. Mwangi. I missed you."

He held out his hand and she slid into the chair next to him.

"This is the place to meet, huh?" She looked around. The massive glass windows arched inward to build a huge bowl-like ring of glass that felt organic even as it manifested a futuristic shape, filling the eye for as far as you could see.

"It really is. Thank you for meeting me."

"Of course, Kuras. I've really loved your letters."

"Well, I've loved writing them. I feel like I've abused your professional courtesy for so long, pouring out my soul in letters."

"Well, I admit that I look forward to them. It looks like they're coming to an end, though?"

"That's what I wanted to talk to you about." Kuras put his hand over hers.

Lelei winked at him. "Where is she?"

Dr. Singh stood up and made a motion. A woman a few tables away started over. She was older, with grey hair. She wasn't slim, but certainly not fat, either. She looked like an iconic grandmother. And her face opened up into a wide smile as she sat down, shaking Lelei's hand"

"Dr. Mwangi."

Lelei looked at Kuras and then pumped the woman's hand. "It's so nice to finally meet you."

Kuras put on his prescriptionless glasses and nodded. "She has something she'd like to say to you."

The older woman took a deep breath and folded her hands in front of her.

"I want to thank you for how much you helped Dr. Singh help me. Everything you told him, the things you did, said, recommended, all of it. It means so much to me."

Lelei put her hands over the woman's. "Florida, I waited a long time to meet you. I'm so happy to have been a part of what helped you."

"I don't have any way to repay you, or the doctor here."

Kuras interjected, "Florida grew up not far from here. This area was her home. She's been assisting me for so long. And doing a wonderful job, I have to add. It's nice to have another Salvado, as you say, helping."

Dr. Mwangi thought for a second. "You know that Dr. Singh will be going away, right?"

Florida nodded. "I'm sad. But I feel ready to change and stand on my own two feet, really. I'll always owe him everything."

Lelei leaned in. "Florida, how would you feel about coming with me to Albion and being my assistant? Working with me?"

Florida looked at Dr. Singh. He nodded.

Her face broke into a smile. "So this is your plan, huh, Doctor?"

"I think you will find that it's pretty rewarding working with Dr. Mwangi."

"I don't know what to say. This is amazing. I'm so... in Albion."

LeLei lowered her voice. "My main office is in Manchester. You really should see it."

Florida nodded. "Oh, I bet it's beautiful. And I could learn from you?"

The doctor nodded. "Absolutely."

"She's like a sponge. She could learn a lot from you.

Florida looked around. "I promise I will. I won't let you down."

Lelei laughed. "I know you won't. It looks like we should get to know each other."

***

I had set up Jamie, Leah, and Martine's room myself. I know they needed space. I thought about how that sounded and laughed a little as I knocked on the door. It swung open with a whirr and I saw Jamie in a set of white cotton pajamas. On the couch, going over the mission materials.

She looked up at me. "Hey, Anjo." She waved me in. "Nice find. I didn't even know this room was here."

I put down the box down that I was carrying and slid onto the couch across from her. "I feel like I visit here more than you sleep here."

"That's probably true."

"The box is full of various information I've collected on this. I don't suspect it's anything you don't know already."

"But, yeah. Just in case."

"How are Leah and Martine taking all this?

Jamie looked up at me. "Great, really. I've been trying to be delicate, explaining how potentially dangerous this is but they just seem all in."

"Well, that's great."

At that moment, the two of them came in, wrapped in towels. Leah sat down next to me while Martine kissed Jamie on the head.

Leah pushed me. "You guys are talking about us."

Jamie pulled Martine close. "Yes, we are. He wants to know if you munchkins are really up for this."

Leah shot back. "100%"

Martine nodded and added, "we are, but I have to admit, why me? What am I adding here?"

I could answer that. "You three are my best explorers. I know you only do it for fun, but the things you've gone and found. It's amazing. I don't think you really realize how good you are."

Leah squinted. "I thought everybody does that?"

I shook my head. "They try. You guys do. Every time. We need that."

Martine lifted her arms. "Yay, us."

Jamie snickered. "It's going to feel a little different on Mars than underwater."

Leah leaned in and put her arm around me. "Ooh, how will it feel? This is nuts."

I pulled out my bracelet. "Devilboy, how will it feel on the surface of Mars?"

Devilboy's reassuring AI voice rang out. It seemed to come from everywhere. "Okay, for you, Angel, or for regular old creeps?"

I smiled, "For Salvado like me."

He continued. "Okay, according to the very attractive Jamie Symone, one of the five Salvado that have been on other planets, it is an eerie sense of nothingness."

Jamie smiled and pretended to do a little bow. "What else did I say?"

"Oh, you also said that the pressure is incredibly low, the opposite of the pressure underwater. Ebulism would cause fluids to come apart at that low a pressure, making it look like they were boiling, no matter the temperature. So you won't feel any moisture. But you know Jamie, she's a big fat liar, so..."

"Hey. I'm right here." Jamie threw a wadded up piece of paper at me.

"Ok, Devilboy, what happens to clothing and stuff we bring?"

"It's varying levels of fucked, really. Seriously fucked are anything with air pockets. That just explodes. Slightly less fucked are things that need to be galvanized, rubber, etc., because without atmosphere cold is super cold and hot is crazy hot. Ironically, you are probably best off in a light linen pair of pajamas, such as those currently modeled by the delightful Jamie Symone."

"Your AI is obsessed with me."

Leah laughed. "We all are, baby."

Martine's eyes went wide. "Holy shit." She ran out of the room.

I glanced over at Jamie. "Does she do that a lot?"

A second later she came back in. "What did you call your AI?"

I smiled. "It's Devilboy. I'm Anjo —Angel, so —"

"Right, got it. Can I see that?"

"My bracelet?" I held it out to her. It wasn't incredibly common to engrave the name of your AI on bracelets. It just made me laugh.

She opened up her hand. In it was a tiny piece of metal, with the word "EVIL" engraved on it. She held it up to my bracelet.

The lettering was an exact match. It could have been a piece of my bracelet.

"Where did you get this?"

Jamie stepped over to look, holding the metal up to my wrist. The metal matched. And the word "EVIL" was clearly written in the same type, engraved the same way.

"When we found that piece on Azores. We found this first. It wasn't what we were looking for, so we ignored it. We just assumed it didn't mean anything.

Leah and Martine threw some clothes on and we made our way to the lab on this floor. Yazmin met us inside and we ran the piece of metal through some experiments.

We didn't learn much.

Yazmin held it up to the light. "Well, first thing, it's the same metallic composition. The engraving is the same. Like exactly the same." She waved her hand and two holograms popped up. She zoomed in and we could see the "E" in both the metal and my bracelet.

"You see that little imperfection, and this one here. The odds against both of them being present in both are insane. I mean, not-possible insane. The level of corrosion doesn't tell us anything, really. We don't know what happened to it before it hit that water. But here's something."

She waved and we saw a close up of the metal piece at the microscopic level. "See this little guy? He was, once, a unicellular creature. He basically got stuck to the surface with a bunch of his friends and died. Radiocarbon dating shows that happened 700 years ago. This thing is at least 700 years old."

Leah asked cautiously, "at least? There is no way to date metal?"

Yazmin shook her head. "Not really so much. This is a gift, really."

Martine stared. "Holy shit."

Jamie shook her head and laughed. "Yes, you said that."

"What is happening here?" Leah looked confused.

Yazmin looked over at me. "Have you ever owned another bracelet like that?"

I shook my head. "No. I've had this one forever. The one I got after we all got back didn't have an engraving."

Jamie sighed. "Did they make a prototype and then throw it away -- a reject?"

"Not 700 years ago." My head was hurting.

Jamie looked up. "Okay, this is probably a black suitcase."

Yazmin nodded. I was confused. "What does that mean?"

Yazmin explained, "Jamie and I have talked about this. This is about the coincidences around us. The ones that build with time, with age. Her mother hated black suitcases. The nuclear device Linus saved the airport from was in a black suitcase. "

I nodded. "When I went to XenoVera, all I took was one black suitcase."

Leah spoke up, "okay, so we can't let ourselves get derailed by coincidences, like you said."

Yazmin handed the piece of metal to Martine. "Exactly. That's what I think."

And I don't think I believed her.

***

I could tell Jamie was trying not to think about the Sargasso two weeks later as we climbed into the Euphrosyne. We had just that week painted the "E" on the side of the ship, christening her after the ancient Greek goddess of mirth and good cheer. Ironically, despite the fact that this is one of the most science-dependent things you can do, it doesn't matter who you are, when it comes time to go into space, you are superstitious.

And the goddess of mirth was watching.

Poni helped us inspect the main cabin. It was clear he was looking for any reason to postpone this, to stop it for now. He ran his hand over the seats, the connections. But there was hardly anything at all in the ship to disqualify it. He stood there disapprovingly staring at Yazmin. He reached into the baggy pockets of his pants and pulled out a small round object

It was an orange.

Yazmin laughed. "You're crazy. And I love it."

Poni put it into her hand. "This means be safe." He looked over at me. "Scurvy is real, you know."

"I know." I hugged him tightly. "I know."

He kissed Akana on the forehead and turned around. I felt it in my stomach when he stepped out the door. The door clicked and we were locked.

The seats in the center were arrayed like a six-pointed star, but facing inward. The respies we wore were similar to the clear face guards used to spend time underwater, helping us to not breathe, carrying our words around to earplugs. The only other thing in the capsule was Jamie's Captain seat, in front where she sat already, examining the instruments.

For future reference, this ship is about to do something really stupid.

We were closer to Mars than we'd ever be again this year – a little over 54 million kilometers. The hull of the Euphrosyne is radiant material, the kind you'd find in a lightsail. And the base of it is, essentially, a timed high-yield nuclear explosive. The framework around us channels that explosion and the hull material builds energy as the explosion is released in increments over the course of 600 seconds.

So, this is what that looks like to us.

In the first 600 seconds of flight, we will accelerate to our travel speed, which will be one-half of one percent of the speed of light. Because of the speed of that acceleration, if it's kept constant and gradual, we will experience dramatic acceleration artifacts that will feel like 255 gravities. That is 255 times the gravity you experience standing on Earth. That will be pulling us and everything on the ship down. This would instantly pulverize a baseline human being, who can, for short spurts, handle 10 gravities.

At that point, we will be in space, with all the navigation prowess of a just-fired bullet, waiting to land. But because there is no resistance of any kind, we won't slow down automatically. So, when we are near Mars, we will detonate another high yield nuclear explosive and perform the operation in reverse, slowing down.

If our speed were steady, we would make it in 10 hours. This is an insanely short period of time and it still blows my mind.

Due to artifacts from acceleration and deceleration, though, it will take about 24 hours –one full day. The first ten minutes and the last ten minutes will be brutal, impossibly rough on the ship and anything in it, and subject to the whims of large-number mathematics.

For the rest of the time, we will feel, essentially, like we are coasting.

I reminded myself one more time that there were 134 trained physicists, mathematicians, and engineers in the building we were leaving who thought it would work. That didn't include Jamie and Yazmin, two of the most experienced astronauts on earth. There is one thing they all agreed on, though.

Landing would not be trivial.

So, our plan was to land far enough away from the target area so that we wouldn't potentially destroy it. Everyone decided that would be about 30 kilometers. Which, if the ATVs survived the landing, would be about an hour away. Then, we find Linus, we turn around, and we drive on to Arcadia Planitia, meet some new people, and wait for a shuttle home.

That was the stupid plan.

***

I sat between Yazmin and Akana, holding their hands for the first ten minutes, but I watched Martine and Leah closely. Surprisingly, they handled the acceleration really well, despite the strangeness of it. We could all hear the seat joints creaking and i tried not to imagine the forces pulling at them.

Once the initial acceleration had passed, there was almost no discernible pressure or gravity. I though for a moment about what we had just endured and was amazed, once again, about what these bodies could tolerate.

Jamie called out, "You all okay back there?"

Leah laughed and shot back, "you know we are."

"Well, don't make me turn this thing around. Mostly because I can't." Jamie swung her seat around and faced us. It was still a good idea to stay strapped in, but at least she could be part of the group.

Dr. Singh had seemingly loaded up with an endless supply of dirty jokes to make the time go by faster. We all decided that having Akana translate them one at a time into Japanese made them so much better. She laughed and blushed repeating a story in Japanese about a young man who shrunk so he could better climb inside his girlfriend's privates to service her. I'd never seen that look on her face before.

She looked happy.

Kuras definitely earned his keep on the day out, telling jokes, leading us all in telling stories, even talking about all the Martian creatures he was going to take home and make pets out of.

Part of me felt bad knowing that Yazmin was doing most of the worrying for us. We were in a tiny shell in deep space. If it exploded, we'd be scattered across the solar system.

Alone.

I knew Yazmin well enough to know that this was what the demons in her head were parroting back at her. So, I joined in with the Doctor to make her laugh.

We got a few out of her.

After 20 hours, we all started emotionally preparing for landing. We knew that there would be ten minutes of chaos, followed by...

Something.

A hologram in the center of the ship showed our descent to mars. It seemed impossibly fast.

I saw Jamie hit the series of switches that would set off the explosions needed to land.

There was a lag. Maybe it wasn't a huge lag. But there was definitely a pause between pulling the last of the switches and the rumble from the first explosion.

I looked at Yazmin and tried not to panic. I could see in her face that she caught it, too. No one else seemed to have.

I looked over and saw Jamie shaking her head. At this point, there wasn't much she could do. The hologram got larger. I saw the green x of the landing spot and squinted.

It was below the surface. It was about 40 meters below the surface.

Jamie called out. "Okay, everyone grab on. We're going to hit hard."

Yazmin held my arm tightly. "Hold on to each other. Nothing in this ship is worth anything. Just us. You want to close your eyes but don't. Watch."

That was good advice. If anyone was thrown, we needed to see it. There was a whirr over the explosions that meant the landing gear was engaged.

It wouldn't do us any good.

The front of the ship hit and we could feel it digging into the ground. The straps holding me to the seat gave way and I felt myself flying upward through the holographic Mars image, landing hard on the ceiling. I was able to catch Akana before the seats slammed into us. Everything in the ship seemed to come apart and pour into the space around me on the ceiling. I followed Yazmin's advice and kept my eyes open, watching. The hull appeared to have survived intact, but everything inside was stripped away, leaving an empty space.

Finally our movement stopped. The ship was upside down and we were lying in junk. I stood up and looked down. There was a layer of pulverized metal a few centimeters deep beneath me. I tried to imagine how hard we had to hit to atomize metal like that.

We climbed out of the ship, leaving us still about ten meters underground. There was a column of red dirt and sand threatening to collapse in on us, forcing our hand. We could work to pull out the ATVs, but we'd be buried by the time we got them from the hold.

Or we could climb out now.

I helped Leah and Martine out and Jamie, Yazmin and Kuras made their way to ground level with ropes to pull us up. Akana was the first one up. By the time I ascended, the dust was nearly covering the ship. We stood around the pit and watched the winds fill in the hole.

Making matters worse was that we were currently in the middle of a windstorm. The air pressure was so low that it couldn't really affect us too much – even the harshest of windstorms. But it could stop us from seeing anything.

And it did.

It took me a minute to process that I was standing on an alien planet. It didn't feel all that different to me, but I hadn't thought it would, really. Yazmin and Jamie were talking. I moved closer to hear. It was impossible to see more than a few meters around us.

But all seven of us were there.

They called us all over and we gathered. Yazmin started, "ok, we lost the ATVs so we're on foot. Akana, do you have the two points?"

She nodded and pointed. "This one is about 12 kilometers away." she pointed straight ahead. "And this one is about 20." she pointed to the right.

Yazmin was anxious. "Can you tell the difference?"

Akana shook her head apologetically.

Jamie let out a sigh. I realized why. We were supposed to be 30 kilometers from the mons Mosaica, where one of those blips were. This way, we honestly didn't know where we landed. And until the dust storm cleared, we wouldn't.

It seemed to make sense to move toward the one 12 kilometers away. We could cross that in a couple of hours, even with the shifting dust. Jamie took the lead and we walked.

The respies were helpful and we could flip them up to cover our eyes, too. This meant no dust in the eyes or mouth. Plus, we could talk easily, even though seeing each other was a bit harder. Akana was stopping every kilometer or so to try and sense the signal. It was moving, but slowly.

We still didn't know if this was Linus or the other, unknown one.

After about an hour of walking, we turned a little to the left, based on Akana's feedback. The blip was moving and the sandstorm seemed to be getting more intense. About 20 minutes later, I was staring at the back of Jamie's head. Suddenly, she seemed to disappear. I called out but a second later, so did Yazmin. I pulled Kuras back and yelled for them.

"Jamie! Yazmin!"

Kuras held his arms out. "It's a basin. Filled with sand from the storm."

Martine ran up. "We have to follow them."

I grabbed Akana's hand. "Everybody grab hands. If we go in, we need to not get lost."

I felt the ground fall away under me as I slid to the bottom of the basin. The dust was up to my chest as I sat there, flailing, reaching for the other's hands. I saw the black of Jamie's hair as she crawled toward me. I was holding Martine's hand in one hand and Akana's in the other.

Yazmin crawled back to us. "Who's missing? Where is everyone?"

I yelled. "Call out."

We heard Leah's voice a little to the left. Jamie called her to come join us. I felt her squirm by me and I tried to grab on.

We sat there and held on.

I heard Jamie's voice. "We have to hold on and move together. We need to crawl. This entire basin could fill up and we'd be covered. Everyone link hands and move toward me."

We were crawling like that for at least an hour. I had no idea how fast we were going but the time seemed to pass interminably.

Jamie pulled us forward into a cave. It was near-dark as we crawled into it. I wasn't sure how much of that was the time and how much was the sand. We pushed toward the back of the cave and around a slight curve. The sand seemed to die down around us. Jamie counted us all out loud and fell to the ground on her back. We'd been crawling forever.

Yazmin pulled away and sat in the back of the cave, rocking back and forth. She had her head down, crying. The cave was cramped and there wasn't enough room to stand. I crawled over to her and held her.

"I lost everyone. I almost... I lost everyone. How could I do that? How could I lose...?"

I pulled her closer and squeezed. "You didn't lose anyone. There's seven of us here. We're here. We're in here. We're all good."

She looked at me. I'd never seen Yazmin really cry before. I'd never seen her look so lost. It was crushing.

She fell into racking sobs and I just held her until I heard Jamie's voice whispering. "Anjo."

I glanced back. She was pointing to the far end of the cave. I saw a little movement. Darting back and forth was a shape.

I looked at Akana. She nodded.

The figure was lost in the shadows of the cave, but for a second I thought I saw blond hair. I tapped Yasmin and pointed. She started breathing heavily. Jamie moved to the front of the cave and pulled Kuras back. Yazmin crawled toward the shape. He shifted out of the shadows.

He was naked, covered in red dirt. He was breathing hard, crawling back and forth as we invaded his cave.

But it was Linus.

Yazmin let out a moan and crawled faster. "Please, please. It's okay. It's okay. It's me."

Linus reacted like an animal. He pulled back, spinning, trying to get away.

"Please, please, Linus." She called to him. But the air was too thin to carry sound.

Kuras crawled next to me. He took off his respie and advanced. Linus saw his face. I realized that he didn't recognize the human faces under our devices. I pulled mine down. He stopped.

Yazmin pulled hers off and dropped it, moving toward him. Suddenly, it looked for a second as though he recognized her. He put his hand out and she took it pulling it toward her.

Kuras put out his hand face-up and Linus gave him his other hand. Kuras pulled him closer and wrapped his arms around him.

Slowly, the back of the cave filled with an orange and white light. It built up in the space between Kuras and Linus. I watched as it burned its way into my eyes. Somehow it wasn't oppressive or blinding, even as it filled the space completely. I watched the two men as their skin seemed to turn incandescent and the light finally faded off, leaving them in a gentle hug. Kuras smoothed Linus' hair back and placed the respie on him.

His eyes adjusted to the newly-darkened cave and he saw Yazmin. He crawled over to her and fell into her. She sank into his arms and cried, running her hands through his hair. We could hear him breathing into the respie and whispering softly. The two of them had turned into one piece, one lump in the center of the cave as he held her and whispered.

"You came for me, little fig."

10 - Mosaica -
The Rise of Tharsis, Mars - 3220

The question under the surface of all the Terminator films is, "are we in a universe where we can change the future?" From there it's just a matter of how. The choices sometimes look binary. We can do this or we can do that. Choice A or Choice B. Now, it's just about WWSCD.

What Would Sarah Connor Do?

If that sounds like feedback you might get from Devilboy, it's because it is. We waited out the sandstorm in that cave, asking my AI various questions about Mars.

And, of course, finding out what Linus had been through. Kuras took off his undershirt and made a makeshift pair of shorts for him, cleaning him up as much as was possible without water and a bar of soap. He barely remembered the last half-century since his mind had effectively shut down. But the time before that was uneventful. Ironically, he never knew there was a colony here, built after he landed. He could have reached them. He could have returned home hundreds of years ago.

It was best not to focus on that, though. The colony was such a small, infinitesimal part of the planetary surface that you could walk randomly for two millenia and not find it. And the colonists had been looking for him, but, again, with him hiding they would never have found him. Sometimes we can be so close but never find each other.

Worlds were big. Mars was big.

And our big deal now was the choice in front of us.

We could start out toward Arcadia Planitia – a 40-day walk – and then wait for a shuttle. Or we could go to Mons Mosaica and find out who or what that other blip was. What would Sarah Connor do?

"Sarah Connor would go to the Mosaica. There could be someone there with real answers." Leah was still excited about all of it.

And in Jamie's mind, too, this was part of the Mission. "It's really a short detour."

Kuras played devil's advocate."Look, I'll go along with whatever you guys say, but we can come back any time. I say this mission is done."

Yazmin had her hand wrapped tightly around Linus's. I could tell she was inclined to agree. But it was Linus himself that made the winning point.

"Guys, if someone else is here, alone, we have to get them. We don't have a choice."

Kuras nodded. That was an argument he couldn't fight. And as much as Yazmin wanted to, she couldn't, either.

The air was clear and still now, as we walked out of the cave. Our diagonal to the cave had only added about 5 kilometers to the trip, giving us about 25 kilometers to cover. Akana confirmed that the other blip was stationary. While it was moving, it wasn't moving too much.

This was going to take us about eight hours. I thought back to all the long distance walking the people in this group had done in the last millennium and considered the lost pedometer sponsorship opportunity.

Finding Linus had raised morale considerably. As the rest of the team were getting to know him, they saw a little of what he did. He was kind and willing to be a little silly. He tended to see the upside of nearly anything and that made walking a lot lighter as we used the opportunity to explore an alien planet.

The effect he had on Kuras was immediately obvious as well. Kuras the doctor flowered in the presence of a patient. He doted on him, constantly checking in. At the same time, he took care to see to Akana, now that Yazmin was focused on Linus. He and I took turns helping her over the bizarre half rock half sand terrain of Mars.

One sol on Mars was just a little under 25 hours. It was still daylight when we got to the Mosaica. At first, there was nothing to see. The area was a large lump, covered entirely by sand. It was obvious enough that Linus could confirm it wasn't there when he landed.

Climbing to the top of the lump wasn't easy. The sand shifted and flowed under us, falling away. So much so that, after about an hour of climbing, Jamie noted that, at this point, climbing it and digging it out were essentially the same thing. Leah and Martine laughed and dove into it, determined to be the first ones to unearth something.

And they were.

The metal wall beneath it was smooth and silvery, with a slightly orange tint when you looked at it from one side or the other. There was no entry we could find yet, but we kept digging it out. I turned to Jamie, Yazmin, and Linus.

"So, we think our blip is in there?"

Yazmin glanced at Akana. She was helping to dig. "Well, she seems to think so."

Linus nodded. "Whoever they are, they're inside somewhere, so that's good news."

Jamie interjected, "or whatever, right? We don't think that the other blip is human?"

"If they're human, they fell off my radar. I have my list of the 1936 original Salvado. And when it's passed on, it's complete. The number doesn't go up or down. This one is not from Earth."

We heard Martine's voice resonant in the earpieces. "Door!"

She stood at the top and pointed below, to her feet. She was near the center of the lump. We climbed up to where she was standing. There was a round portal, solid, featureless, barely recessed in the metal around it. There was no handle or visible way in.

But it was definitely a doorway.

On a whim, Kuras knelt down and put his hand on the portal, directly in the center. For a moment, we saw nothing. And then, there was a glow, like in the cave. It got brighter, illuminating the bones in his hand, rendering it bright red and then white. As the light faded, we could see the doorway slide into the metal around it, without a sound.

Kuras looked up at me. But I had no answers. I didn't know what this meant.

Jamie was the first one in, jumping into the hole left by the open portal. She called out and the rest of us followed.

The floor below us was about eight meters down. The area was open and spacious, reminding us that the artifact was mostly sunken. All eight of us made our way into the artifact. The doorway appeared to be in the middle of a long hallway, one that extended in two directions, to our left and to our right.

As we filed into the hallway space, a row of recessed lights above us slowly began to glow. There were symbols etched into the walls, recessed, unpainted, like strange colorless tribal tattoos. None of them was in any kind of language we could read. The light was vaguely warm, leaning towards yellows, but besides that it felt normal. It all felt too normal, really.

Jamie looked around. "Okay, this is not a human artifact. It's either a ship or a habitation center. The sizes seem about right for human size, though, and the lights suggest a similar visual range."

I realized that her educator's demeanor was a cover up for how little she knew right now. Jamie had been alive for 1200 years and the depth of her knowledge about things like this was nearly infinite.

But this was beyond her.

Yazmin interjected, "is there anything you see that might suggest a purpose for this or, more importantly, if there is an aggressive or warlike component to it? Does anyone recognize any of the markings?"

Kuras looked like he wanted to say something. I turned to him. "Doctor. Do you see anything?"

He shook his head. "I don't... Okay, this sounds crazy. But if I blur my eyes, these writings look familiar."

Leah asked, "familiar, like how. From where?"

He let out a long breath. "My brain could be making this up."

"Go on, "Yazmin urged.

"My whole life, I've felt like it's talking to me. The Gorukai."

I explained to the group, "that's what he named it. A long time ago."

"That's just it. I think that's the name it gave me. It's the Gorukai. This power."

We all looked at Kuras. He pointed to a symbol on the wall. It looked like a kind of crown with three points. Or maybe a squared off bird rising upward.

"And that's its name, written."

Jamie surveyed the room, "That's the third sign we have that they're connected – the blip, the fact that we could open the portal – that symbol."

I didn't want to say this. But I did. "But what if the blip is unconnected. And the portal could have opened for any energy source. And, no offense, Kuras, you might be..."

Kuras finished my sentence. "Wishful thinking. I know. It's possible."

Leah affirmed. "Yes, but what if he's right. The odds."

Martine spoke up. "So, odds are good that when we find this person, they can tell us more about it?"

Yazmin looked at Akana. "So, which way?"

She nodded her head to our right and started walking. We all followed. As we reached a new area in the hallway, the light slowly started to glow.

Kuras started. "To answer a question from earlier, what I'm seeing, and tell me if I'm wrong, is a kind of gentleness everywhere. The walls are curved. The floors are comfortable and flattened, rubbery for ease in walking. The markings aren't brash or jarring. The lights are organic and smoothly activated. This is the kind of space gentle people build, not warriors."

Linus laughed, clearly considering that good news. "Well, I'm sold."

Yazmin asked, "Do you recognize any other symbols?"

"I do not."

We walked for a few minutes. At this point, it was clear that there was a slight downward grade to the corridor. We were going down and had no idea how much. I asked Devilboy.

"Can you place our altitude?"

His voice sounded odd in the hallway. "Good question, Mole-boy. You're underground right now but for some reason I can't estimate how far. I'm also having trouble estimating time exactly and location. And, for some reason, it seems to be getting worse as you descend."

Linus responded right away. "So, your AI device says it can't even estimate the time for us. And it's worse the lower we go?"

Jamie speculated. "This could be a sort of effect that this space uses to disorient invaders when they come aboard. It's also sort of gentle. Like it's a defense, maybe? But not a destructive one?"

I added, "that makes sense. Disorient them enough so that they can't really do anything and have to ascend. But no one gets hurt."

Yazmin chimed in, "at what point are we just guessing?"

Jamie laughed. "Oh, these are all guesses. Everything past that door."

Martine found it first. There was a door to our right. "How about this door?" It was round, similar to the one on the hull. Possibly just a little bigger. Just as recessed.

Yazmin stepped forward. She shrugged and placed her hand close to the center. For a moment it looked like nothing would happen. Then we saw a faint glow coming from her palm. It enveloped her hand and burned bright red, exposing the bones beneath, before becoming white, then clear. The door whirred open.

Something I noticed right away was that it felt good to be in the presence of the light. I realized I had felt it when Kuras did it, too. I felt alive, free.

I felt strong.

She stepped into a large room. The walls were far enough apart that I began to wonder if we were still on Mars. Was all this underground?

And how far did it go?

About 30 meters away we could see a kind of column in the middle of the room. From this distance it looked grey and blue as though it might be made of water. As we came closer we could see what it was.

Jamie stared, walking around it. "This is a holograph?"

Leah was transfixed. "It's really beautiful."

It was. There were scenes playing out, shifting, ending starting, like cameras rotating around people. Most of the scenes included a single person, someone alone, someone in crisis.

Martine stepped back. "That's me." She pointed.

I could see Martine in the holo, a tear in her eye. Lifting her head and stepping out into the street. One foot first, and then the next.

We all felt it when a bus tried to stop, failing and crashing into her, dragging her body 10 meters until it finally stopped. Martine stared at her body, crushed and broken in the hologram and let out a whimper. An elegantly dressed man stepped from out of the crowd. He leaned down and laid his hand on her. And the hologram shifted, almost as though someone fast forwarded and put in a new video. This was a woman cowering in a closet. Trying to hide from a man who towered above her, angry, in a black t-shirt. He grabbed her and pulled her out, pouring a liquid on her face from a mason jar he carried. She screamed. The hologram fast forwarded to show her, burned, face disfigured by acid, in a hospital bed, pouring out pill after pill from a container and swallowing them all.

"LaToya Masterson, 38." I started to cry. I had met her. I knew all this. But it was hitting me all over again. Her pain. Ten years in hospitals, having her features reconstructed, with no hope of being herself again, she believed.

Until Savior Day.

The hologram changed. It was Linus, so confident, walking toward the beach, His face, though, it looked empty. It looked like a horrible cartoon of the joyful face we knew. This was a man with nothing to care about. Until he made something.

The scene shifted again to a woman, older, a grandmother. Her skin had grown lighter with age, like her hair. And so had her mind. She took a moment of clarity and stepped into the car, closing the garage door and turning it on, lying back to sleep.

Just to sleep.

I looked at Yazmin and whispered. "Rose Ediboiyo, 67."

I knew these stories. There were over 1936 of them now, new ones, different ones.

Suddenly I saw myself. In the truck. I looked over and Savi was there, next to me. The police chased a man into the parking area in front of the vehicle. I stepped out of the truck. Savi was asleep.

He looked so young, so perfect. I reached up to the hologram as the other version of me reached up to protect myself from the bullets. My phone fell, bouncing under the car. I felt myself fall away like I did the first time. The blond policeman. Asking me what Savi's name was. This time I smelled the blood first. I was on the ground and he was on top of me.

I smelled the blood.

The holo wrapped around me and I was in it. I dropped to my knees. I fell to the ground. Both versions of me were breathing hard, listening, confused. There was yelling. I heard Jamie call out, but then I heard the paramedic.

It was time of death.

I tried to scream. My eyes slammed shut as I did.

I opened them. Savi was gone. The hologram was gone. I was in a clean, empty white room. There was a figure standing there just a few meters away. A man with dark hair. He smiled at me.

"Hey, angel baby."

I stood up straight. He was dressed in a pair of jeans and a ripped up red sweater. "Do I know you?"

He laughed. And that was familiar. He pointed to the red sweater. "I'm Devilboy. I should have worn the horns. That would have been a giveaway. I'm too subtle."

"The AI?"

"Well, it's more complicated. But, yeah. I'm part Devilboy. The owner of the ship is interfacing with me so we can talk. It's not sexual. So stand down. I'm still a virgin."

"You're the Gorukai?"

"I'm something different. But I've been connected to it. I was part of it once."

"Where am I?" I looked around. There was nothing.

"The big question is who? Who are you? I can talk to you because you're the…"

And then he said something I couldn't understand. "I can't understand."

He laughed, "but, dude, you try. That's all that's important. I'm sorry, you are the storykeeper."

I thought to myself about how I tried to explain that I just collected the stories. I was shit at telling them. "Is that what I am? That doesn't seem like much. I'm an archivist. I'm not even a storyteller."

He stepped over and put his arm around me. "Anjo, not every story needs to be told. Some get kept, felt, remembered. The keeper remembers. Even the secret ones. The keeper is empathy."

"Empathy."

"This is how I'm talking to you."

"So is this a ship? Are you on this ship?

"I'm not anywhere. And, really, neither is this ship."

"That makes no sense. Were you going to Earth?" I tried to wrap my head around this.

"Okay, here's where this gets a bit fucked up. That's just it. I wasn't. It wasn't me. "

"What does that mean?"

"The Gorukai. It was meant to be here -- there. Let's just assume we're talking about earth. It never made it to earth. Are you okay, Angel-boy?"

I nodded, "The ship?"

"Malfunctioned. On its way to a number of places. I was bringing it here. This ship. It's hard to explain, but it goes everywhere. And when."

"But It wanted to be on Earth?"

"It needed to be. This is how it's been for people, since the start." He started walking with me. A row of white video games popped up. Right near them was a bench. I sat down on the bench while he slipped behind a game. He started moving the joystick around.

"I don't get it."

"Hm. You should play. It's no fun if all the high scores are me. I mean, they will be anyway. but…"

"Why does the Gorukai want to be here?"

"He looked over. I could hear the game end,. He wasn't focused. "It's what's missing. It's how people all over the universe survive, grow old, build great cultures."

"Using the Gorukai?"

"Yep." He patted his pockets. "Never a virtual quarter when you need one." He leaned against the machine.

"It's how cultures remember. It's how they come back after they fail. It's how they patch up mistakes. It's how people who have a moment of weakness survive."

I turned to him. "Someone strong shares their strength."

He hit the knobs twice and shook the machine. It lit up again. "Cheat code. Yes. It's the way of the universe. You can feel it, can't you?"

"I think so."

"Baby, we were never supposed to be alone. None of us. We're trapped in our heads, caught up in our lives, there is a quicksand in all of us that can suck us down. But we weren't meant to deal with it alone. We were meant to seek out people in that one moment and give them what they need. You've seen the stories. It's happening all over the world."

"So they could survive."

A buzzer went off and Devilboy raised his arms and then waved them. "YES! Sorry. I don't usually have hands."

He walked over and sat next to me. "It's the talking stick. It's the rope. It's the basketball. It's the way out and we learn to pass it around, just like my culture did. And then we bring it where it's needed."

"So it wasn't about you coming here?"

"No. But talking to you in the flesh was worth all this for me. And a game or two."

"What do I need to do?"

"Well. First of all, you need to say goodbye."

So I closed my eyes and did. And I felt myself falling. I don't know how long I fell or how far.

A second later, I was on the ground. Kuras was over me, helping me up. "He's ok."

I looked around. Yazmin was to my left. "What just happened, Anjo?"

I took a deep breath. "It's like I went somewhere. Something explained things to me. What is happening. Some part of the Radiance. But they explained it. How long was I passed out?"

Yazmin looked relieved. "Just for a moment. But we found him. The blip. Right when you fell."

Kuras nodded. "He just walked in." He pointed.

I tried to stand up and failed. I sat there and followed his finger. Standing behind Jamie and Leah was a man with a short shock of dark brown hair in a silvery suit. He looked human. He looked normal. I turned to Yazmin.

"That's my dad."

We followed my dad to another room with a big wide metallic table. We all sat around it. I still hadn't been able to talk to him. I didn't understand how this was possible.

Jamie looked around the table and then at him. "So, you're Jon Riley Killean?"

He nodded. "Well, yes. I am about to be."

Linus laughed. "Okay, that clears up everything."

She went on, "I mean, I've read your books."

"Okay, this is awkward. I haven't written any books."

Yazmin cut in, "you mean yet?"

"I think that's what I mean."

Yazmin looked over at me. "Anjo, is there anything...? I mean..."

"Yes, so. Hi. Jon Riley Killean is my father. He met my mother, Mari, and they got married and had me a little over 1200 years ago. And that's... well, there's more story, but, that is..."

Martine added, "he wrote some books."

"I did. I guess. I did all that. This gets complicated."

Kuras asked straight out, "let's try this. From your perspective, sir, who are you?"

"Okay. That's a good question. To me, I'm Keari. I'm from a planet called Xioa, so I guess I would be a Xioamite."

Kuras followed up, "okay, and you have the Gorukai in you?"

"Yes. As do all of you. I think I'm starting to see why. For me, you're in the future."

Jamie squinted. "Which doesn't surprise you... why?"

"Jamie, right?"

"It lets you know our names?"

"Sometimes. For me. It's my strength, really." He looked around and his eyes landed on me. I couldn't believe what I was seeing. From all of Ron's videos -- this was my dad. His smile. His slight accent. The way he talked. It was him. He smiled at me. "And you're the storykeeper."

I nodded. "Yes."

He laughed. For a moment, I saw something wash across his face. Was it pride? "Of course you are." He continued. "This ship is built on what you would call a pendulum drive."

Jamie was fixated. "I've never heard of that."

"Well, the way spacetime works is that it's really elastic and connected. If you stay absolutely still in time, you can travel more quickly through space. If you are absolutely still in space, you can travel faster in time."

Yazmin nodded. "This much we know."

"One of the things that falls out of that, after a lot of research and lost ships, is that you can make traveling in time generate space-usable energy and traveling in space generate time-usable energy."

Jamie shook her head. "That much makes no sense."

"I mean, I can show you the math. But you will figure it out one day anyway. At any rate, if you alternate, you can get the energy to go anywhere. This ship is called ......"

Linus spoke up. "That really didn't come through."

My dad continued, "okay, what do you call this place?"

"The Mosaica." Martine responded.

"Ok, so let's call the ship the Mosaica. It's a modular ship. That can move back and forth in time, in parts, like a pendulum, to generate the power to move incredible distances in space."

Jamie's face went white. "A modular ship."

Leah grabbed her hand.

Keari went one, "Yes. Is that ok?"

Yazmin sighed. "It's a long story."

Jamie shook her head. "I'm sorry, go on." I could tell that the ghost of the Sargasso was clawing at Jamie.

He took a breath, "and when it builds up the energy, it shoots the pods out and they travel to the far edges of the universe."

We heard Akana's voice for the first time at the table. It was light, but clear. "And carry the Gorukai all over?"

My dad paused. "That's right. It's meant to be passed around. Each of these pods are supposed to contain 2 or 3 people. And they travel to worlds.

"In my...vision... Devilboy told me that we were supposed to have it."

He looked at me. "You are, son. Everyone is."

Yazmin looked thoughtful. "How come it's only you on the ship?"

"That is one of the stranger things about this ship. If you go to the farther areas, time shifts, it changes. I came back here to the main pod section a couple of hundred years ago and I was alone. I've managed to fix four of the pods from the crash. But the other people I was with may be lost in time in the farthest parts of the ship."

"Ok, so we don't wander. Good to know. What do these pods look like?" Yazmin asked.

He stood up. "I'll show you mine. The others are right near it."

We followed him just about 350 meters further down the hallway. There was a round room with doors all around it. There were orange lights lit on 4 of the doors. The rest were powered down, apparently. He moved to the closest of them and pressed his hand against the door. After a few seconds of illumination, the door whirred open.

We walked in. The pod was barely large enough for all nine of us to stand in it. It was smooth and metallic with three chairs and what looked like a large bed in back. I looked around.

"There's not much to this?"

"Well," Keari answered, "people like us don't need much."

That made sense. There were screens all around. They took the place of windows, I guessed. I looked down to see another small door. "What's this?"

He stepped over. "Oh, it's a smaller pod. It's an escape pod."

At that moment, Martine let out a squeal. We all stared at her. She pointed to the hull, an area right behind the chairs.

Leah laughed. "No fucking way."

I saw it now. Jamie fished through her pocket and pulled out the tiny piece of metal. She'd been carrying it for luck more than anything else. She handed it to Leah.

"You want to do the honors?"

Leah stepped over to the hull and looked at my dad. He nodded as she etched into the metal of the pod wall the words "Leah loves Jamie & Martine"

She stepped back. I realized that this would be my pod. And I knew where it went.

***

Back in the conference area, we all sat around the table.

Yazmin stood up. I had stopped thinking of her as little a long time ago. Today she looked huge, towering. Linus was right next to her and she slid her hand into his and started speaking.

"I don't know how to do any of this or even say any part of this. Some of the people in this room, I owe you for over a thousand years of friendship. That's a lot of power. We're a lot of power. We have the chance right now to take that power where it belongs. And that means one last big trip with no guarantee of what the end looks like. These pods are set to go places I don't even understand. The people at the other end are people I don't understand. If anyone doesn't want to do this, there is still Arcadia Planitia and a ticket back to Earth. If you do, though, there is complete unknown.

Leah asked, "can the three of us stay together, in one pod?"

Keari nodded.

"Linus and I will take the far one." Yazmin reached for his hand.

Keari cleared his throat. "Anjo. Son. Would you go with me?"

I nodded and stepped over to him. I put my hand in his and sat down.

Kuras laughed and knelt down next to Akana. He opened an imaginary box. "Akana Tanaka, would you do me the honor of accompanying me on a weird one-way fucked up spaceship trip?"

She laughed and pretended to take the ring. She held the imaginary ring up to the light and examined it, moving her hand a bit.

"Yes."

We all cheered.

Devilboy managed to patch into the speakers and turned the music up.

It seemed like it was coming from everywhere. We danced, because we had to. And we held onto each other, because we would never do that again. And we talked, into the night.

And when we climbed into our pods, I had the chance, finally, to talk to Jon Riley Killean. He would ride the pendulum with me until the right time and then take the smaller pod. I don't know what kind of universe we live in but this one needed him to be somewhere.

I hugged him and flopped onto the bed in the pod as we watched the swirl of colors herald the launch. I leaned back and we both talked, staring upward.

"I think that mom is waiting for you."

"You know, son, like this, I can't... I can't have children."

"I know. I think I'm waiting for you, too." I thought about Ron and how we looked alike. How he was an archivist like me. A storykeeper.

I turned to my dad. "When I'm born. I'll be... Well, it'll seem like I'm a little girl. But don't let that throw you."

He smiled and touched my face. Like I imagined my father would. He shook his head. "I won't."

"I'll be me. Waiting to grow up and spend as much time with you as I can."

"I'll be there, son. My boy."

"I love you, dad."

He gave my face a little slap and messed up my hair. "Of course you do. You're not insane. I love you, too."

I wish I could tell you what was happening inside the other pods. I wish I could sit here and say that Jamie, Leah, and Martine had turned up the music and were dancing together, laughing, celebrating the greatest exploration of their lives as the pendulum swung, sending them far away together. Martine and Jamie might remember for a moment that they almost walked away from this life and all the things in it. Then they would dance until they fell to the ground, cuddling, laughing, just being people in love that could turn any place into a bedroom or a retreat, or an exotic getaway.

I wish I could. But I wasn't there. That was their space.

And I wish I could tell you that Yazmin and Linus just sat there, holding hands, sinking into the cushions of that strange ship while she shared stories about her life, the incredible things she did, while he laughed approvingly, reassured that she was every bit as remarkable as he thought she was way back in that Ramla prison. That she was worth it.

Or that I could give you some insight into what was happening in that pod with Kuras and Akana. How the wildly charismatic doctor would charm the demure beauty, coaxing from her every smile she had kept hidden out of propriety for the last 1200 years, every loud sound, every gesture, making this woman who had spent her nearly endless life living for other people the center of all of his attentions as their ship disappeared to...

To where?

Jamie, Martine, and Leah's part of the ship spun off and seemed to lose dimension, folding itself sideways somehow, getting smaller until it disappeared. Moments later, Yazmin and Linus's did, too. I put my hands against the view screen and squinted.

Gone.

Dad's escape pod disappeared from sight so quickly, too. I pressed my face against the poly glass screen, feeling the vertigo as my body imagined it was a real window, and I was so high up that there was no down anymore. I pushed off, trying to see the pod from any angle.

It had faded toward Earth. Of all the ship sections, Akana and Kuras's was the only occupied one left. I stared at it, trying to see it grow smaller, but I couldn't figure out where it was going. It seemed to move in a dimension I'd never seen before.

I imagined Dad crashing on earth, just less than a mile from my mother, waiting for this great love story to begin, and I was suddenly so happy to have had this last day. It all seemed so accidental, but I knew, in my heart, it wasn't.

There was no way to feel the sped-up motion through time but I tried to pretend I could. I felt presidents born and elected, assassinated and interred, people living whole lives as the great pendulum arc of the ship slowed. Countries rose up and fell, entire languages came to prominence and disappeared as the ship bobbed across the 25,000-year gap built into its machinery. I felt the pendulum move.

This was the final arc, it seemed, and I now realized where the center was. I laughed, thinking about being young and wanting to travel across the galaxy, across time, across space, just to find myself coming to rest...

At home.

I know it was impossible for me to feel the radiation burn, but I did.

The ship jumped again. This time the jerky epileptic movement was worse than before. My head slammed back into the control panel behind me and I laughed. It was getting hard to feel specific instances of pain through the pain. Pain was new and exciting again. It was raw and real.

And everything was pain.

But pain is so different when you know. When you realize there is no death on the other side of it. Now it's just a fleeting, passing thing that is meant to wake you up, raise you from some kind of material sleep. As the last sweep of the pendulum began, I began to sympathize with this poor ship, built to weather anything, torn apart by time.

In a way, this ship was me. Maybe I had been conditioned by Devilboy to think of all mechanics as friendly, anthropomorphized, whiny musing wonders of material invention.

I looked out the massive port window and I saw it. The stars were beginning to organize in a familiar way. I'd seen that configuration before.

And here's where everything made sense.

I was glad I had said goodbye to Devilboy. So he could laugh at me for starting this trip, but secretly mourn with me for the end of our epic friendship, one that lasted more than a millenium. I always knew what he would say, making some kind of joke about how I'd left the oven on or how I'd forgotten some vitally important thing that was now to be lost to history. He faced death the way he faced everything, with a wry piece of sarcasm and then a sympathetic wink. I won't give you the exact words, because that was our conversation.

I felt my other friendships like blood inside me, nurturing me. I remembered Savi at my shoulder playing free video games and what that meant. I remembered him sleeping in the truck next to me so I wouldn't be alone and the joy I now recognize in his eyes when he saw I couldn't be hurt anymore, as though the idea of me being hurt was painful to him. His friendship had only grown in my eyes since he was gone. It protected me.

I felt it inside me.

The Gorukai.

I let go and breathed it. It infused the air around me. I wish I'd spoken to it, learned from it like Kuras had, gotten to know it. I wish I had understood how it worked. I could feel, deep down, that it had a life of its own. It clung to me as the ship fell apart, aware of my need.

But my need was nothing, compared to the people below me.

My body was pulling apart, atom by atom, but it didn't matter. I closed my eyes and smiled. In the back of my head, maybe I saw this coming and I leaned into it. I didn't bother looking down at the date on the panel.

I knew what date it was.

I spoke to the Gorukai now and explained the need all over again. I tried to remember as many of those 1936 people as I could, imagining the few who were never found. I thought about Jamie and Kuras and wonderful Lian, Akana, Yazmin, Lelei, and all the rest of them, down there right now.

In need.

I looked up at the part of the wall that said, simply, "Leah loves Jamie & Martine." It was beautifully lit in the pod, like a mandate to the universe. In my head, I blessed this part of the pod with the knowledge of where it might land when it all came apart. I smiled at it in the hidden knowledge we shared. It had purpose, too.

I used to think this was all about someone wishing on a star. And that star, the Savior Event, just mindlessly followed through, delivering 1936 people to a place they needed to be.

But I realized now it was the star's own wish. And I knew I was down there somewhere, right now, falling, just as I was now. In a way, I'd been falling for over twelve hundred years, waiting for this moment, waiting to let go and disappear.

Maybe 1936 people had to be the explorers, the ones to make it to the other side, to be the ones that reported, in the end, on the truth. Maybe, just like me, they had to step away from the painting a little to see all of it, to realize how beautiful and glorious this life was, to see inside all the moving parts, to outlive the pain, and put the gun down, stop the jump, vomit up the horror.

And we did it. We explorers, we came back to this moment, just like I was doing now, and we testified. We learned that this shell of despair had to be broken through, cracked open to reveal the love, the art, the patience and prospects, the visions that played out when you looked it all in the eye and told it to sit down so YOU could talk. It couldn't just be thrown away.

I was so grateful to it and I could sense it now.

It knew.

It slipped from me and filled the ship. It wrapped itself in the reddish-orange trail and shone down brightly, piercing the veil around the planet and seeking out the people who needed it today. It left me, just as my body began to dissolve, floating above a world in greater need.

I felt parts of me fade away in that blood-orange glow of the ship's descent and smiled at the thought of my face, thousands of feet below me, looking up into the sky confused as I stood at the foot of that mountain, absolutely unready for anything that came next.

But doing it all anyway.

Epilogue
2028

Mari was sleeping in the front seat, shoeless, when the truck split their car like an overripe apple and sent pieces of it flying across the bridge. By the time she woke up, Jon was braindead, showing no sign of higher-order brain function.

The X-ray machines were less than effective in piercing her skin. The doctors were confused, assuming she was torn apart on the inside. This tiny Montana hospital had sent away for an MRI machine to find out more about her. But Mari knew that it would yield nothing.

She was fine. She was fine, and her Jon was dead. His breath still cycled through the plastic tube in his throat while his chest lifted and fell. The machines counted off beats of his dead heart in deceptive couplets, trying to deny the evident, the obvious.

Mari knew he was gone.

She still tried. Over and over she tried.

She held his hand in the hospital, feeling the shattered bones of his fingers and tried to pass the Gorukai back to him.

This was his moment of need. She tried to feel for it. Surely he needed this. No matter what, his body had to recognize it. It would just flow from her back into him

It just didn't work.

She remembered back, a year after Anjo was born, when she had taken the pack of twenty razor blades and slid them out onto her belly in the bathtub, grabbing at one and pulling off the tiny brown cardboard wrapper and plunging it into her wrists, one after another.

It didn't hurt at all. And the water was so warm, wrapping around her. Thick black vignettes around her field of vision contracted as Jon rushed into the room and sat next to her on the floor. He talked to her and held her. She closed her eyes and breathed in.

And finally nodded.

When he passed it to her, it felt like a cool rush through her system, almost as if she had been injected with cold water. Her eyes opened and she began choking.

Jon held her until it went away. And just like that, the blood pooling in the tub fell away from her and the tiny, angry lines on her wrists closed up, like little thin-lipped mouths falling silent forever.

For the last three years, she had carried it, feeling stronger, more powerful. More capable. Anjo seemed softer and lighter on her hip, protected by her. And even Jon looked lighter.

She was protected, too. That was all he needed.

But now Jon was gone There was no "him" left in there to pass it to. She could feel that, all over the world, there was no more Jon Riley Killean anywhere. This planet, full of every kind of resource imaginable, was bereft of what she needed most right now.

At the far end of the room, Ron was asleep in the chair, Anjo on his lap. She moaned quietly, trying to avoid waking him up.

Even before she had explained it to Jon, he knew Ron was Anjo's biological father. But he never once pushed him away or tried to force him out of their family. Jon's unique senses could read Ron, this shy, simple man, who was just good. Ron was incapable of anger. He was not able to hate.

As much as Jon loved Mari, he knew that what Anjo inherited from her was a kind of sickness. His people called it the ending. He knew Mari fantasized about it, thought about it, planned it. And he could feel it in Anjo, too.

But the child also had an inheritance on the other side. Ron knew only how to love, only how to be loyal. So much so that he stood up next to his best friend when she married someone else. He nodded and hugged her as they ended their playful high school-born physical relationship. He let Anjo grow up thinking of him as a kindly invested uncle while Jon acted every bit the father he was intended to be.

And he never once thought about leaving. Ron videotaped their friendship, documented it, celebrated it. He was there on every birthday. He was there when times were good and when they were the other thing, even more so. When Mari drifted away, when she went somewhere else, he held up a light for her, too. And he came to love Jon.

Mari's lungs worked to pull in enough air to live, so close to her dying husband. But she knew what to do. And she knew Ron well enough to trust in that decision.

She couldn't pass the Gorukai to Anjo. She was so tiny. She needed to grow into who she was. Jon was sure that she would make choices soon that would change her, let her be her authentic self. Mari didn't know how he knew, but she never really knew how Jon knew anything. She trusted him. In her mind, she had started already thinking of Anjo as her little boy. And so had Jon.

Jon. Her strange love from the stars. Who had traveled across the universe, just to make her happy, to adore her, to be a satellite to her and bring her back to life, not just that one time but every single time. This spaceman who showed her what love looked like so expertly that she never doubted anymore. And was sorry she once did. She had come to really believe he had followed her here, after the crashing of his tiny escape pod. He had told her he would follow her anywhere. He called her his firefly, his lighting bug, his light.

And he followed.

She padded over to Ron, sleeping as he cradled Anjo preciously. He would watch her little boy grow into a man. He would understand it and make it easy. He would tell him that he was loved.

She put her hand on Ron's arm and felt it. She wondered how she could give it to him, how she could pass it on, if he wasn't in need. But under this surface, he was entirely in need. She felt his love for her, his love for Jon. She felt his secret wish before falling asleep that this would all be a dream and his people would be there, whole, happy, healthy, when he woke up. The need in him was like a vacuum.

She felt the Gorukai slip into him so easily. He would wake up invulnerable, powerful, capable. He would live so long if he wanted to. He could do anything.

But Mari knew what he would do. When Anjo grew up, the first time he saw him in need, lost, wanting, he would pass it on.

It was inevitable. He would hold onto the Gorukai for her son, passing it on when he needed it. She wondered what that might look like. She looked down at the child, so similar to her, even down to the pixie haircut.

And she laughed a little. It would be a strange trip. She remembered sitting at the bottom of the pool for two hours once, not needing to breathe, not panicking, feeling the absolute stillness of the water.

She hoped he would do that at least once.

Sliding into bed next to Jon, she could feel the sharp prick of his cascade of slivered bones, jutting out from his skin, threatening to cut open every bandage and expose his broken body to the cool hospital air.

She pulled him close and grabbed the syringe, sinking it into the purple line in her forearm.

She pressed the plunger and leaned in, wrapping herself around the man who had once said with such joy that he would follow her anywhere, that she was his light.

She closed her eyes as 200 mg of morphine moved from her forearm to her heart, and then all over her body. It wasn't the cold of the Gorukai that she remembered, but the warmth of the water enveloping her.

She whispered to her Jon and, for the very last time, lit the way for him.

■ ‖ PULSEBLACK ■ ‖